FELIDAE

Akif Pirinçci was born in Turkey but now lives in Bonn, Germany, with his wife and three cats. His non-fiction study of cat behaviour – *Cat Sense: Inside the Feline Mind* – will be published by Fourth Estate in the Autumn of 1994.

FELIDAE

Akif Pirinçci

Translated by Ralph Noble

FOURTH ESTATE · LONDON

First published in Germany by Goldmann Verlag in 1989

This translation first published in Great Britain in 1993 by
Fourth Estate Limited
289 Westbourne Grove
London W11 2QA

This paperback edition first published in 1994
10 9 8 7 6 5 4 3 2 1

A catalogue record for this book is available from the British Library.

ISBN 1–85702–204–1

Typeset by York House Typographic Ltd, London
Printed by Cox & Wyman Ltd, Reading

For Uschi and Rolf, the best!
And Cujo and Pünktchen, the brightest!

THE WORLD IS A HELL! *What does it matter what happens in it? The world was so created that one sorrow follows another. There has been a chain reaction of suffering and cruelty on this earth since its creation. Yet perhaps it is no better elsewhere, on distant planets, stars and galaxies . . . Who knows? The crown of all that is loathsome in this universe and unknown universes is, very probably, the human race. The human race is so . . . so evil, mean, cunning, egotistical, greedy, cruel, insane, sadistic, opportunistic, bloodthirsty, malicious, treacherous, hypocritical, envious, and – yes, this above all – just plain stupid! Such is the human race. . .*

Yet what about the others?

And God made the beasts of the earth according to their kinds, and cattle, and every thing that creepeth upon the earth after its kind. And God saw that it was good.

– GENESIS

CHAPTER

—— 1 ——

IF YOU REALLY WANT to hear my tale – and I strongly urge you to do so – you must get used to the fact that it's not going to be pleasant. On the contrary, the mysterious events I suffered last autumn and winter finally made me realise that times of harmony and tranquillity in life are brief, even for my kind. I now know that no one can avoid the horror that surrounds us, and that chaos threatens at every turn. But before I bore you with a lecture on the beckoning abyss, let me tell you this tale, a sad tale of evil.

It all began when we moved into that damned house.

What I hate most in life is moving and everything that goes along with moving; and since I believe in the theory of reincarnation, I'm convinced I must have hated it in my earlier lives too. The slightest irregularity in my everyday routine plunges me into a deep well of depression, from which I can only escape after prodigious mental effort. But my simple-minded companion Gustav, and those like him, would change their home-sweet-homes every week if they could. They have elevated interior decoration to the level of an insane cult. They consult magazines on moving (which, in turn, encourage them to move on a regular basis), hold heated debates about décor and colour schemes late into the night, come to blows about the shape of toilet brushes for the optimal maintenance of hygiene, and are constantly on the look-out for new and better houses. Apparently, the average householder will move up to thirty times in his life. I have not the slightest doubt that such a practice irreparably damages his mental health. My explanation for this harmful habit is that these pitiful fools have no equanimity, and try to compensate by incessantly summoning the removal men. It's nothing less than a full-blown neurotic compulsion. Surely the Good Lord didn't give human beings hands and feet for the sole purpose of constantly transporting furniture and kitchen utensils from one dwelling to the next?

That said, I must confess that the old flat did have its shortcomings. First of all, there were those billion steps you had to run up and down, day in, day out, if you didn't want to become an urban Robinson Crusoe. Although the building was relatively new, the architect obviously thought the lift to be an invention of the devil and expected the inhabitants of his Tower of Babel to practise the old, tried-and-trusted method of floor-to-floor locomotion.

Also, the flat was far too small. Well, to tell the truth, it was big enough for Gustav and me, but you know how it goes: after a while you want more and more. Your place has to be cosier, it has to be more spacious, expensive, and stylish . . . But I'm sure you've heard all this before. As a young rebel your ideals will be intact (unless you already own the house of your dreams). But later, if you still don't have your dream house and you find out that you aren't exactly the big bad rebel you thought you were, what is your fate? A year's subscription to *Better Homes and Gardens*.

So that's why we moved into that damned house.

When I first saw it from the rear quarterlight of a Citroën CX2000, I thought Gustav was playing a nasty joke on me — which would not have surprised me considering his rather immature sense of humour. For months I had heard him talk about 'an old building', 'renovation' and 'a bit of doing up', but since Gustav understands as much about renovating houses as a giraffe does about stock-market speculation, I thought this was merely a matter of nailing a little name-plate to the door. To my horror, I now realised what he had meant by 'an old building'.

Admittedly the residential area was elegant, even romantic. A dentist would have to convince his patients that they needed a considerable number of fillings and bridges before he could afford to take up residence here. And it just so happened that the sad structure that was to be our home looked like a rotten tooth in comparison to the turn-of-the-century dolls' houses which surrounded it. Embedded in a tree-lined street of houses which were picture-postcard perfect (a street where the renovation mania of all those high-earners looking for a tax write-off had wrought havoc), this majestic wreck seemed to have sprung from the imagination of a horror film scriptwriter. It was the only building on the street which had not been given a facelift, and I tried to keep myself from imagining why that was. The owner had probably been waiting years for a sucker who would even dare to set foot over its threshold. And if we went in there ourselves, no doubt the whole house would tumble down on our heads. I already knew Gustav was no genius, but only now was the true extent of his idiocy becoming clear to me.

The front of the building was embellished with a number of cracked, ornamental plaster baubles, and resembled the visage of a mummified Egyptian king. Grey and weathered, it glowered at you as if it had diabolical intentions for its inhabitants. The window shutters of the two upper floors – which, as Gustav had mentioned, were empty – were partly broken, but shut. Something eerie emanated from these upper floors. You couldn't see the roof from below, but I would have bet my life that it was in a state of complete dilapidation. Because the ground-floor flat into which I and my muddled friend were to move was about six feet above street level, you could only catch a glimpse of the interior through the filthy window-panes, but in the harsh, merciless afternoon sun I could make out stained ceilings and tasteless wallpaper.

Gustav uses only a particularly inane baby-talk with me, which doesn't bother me since I would employ the same primitive language if I chose to speak with him; and now, as we finally came to a halt in front of the house, he emitted some mumbling sounds of enthusiasm.

If you have gained the impression that I harbour hostile feelings towards my companion, you are only partly right.

Gustav . . . well, what is Gustav like? Gustav Löbel is a writer. Yes, a writer, but only by comparison to a telephone book would his work be recognised as an intellectual contribution to the world. He pens 'novelettes' of such clever brevity that the plot exhausts itself within the space of half a page, and gets them published in 'women's magazines'. Mostly he derives the inspiration for his strokes of genius from the vision of a hundred-pound cheque – his 'publishers' would never fork out more. Yet how often have I seen this conscientious author grappling with himself as he searches for an apt conclusion, a spectacular dramatic effect (at least within the bounds of his genre), or a variation on adultery that has never been thought of before? Only for brief periods does Gustav write what he really wants to, abandoning the imaginative world of legacy hunters, violated secretaries, and husbands who never noticed that their wives have been prostituting themselves behind their backs for the last thirty years. Gustav studied history and archaeology, so when he writes what he wants to he composes treatises on ancient civilisations – and especially on Egyptian divinities. This, however, he does at such numbing length that all these tracts sooner or later turn out to be unsaleable, and his dream of some day making a living from them has been receding further and further from reality. Although his appearance is not unlike that of a gorilla, and although he is the most extreme example of obesity with which I am personally acquainted (two hundred and eighty-six pounds), he still retains, to employ a euphemism, a childlike, if somewhat feeble-minded, charm. In his dealings with the world he is placid, congenial, and self-satisfied. Gustav takes care to avoid anything that threatens this holy trinity. Ambition and stress are foreign words to his harmless, easy-going spirit. Mussels in garlic soup and a bottle of Chablis are worth far more to him than a challenging career.

So that's Gustav: my exact opposite. It is no great wonder that we get in each other's hair every now and then. But I'll let the subject go for now. Gustav does provide for me, shields me from mundane inconveniences, protects me from danger; and the greatest love in his sheltered life remains none other than Yours Truly. I do respect him, though I confess it is at times extremely difficult.

Once Gustav had crammed the car into the slot between the chestnut trees in front of the house (Gustav never did understand how to park a car, parking is quantum physics to him), we both got out. While he manoeuvred the entirety of his awe-inspiring bulk up to the building, regarding it the while with such a gleam in his eye that you might have thought he had built it himself, I made an immediate scent check.

The musty stench of this ghastly edifice hit me like a sledge-hammer. Although a mild wind blew, the dry rot in the house smelled so strongly that it sent my nasal receptors into a state of shock. I realised in a flash that this foul reek did not rise from the foundations of the building, but crept down from the upper floors, and was now in the process of extending its stinking fingers into the flat in which we were about to . . . well, if not precisely live with dignity, at least exist. But there was something else as well, something odd, murky, threatening almost. It was extraordinarily difficult even for me to analyse such faint and peculiar smells, and I can claim without false modesty that my two hundred million olfactory cells, compared even to those of others of my kind, are unique in their powers of discernment. Yet no matter how much I moistened my nose, I could not identify these strange scent molecules. I therefore called upon my good old 'J' organ for help. I grimaced, licked the air, then pressed my tongue against my palate.[1]

This had the desired effect. I could now distinguish this ominous smell beneath the dry-rot stench of our new home. Since it had no natural origin, however, I couldn't immediately classify it. Then at last I recognised its source: a concoction of chemicals.

I still couldn't unravel this smell into its constituent parts, but at least it was now clear that synthetic chemicals were involved. Everyone knows the odour that hangs around hospital corridors and chemists and my powerful nose recognised just this smell in the repulsive stink of decay discharged by our corpse of a house. But the unease I felt was barely an inkling of the nightmare that was to descend upon me, and I waited calmly on the pavement beside my friend, who continued to beam with joy.

Gustav rummaged at length in his trouser pocket before finally conjuring up a worn metal ring with numerous keys. He pushed one sausage-like finger through the ring, then raised the tinkling keys up somewhat while stooping down towards me. With his other hand, he patted my head and made jubilant chuckling sounds. I assumed he was attempting one of those rosy speeches that a groom customarily delivers to his bride before carrying her over the threshold of their new home. He kept jingling the keys in his hand while pointing to the raised ground floor to make clear the connection between the keys and the flat. At times my dear Gustav has the charm of a village idiot and all the pedagogic talent of a blacksmith.

As if he had divined my thoughts, a sweet, knowing smile flitted across my friend's face. But before he could decide to actually carry me like a bride into our new house, I streaked out from between his fingers and over to the entrance. While I was padding up the flimsy steps, which were covered with yellowing autumn leaves, I noticed beside the right doorpost a rectangular patch on the brick wall that was a shade lighter than the rest.

Rusted screws protruded from its corners, their heads broken off. I speculated that there had once been a doctor's office or a laboratory in the house, which might also explain the smell of chemicals.

This ingenious train of thought was brought to an abrupt end. For while I stood in front of the door of my future home, my gaze fixed on the missing name-plate (presumably Doctor Frankenstein's), another, this time very familiar, scent penetrated my nostrils. Ignorant of territorial law and without the slightest respect for propriety, one of my kind had left behind his rather importunate calling card on the right doorpost. Since I was about to move in, my status as owner was now clear and naturally I insisted upon my right to obliterate all previous signatures with my own. And so, swivelling one hundred and eighty degrees, I concentrated with all my might and let fly.

The environmentally safe, all-purpose jet that shot out from between my hind legs inundated the spot where my predecessor had left his mark. Order had once again been established in the world.

Gustav smiled idiotically behind me, the smile of a father whose baby says 'goo goo' for the first time. I understood Gustav's little pleasure, because Gustav sometimes seemed to me to be a sweet ickle 'goo goo' himself. His foolish grin breaking into grunts of happiness, he waddled past me and opened the door with a rusted key from the ring. After some rattling, the door swung open.

Side by side, we made our way across a cool hallway to our front door, which gave me the spontaneous impression of a coffin lid. A shaky staircase on the left led to the two upper floors, from which Death himself seemed to waft downward. I vowed I would take the first opportunity of inspecting the upper floors to find out what was going on up there. I must confess, however, that the mere thought of wandering by myself through those rooms made me shudder. Gustav was dragging us into a godforsaken dungeon, and he didn't even realise it.

At last he got our own door open and we marched, in step with each other, into a veritable battlefield.

It was, to be fair, an impressive flat. It just happened to be in a state of utter turmoil. That wasn't the real problem, though. The real problem was Gustav. My dear friend was in neither physical nor mental shape to take on a ruin like this and bring it up to par. (I need hardly mention that he was entirely incapable of wielding any kind of tool with any degree of success.) If he was seriously considering such a plan, the tumour I had long suspected was replacing his brain must have grown to critical dimensions.

Slowly, cautiously, I crept through each room, taking in every detail. Three rooms branched off to the right of the spacious corridor; they competed fiercely among themselves for the honour of being the most striking example of ruin and decay, and were alarmingly reminiscent of scenes from *The Cabinet of Dr Caligari*. These rooms were all quite large and faced south towards the street, so that presumably they would be flooded with sunlight on warm spring and summer days. But it wasn't possible to witness this effect there and then because the after-noon sun had just begun to slip around the corner of the house. At the end of the corridor was a further room that I assumed to be the bedroom. A door opened from this room to the outside. Off to the left of the hallway was the kitchen, which you had to walk through to get to the bathroom.

The rooms looked like they had only been occupied by worms, cockroaches, silverfish, rats and various insect and bacterial empires since the Second World War. Or maybe the First. The notion that human beings had lived here recently seemed absurd. There were gaping holes in both the crumbling parquet floor and the mouldy ceiling. Everything smelled of rot and the urine of certain indefinable creatures that had attained an evolutionary stage just advanced enough for them to be able to piss. In the face of this horror, only my high tolerance of pain and my faultless hormonal equilibrium saved me from suffering an immediate nervous breakdown.

As for Gustav, he had suddenly become schizophrenic. After I had returned to the corridor, bent down with grief, from my survey of the last room, I spied my poor friend standing in the middle of the kitchen and carrying on an animated monologue. To my consternation, I discovered that the enthusiastic conversation he was holding with the ancient kitchen walls concerned not the depressing state of the dump we were in but, quite the contrary, his excitement at having finally arrived in the Promised Land. Somehow, I felt sorry for the man, seeing him there, whirling around again and again, arms stretched out as if in prayer or in the thrall of some mad religious cult, the whole time babbling to himself as if he were delivering a speech to the resident colonies of insects and viruses. He looked like one of those decrepit, alcoholic bit-part actors in a play by Tennessee Williams. But Gustav was no tragic hero, and no audience was going to cry its heart out when he took his leave of life in the last act. Gustav's life had more in common with the deadly dull real-life dramas filmed by television producers to illustrate programmes for the afflicted masses on losing weight and lowering your cholesterol.

Who was this man, anyway? A plump, not particularly intelligent guy in his mid-forties who wrote affectionate Christmas and birthday cards to so-called friends who might visit him once every ten years; a man who had invested all his faith in the pharmaceutical industry in the hope that it would discover a miracle cure for his advancing baldness. He was the perfect dupe for insurance agents. In the course of a miserable sex life he had had a total of three or four miserable sexual encounters with wretched creatures picked up during late-night visits to singles' bars – women who would empty his wallet before slipping away early the next morning while he was sleeping off his hangover.

And now, somehow, he had managed to get his hands on this

hovel. It was one of his great successes, a fact which gave me good cause to reflect on the sorry state of his existence. I began to resign myself to my fate. After all, doesn't everything in this world have an order, a purpose, a higher meaning? Yes, of course. Destiny, that's what it's all about. Or as a Japanese assembly-line worker would say: the way things are is the way things are, and the way things are is good.

But enough of philosophy. Gustav was no Job, and there's no point in making him out to be one. While my friend composed further odes to the splendour of our new quarters, my gaze drifted from him to the bathroom. Both the door and the large rear window were open and, seizing the opportunity to inspect the back of the building, I whipped past Gustav and sprang up on to the window-sill.

The view was simply heavenly. Before me lay the navel, so to speak, of our neighbourhood. It consisted of a rectangle, roughly two hundred yards by eighty, framed by the previously mentioned paragons of turn-of-the-century residential respectability. Behind them and directly in front of me lay an intricate patchwork of variously sized gardens and terraced lawns, enclosed by high, weathered brick walls. In some gardens there were picturesque arbours and summerhouses. Others were fully overgrown, with platoons of climbing plants creeping over the dividing walls into adjacent gardens. Where feasible, miniature ponds had been laid out, tokens of the current fad for environmental awareness – only now squadrons of neurotic urban flies hovered over them. There were also rare varieties of trees, grossly overpriced bamboo sunshades, neoclassical terracotta flowerpots with reliefs of copulating Greeks, batteries of environmental rubbish bins, beds bristling with marijuana plants, plastic sculptures – in short, anything that might be considered the heart's desire of a well-to-do property owner who didn't know what else to do with the money he saved by cheating on his income tax.

Joining company with the above were the sort of garden idylls you would expect to see in the grounds of a tacky Florida motel. These ghastly scenes were obviously the work of people whose hunger for fashionable trends could be satisfied entirely by a visit to Woolworths.

The situation was a little different on our patch. A rickety balcony with a hopelessly rusted railing hung directly underneath me, under the bathroom window, about two feet above the ground. The balcony could only be reached through the bedroom, though I anticipated that the bathroom window would serve as my customary gateway to the outside world. Under the balcony sprawled a broad concrete terrace that looked like it doubled as the roof of a basement extension. Owing to sloppy workmanship, the terrace was shot through with cracks, and bizarre forms of vegetation jabbed up through its numerous crevices. Another rusty railing had been installed fifteen feet or so away on the edge of the terrace, to prevent unexpected late-night descents into the small garden below. In the centre of this garden, which was wholly overgrown, grew an extremely tall tree; it looked like it could have been planted in the time of Attila the Hun and was stripped bare of foliage – this was autumn, after all.

Then I spotted something else in my field of vision: an extremely unusual member of my own species.

He was squatting down in front of the terrace railing and staring down into the small garden. Although he could easily have competed with a medicine ball as far as bodily size was concerned, I noticed right away that he had no tail. Not that he was born that way – someone must have amputated that priceless part. At least, that's how it looked. He was clearly a Maine Coon, a tailless Maine Coon.[2] It is difficult for me to describe the colour of his coat, because it had the hue of a palette used by an artist on the point of a nervous breakdown. The predominant colour could definitely be said to be black, but there were shades of beige, brown, yellow, grey, and even spots of red, so that seen from behind he resembled a huge, seven-week-old bowl of fruit salad. On top of which, this strange fellow stank terribly.

I expected him to notice me soon and launch a major offensive, no doubt because his great-grandfather had once taken a crap on this very terrace, or because he had already received special permission from the High Court in a 1965 landmark case to gaze down at this wonderful garden every damn day from three to four in the afternoon. These types could be a real pain.

I decided to take the risk. What choice did I have?

As if he were some sort of living radar, he swivelled around just as I was thinking all this through, and focused on me – except 'focusing' wouldn't be quite right because he had only one eye; it looked like the other had fallen victim to a screwdriver, or been lost to disease. Where once his left eye had been there was now a shrivelled, rose-red cavity of flesh that had become uglier with the passage of time. To complete the grisly effect, the entire left side of his face sagged, probably because of partial paralysis. Needless to say this did not prevent him from posing a threat. It was clear that extreme caution was advised.

After he had looked me over from top to bottom without showing any emotion, he surprised me by turning his head away to look down at the garden again.

Since I am the soul of courtesy, I decided to introduce myself to this pathetic stranger, thinking I might be able to coax more details about my new surroundings from him.

I sprang down from the window-sill to the balcony and from there to the terrace. Slowly, and with an affected nonchalance, I strolled up to him, almost as if we had once put each other's eyes out in a sandbox fight. He took note of me with sovereign composure, not once interrupting his garden meditation to deign to look at me. Then I stood beside him and risked a sideways glance. At close range, the impression he had made on me from a distance was increased, let's say, to the power of thirty-four. In comparison to this maltreated creature, even

Quasimodo would have had a realistic chance of becoming a male model. As if what I had already witnessed was not enough for my sadly abused eyes, they then had to register that his right front paw had been mutilated. Nevertheless, he seemed to endure his frightful disabilities with a calmness so stoic and profound that he might have been suffering nothing worse than a bout of hayfever.

Apparently, these diverse disfigurements also included some inside his head, for although I had now been standing beside him for more than a minute, he had paid me not the slightest attention, choosing instead to continue staring down. Really supercool. I obliged him by lowering my own gaze to locate the spot in the garden that had cast such a persuasive spell on my confrère.

What I saw there was, so to speak, my welcoming present. Under the tall tree, half-hidden by bushes, lay a black brother with all his limbs stretched out. Only he wasn't sleeping. I couldn't imagine that he would ever engage in any activity again, not even taking a nap. He was, as people of lesser finesse might say, as dead as a doornail. More specifically, this was a member of my species whose corpse was already in an advanced stage of putrefaction. All his blood had gushed from his neck, which had been ripped to shreds, to form a large pool that was now a dry stain. Excited flies circled over him like vultures over slaughtered cattle.

The sight was a shock, but my sensitivities had been considerably blunted by everything I had already seen that day. I now cursed Gustav under my breath for the thousandth time for having dragged me into this neighbourhood of murder and bedlam. I was stunned, and hoped that this was all a dream, or at the very least one of those ingenious, animated films they sometimes make about my kind.

'Tin-opener!' the monster beside me suddenly bellowed in a voice to match his deformed appearance. It sounded like all the people in the world who had ever dubbed a John Wayne film had crackled in unison.

Tin-opener, hmm. Well, what was I supposed to say in return, not being a monster like he and not being quite in tune with the local slang?

'Tin-opener?' I asked. 'What do you mean by that?'

'Just that it was one of those damned tin-openers that did it. Yeah, they dressed up little Sascha with a hole in the neck.'

Associations spun through my mind. I tried to imagine how all this could be connected to a tin-opener – a difficult task, considering the stinking corpse below and the even stronger stench of the freak from the underworld at my side. Then I realised what he meant.

'You mean humans? Humans killed him?'

'Sure,' growled John Wayne. 'It was those fucking tin-openers.'

'Did you see it?'

'Shit, no!'

Anger and annoyance flashed across his face. Something seemed to make him lose his cool. 'Who else except for a lousy tin-opener would have done something like this? No one. Just a lousy bastard of a tin-opener who's good for nothing but opening up tins for us! Shit, yes!'

He had hit his stride. 'This is the fourth cold sack already.'

'You mean, what's down there is already the fourth corpse?'

'So you're new around here, huh?' He roared with laughter, perfectly cool again. 'You moving into that shit-heap? Nice place. It's where I always go to take a leak.'

Ignoring his laughter, deafening though it was, I sprang down from the terrace to the garden and approached the corpse. The scene was both shocking and sad. I examined the fist-sized puncture in the neck of the deceased and sniffed at it. Then I turned around to face the joker on the terrace.

'It wasn't a tin-opener,' I said. 'If tin-openers want to bump someone off, they have plenty of nifty instruments of murder at their disposal, including knives, scissors, razor-blades, wrenches and, yes, even tin-openers. But the neck of this brother has been clawed open, practically torn in half.'

The monster sneered and turned to go. But what that pathetic creature did couldn't be called walking – it was more of a mesmerising mixture of hobbling and staggering which he had perfected into an athletic discipline.

'Who gives a damn!' he shouted defiantly, and hobbled and staggered over the next garden wall, most likely in the direction of the nearest home for the disabled. After his first few steps, however, he stopped in his tracks, turned, and leaned down towards me. 'Hey, clever bastard, what do people call you?' he asked, maintaining his cool air of unconcern.

'Francis,' I replied.

CHAPTER

—— 2 ——

T HE FOLLOWING WEEK was gloomy. The depression that came with the move hit me like a steam press and paralysed my brain. I descended into a dark valley of woe, and everything that got through to me had first to suffer its way through a murky cloud of melancholia. What did seep through gave me little reason to cheer up.

Possessed by a destructive demon, Gustav carried out his threat and really did begin renovating. His first move was to rip up the rotting parquet floor and throw the refuse into a rented skip parked in front of the house. He had actually got the idea into his head of laying a new parquet floor! I'm not joking. This is rather like a deaf-mute auditioning to replace the host of a chat show. To cut a long story short, Gustav didn't accomplish much after his daring feat of demolition: he bought an exorbitantly expensive book on floor laying, panicked when he saw how complicated the work was, and decided for the time being merrily to carry on his slum clearance holocaust. I was beginning to be afraid that, deluded as he was, the maniac would tear the whole house apart.

Finally, just what I could have predicted to him at the

beginning came true: he had to admit to himself that he couldn't manage a renovation job of such proportions. This was not only annoying but also, as usual for Gustav, tragic. In the night, I could hear my mentally deficient friend weeping quietly to himself in the army cot he had set up provisionally in the living-room.

I, too, was on the brink of tears, for the shock of seeing a murdered brother in my new neighbourhood had not exactly made it easy for me to make myself at home. Yet I decided to take a look around anyway. After the monster – whose real name I still didn't know – had disappeared, I inspected the corpse and the scene of the crime with a little more care.

One thing was sure: there hadn't been much of a fight. True, the victim had put up a strong defence, as the scuffed-up earth and bent blades of grass around the lifeless body attested, but only when he had already felt teeth ripping deep into his fur and neck. From this I deduced that the victim must have known his butcher well – so well that he must even have felt free to turn his back on him. After the surprise of the lethal bite, there had been some desperate resistance, ending after only a few seconds with the helpless victim twitching on the ground.

Something else caught my attention: at the time of death, the victim had been about to follow what is poetically termed 'the call of the wild'. Since he had not been a member of that convivial club of the happily castrated, which was itself a wonder considering how prim and proper the middle-class neighbourhood was, the scent of the wide, wide world of lust still clung to him. He had also left behind his pungent signatures here and there in the garden, evidence that he had not been able to restrain himself from engaging in a little amorous play before his murder. I gave his genitals a brief sniff. It confirmed what I had suspected. He had just attained the peak of sexual excitement.

Had he had a rendezvous with some beauty? Was she the last to admire this 'stud' while he was still alive, or was she the one who gave him the kiss of death that transformed him into a 'cold sack', as the monster had put it in his straightforward way? Considering the flaky behaviour and limitless aggression our angelic sisters show after a lovers' tryst, that would hardly have surprised me.[3] But it was still too early to draw any conclusions before more details were known on the three other corpses that that crippled John Wayne look-alike had so generously mentioned.

A day later, Gustav discovered the corpse, which had already begun to stink terribly, made a great many infantile declarations of grief, and then buried the body on the spot where he found it.

But what did I care about this Raymond Chandler crap, about this Jack the Ripper who produced one 'cold sack' after another? Didn't I have enough problems? In the next room my companion was weeping over his inability to decipher the cryptography of a sixty-pound manual on the art of laying a floor; and as far as I was concerned, I had more than enough to do fighting off fits of depression in this filthy hole of a flat.

Yet, as always in life, after a while everything got straightened out. It got straightened out in a nerve-racking way, but it got straightened out. And as always in Gustav's crises, rescue came in the person of Archie.

Archibald Philip Purpur is, as he likes to call himself and as others like to call him, an optimist. Although a tiny pinch of pessimism wouldn't do this magnanimous man any harm, Archie can't and simply won't be a child of sadness. Wherever he is and whatever he does, Archie seeks and collects trends, intellectual fashions, and 'life experiences' with great enthusiasm. No one quite knows what this marvellous man does for a living, nor even what he is doing or what kind of a trip he happens to be on at any given moment. And yet everyone knows Archie and can reach him whenever they want. There is nothing whatsoever, really and truly nothing, that Archie has not been through in his awesome life.

If after years and years you should happen to dig out your

dusty old Woodstock album to indulge in memories of those sweet patchouli days, before you know it, good old Archie will be around with something to say on the subject. He'll take a yellowed festival ticket from his wallet and proudly show it around. If you don't believe it, you can even see a younger Archie – complete with ponytail – passing around a hash pipe in one scene of the famous film. As far as I know, he has a sworn statement from Mick Jagger that he was present at the recording session of 'Sympathy for the Devil' and uhh-uhh'ed in the uhh-uhh chorus. Primal scream therapy? Old hat for Archie. He already screamed his primal scream ages ago, discovered during a reincarnation experience that in a former life he had been Valentino's house pansy, and happened to arrive at Poona just in time to put the Bhagwan's teachings into writing. These, as everyone knows, sell millions of copies nowadays. Archie was one of the first organic farmers to bake his own bread, and he was also one of the first to take his girlfriend's temperature for natural birth control. We had just found out what 'punk' meant when Archie surprised us with his new Mohican haircut, guzzling down copious amounts of canned beer and doing his best to belch out full sentences. Did anyone say that surfing was in? No doubt Archie was already riding the waves off Malibu on a surfboard that the Beach Boys had immortalised with their signatures. From hippie life on Crete to yuppie stress in SoHo, from coca-leaf chewing to Calvin Klein jeans, Archie had already done it and much, much more – except perhaps joining the NASA boys for their moon landing, which, to be honest, does disappoint me a little.

Actually, the question is not whether Archie has ever missed out on anything in life, but whether he even exists. Because everything that he appears to be seems to be merely appearance. Since he obviously owes his existence to the imagination of a fashion-magazine editor, you inevitably become suspicious that Archie disappears into thin air the moment you turn your back on him. In the final analysis, Archibald is empty through and through, a non-person trying to forget the abysmal emptiness in himself through incessant trend-setting. Nevertheless, he is Gustav's best friend and helps him whenever he can – and, believe me, he always can.

On the fourth day after demolishing the kitchen, Gustav called up Archie and discussed the state of affairs with him. Five minutes later Archie stood in the bomb crater that Gustav insisted on calling our home and drew up a plan of action. This time around the chameleon had transformed himself into Sonny Crocket of *Miami Vice* and constantly toyed with the plastic cord of his new shades. As expected, he proved to be an authority not only on laying parquet floors but also on everything else to do with renovation. Despite the danger that the final product would be a hotchpotch of ultra-modern baubles and gewgaws, Gustav agreed to let Archie be the boss while he acted as errand boy. He had no other choice. The two of them got to work the very next day to start the actual renovation of Hotel Higgledy-Piggledy.

A dreadful, never-ending pandemonium of hammering, drilling, rattling, cracking, crashing and clattering surrounded me from then on, which did not exactly help me get over my depression. Quite the contrary. Although Gustav had put a huge old ghetto-blaster in the bedroom where I dozed most of the time away and although he played my favourite music, Mahler's 'Resurrection Symphony', I just couldn't escape my dismal state of mind.

I ventured out on to the terrace just once, but that was enough to land me promptly in the middle of another hopelessly stupid situation. A heap of flesh and bones, pretty well advanced in years, strolled up and down the garden wall and watched with sad eyes as birds he would now never be able to catch fluttered high up in the branches of the tall tree. He had gone completely grey, and had that hate-filled expression that nearly all of the old assume when they realise that time will soon run out for them: an expression of unadulterated envy. Envy of the young, of youth, of all that he once was and could no longer be. I asked myself whether I too would be like that some day, a question that perfectly matched my mood. To smell poorly, to see poorly, to hear poorly, to have poor memories of long-past sexual adventures. Oh, how sad life was! You were born, visited a couple of boring cocktail parties, and then you were already gasping out your dying breath.

But gramps over there on the garden wall seemed to want to set me right. As soon as his ageing eyes sighted my humble person he let loose a string of murderous invective as if someone had stamped on his tail. His entire personality suddenly seemed to be charged with something like divine energy. He was downright electrified, fired up with even more hate and enmity than before.

'This here is my fucking patch,' began the doddering old fool. 'Did you hear me, you scum? My patch! My patch! My patch!' and so on, as if he were an over-wound talking doll. Then he puffed himself up and ran up to me.

Before things came to a confrontation, I sprang from the terrace directly on to the window-ledge. He halted in the middle of the terrace to enjoy his triumph.

And once again the old parrot babbled on: 'My patch! My patch . . .'

I was now completely fed up with the new neighbourhood.

'Take your patch and shove it where the worms will soon be gathering!' I told him, and strolled back into the flat through the bathroom window. It would have been a cinch for me to have given that old fool the beating he so well deserved. But why should I? What would have been the point? The world was a vale of sorrows, and anyone who failed to realise this and worried about something as meaningless as territorial boundaries was a sad clown indeed.

What else could I do in these hostile and ugly surroundings except creep back once again to that mausoleum of a bedroom and nod off to the soothing sounds of the divine Mahler . . .

. . . and dream.

It was a bizarre, really haunting dream. I dreamed I was strolling leisurely through our new home, which – wonder of wonders – Gustav and Archie had finally finished doing up. But the result of their labour was more than just peculiar. As if in a funeral parlour, jet-black velvet curtains covered all the walls, and gloomy lamps, far from illuminating the rooms, made them seem even darker. The furniture seemed to date from the time of some eccentric French king, and had been lacquered either in black or in the darkest of shades. Black silk scarves were draped over the bed and sofas, and even the small accessories – vases, ashtrays, ceramic figures, picture frames – which every house needs to become a home bore the colour of death. In short, it looked like an extravagant family tomb, right down to the raven-black marble tiles.

I was standing in the hall and had an unobstructed view of the living-room through an open door; need it be said that the living-room had also been given the 'black magic' touch? Gustav and Archie were dressed ceremonially in tuxedos and were dining at an oversized black marble table. They were surrounded by innumerable huge candelabras, with thousands of flickering candles casting a ghostly glow on their faces. Using costly silver cutlery, whose shrill tinkling echoed into infinity, the two of them toyed with black, fur-covered clumps on their plates. They cut small, shiny bites out of this indefinable mass, and gracefully conducted them to their mouths. When they noticed me, they stopped, turned towards me, and stared at me with vacant expressions.

At that very moment the flat door flew open and slammed against the wall, letting in a strong gust of wind. I heard a strange sound, a mixture of wailing and weeping, which seemed to come from far away.

I tiptoed to the door and tried to determine the direction from which the weeping came. Although it sent a shiver up my spine, I couldn't resist the temptation to follow it. Some unfathomable impulse, part morbid curiosity and part suicidal courage, made me slip out into the gloomy hallway and creep very slowly up the rotting wooden staircase.

My heart pounded frantically in fear, and when at the half-way point the staircase made an abrupt 180-degree turn to the right I nearly returned to the flat. Something was extremely odd: the higher I climbed the stairs, the brighter the dark stairwell became.

Finally I got to the first floor, where I found myself in front of a half-open door. A glittering light poured out from the door-way on to the stairs, and made everything as bright as day. The strangely distorted howling became louder and stronger.

Now that I had come this far, it seemed my fate to have to trudge on into this white nightmare, so I mustered my pitiful reserves of courage and entered the flat. Unlike the one below, it consisted of only one large hall – no, not really a hall, but a simple nothing, a blinding white nothing. I found myself in an otherworldly realm of whiteness in which neither borders nor dimensions seemed to exist. Now and then, glowing points of light blinked in the distance like mysterious stars in a white universe. I was just beginning to focus on the outlines of objects that looked like bits of highly complicated technical equipment when they became moving silhouettes that vanished from view after only a few seconds. Through all this whiteness echoed a whining voice, intense and piercing, and suddenly I realised that the heart-rending pleas for mercy were being made by one of my kind.

In the midst of this strange scene, a man in a long white coat suddenly appeared out of nowhere. What terrified me, however, was not his abrupt appearance: when he turned his head towards me, I saw that he had no face.

He held something in one hand that looked like a leash or a collar, and it shot out even brighter flashes of light than the gleaming stars around it. Fascinated by the strangeness of my own dream, I approached the man without a face, who had begun swaying the gleaming collar back and forth like a pendulum. Then, in a gentle voice that could have belonged to the gentlest of angels, he began to speak. It was a captivating male voice, as smooth as the finest silk, as pleasant sounding as a chord struck on a harp. Although my deepest instincts shuddered at this unreal voice, I was all too eager to let myself be hypnotised and do what it commanded.

'Come here, my little one,' the man with no face said seductively. 'Just come over here to me and see what a nice thing I have for you.'

I remained standing in front of him and stared upwards, mesmerised. In his hand glittered a silver collar studded with thousands of shining diamonds. I had never seen anything so extravagantly beautiful. I detest collars, and I adamantly refuse to wear one. But this collar was tantamount to a revelation. The radiance of the diamonds dazzled my eyes so much they began to hurt. The man with no face bent smoothly down to me and held the collar in front of my nose.

'Well, what do you think of this?' he said softly. 'It really is a splendid piece, isn't it? Wouldn't it please you to wear it? Look, I'll just give it to you. Just like this . . .'

And before I could utter a sound he circled my neck with the treasure and snapped the lock shut. Then, while I was still trying to comprehend my stroke of luck, everything around me darkened. At first the whiteness turned grey, and then, very gradually, black. Only then did I notice that a rusty chain was attached to the collar, and that the man with no face held one end in his hand. As the profound gloom gathered around us and all the glittering stars died out, he pulled tightly on the chain. The collar had turned into a noose, tightening around my neck and choking my windpipe.

I resisted, cried out, tried to escape the man with no face. But that made everything much worse, because my resistance only tightened the noose. Within seconds I was out of air and in panic began to flail. But the man with no face only jerked the chain more tightly towards him and pulled me up so high that I lost the floor under my feet, my throat throbbing in pain.

Gasping, and aware that I would die soon, I sought his face in the dark, ungodly emptiness where it should have been. Suddenly, two phosphorescent yellow eyes shone out. They were the eyes of one of my kind, and they were brimming with tears. Tears as thick as pearls ran down from the eyes and fell very slowly to the floor, like hot-air balloons coming in to land. Finally I knew where the weeping and crying had come from. But why was that so important now? The noose had completely throttled my windpipe, and I'd used up the little oxygen still left in my lungs. Everything around me began to dissolve, like a mosaic exploding in extreme slow motion. I died without discovering the secret of my dream.

I wanted to scream when I returned to the world of the living. But my throat was completely dry, which explained why I had dreamed of suffocation. My heart raced wildly, as if I had just taken part in a marathon, and my entire body was as cramped as if it had been through a scrap-metal press. I saw those weeping eyes before me again as clear as day. Tortured, tormented, suffering eyes. At the same time I knew they were the eyes of a murderer. But why were they weeping?

I looked around the bedroom, unsure whether Gustav and Archie had really given the room that weird cemetery look. That was silly, but it confirmed how deeply the nightmare had got under my skin. Then the horror gradually diminished. Nothing had changed. The bedroom still looked as if it were the prize-winning montage of a schizophrenic artist in household rubbish.

Although my circulation had had enough stimulation for the day, I did one of my simple but indispensable callisthenics: I stood up while yawning, curled my back, and shook out and stretched my front and back legs.[4] I was just about to begin my washing routine when an ugly head pushed its way in through the balcony door, which had been open a fraction.

You would not have expected that monster's disfigured head to be capable of revealing his no doubt exciting inner life, but now that toughened physiognomy was clearly moved by concern. Although he did everything possible to betray nothing and to act as if this was a quick, routine inspection of one of his official piss-stops, his one undamaged eye, now blinking fiercely, and his ears, flattened against the side of his head, showed his fear and uneasiness. None the less, he simulated cool lack of interest at first by not even condescending to look at me.

'Another cold sack?' I asked him, not wanting to beat about the bush.

I had caught him by surprise, but in seconds he composed himself and assumed a stoical Humphrey Bogart look.

'A cold sack,' he admitted after a brief pause.

My right back paw jerked upwards, quick as a switchblade, to scratch my neck.

'What member of our god-fearing community got it this time? Stop, wait a minute. It was a guy, wasn't it? Just like the other four corpses.'

Now he showed open astonishment.

'How the hell did you find that out?'

'Just a guess.'

I had given my neck enough treatment. I went on to my chest and cleaned the fur thoroughly with my tongue. In between, I clamped my teeth in my coat and combed through it for parasites.[5]

The monster limped into the room, snorted, then crouched down beside me with a worried expression on his face.

'This time it was good old Deep Purple who said his last goodbye. His neck looks so bad you'd think someone had used it to try out his new ice-pick. As far as I'm concerned, they could have turned that shit-for-brains into dog food, but all these stiffs are beginning to give me the jitters. Who knows, maybe the bloke with the strange hobby will some day have the pleasure of sinking his teeth into my neck.'

'Who was Deep Purple?' By now I had worked down to my tail. I bent it into a perfect U and set about licking it from the root to the tip.

'Deep Purple? A bastard who could have made the Guinness Book of Records for having the world's tightest arsehole. If nobody knew what it meant to be grouchy, then the word would have been invented just to describe him. He was strictly major league in that department. He is, I mean he was, incredibly old, but he had enough juice in his batteries to remind you day and night of our venerable code of behaviour. He was a real pain and made life hell for us with his holier-than-thou lectures.'

'Why was he called Deep Purple?'

'His owner is the exact opposite. He baptised good old Deep Purple Deep Purple because he's a heavy-metal freak. He's sort of an Easy Rider with a salary. As soon as he leaves work, he throws on this heavy leather get-up, plays one of those weird Black Sabbath oldies, tattoos a skull and crossbones on his arse, kicks in his own window with his king-size leather boots, throws empty beer cans at people's heads and, when he's finally calmed down, rolls himself one mellow joint after another and gets wrecked until he blacks out.'

'What does he do for a living?'

'Post office clerk.'

'That makes a lot of sense.'

For the grand finale of my general clean-up, I licked my front paws one after the other until they were moist, then rubbed them over my face and ears. Dealing with a case as muddled as this, I might at least keep my head clean.

'Sure. That tin-opener never did have all his marbles. Anyway, Purple always got really pissed off whenever he saw this grizzled Dennis Hopper character, even if he was a mile away. He didn't exactly conform to Purple's idea of good behaviour. But what choice did he have? You can't pick out your own tin-opener, can you? And seeing both of them together was a real horror show. On the one hand you had Deep

Purple, model of respectability, twenty-four-hour vigilante on the watch for anyone likely to leave a pool of piss on his turf. From morning to night he was on the brink of a nervous breakdown because the Born-To-Be-Wild joker never could get used to the idea of regular feeding times, and because the youth of today doesn't stick to our traditional greeting rules. On the other hand there was his freaky owner, who already has one shattered eardrum because he listened to the new Motley Crue CD through headphones with the volume all the way up.'

'Let me ask you a question. Was Deep Purple castrated?'

'Purple? Castrated? Christ, that freak would sooner have become a dyed-in-the-wool Frank Sinatra fan than have his little darling castrated. But Purple never got into fun and games. Like I said, he was about as old as an oak tree, only he looked a lot older.'

He stood up, turned his back on me and, lost in thought, looked up at the sky through the filmy window of the balcony door.

'Strange,' he said sadly. 'Now I feel sorry for both of them. Although you couldn't have got two more different types than that uptight tosser and that phony heavy-metal freak, they must have liked each other some way or other, seeing as they'd been together so long. Yeah, they were the odd couple, Deep Purple and the post office clerk. What's this tin-opener going to do now without Purple? Is he going to find himself a new housemate? And what kind of name is he going to give him? Judas Priest?'

I had an uneasy suspicion about Deep Purple's identity. After I had finally finished cleaning myself, I turned to the monster, whose burst of unexpected talkativeness had come to an end.

'Where's Deep Purple's corpse now?'

'In Peter Fonda's garage. Do you want to go on with your clever investigation?'

'If you have nothing against it. How about showing me where it is?'

'Why not,' he said, yawning. His inimitable coolness had

29

returned, as if the preceding fit of melancholy had been a sign of weakness that now had to be concealed under a cloak of silence. He turned to go, but before he could quite get into gear, I caught up with him with a smart leap and looked deep down into his one uninjured eye, the eye that sparkled all the more brightly because it was the only one he had left.

'You never did tell me your name, clever bastard,' I said. He smiled wearily, then brushed lightly past me and through the balcony door.

'Bluebeard,' he said outside. 'But don't ask me who my tin-opener is or I might have to puke.'

I followed my limping monarch out on to the balcony, and from there down to the terrace with a big leap. Autumn had made considerable advances in the last few days, coating the picturesque garden with a morbid sheen. Like an invisible vampire, it had sucked all the green out of the trees and other vegetation, turning them into yellowish-brown, bloodless ruins. The sky was overcast with ominous, lead-coloured clouds, between which the setting sun cast a few pale, reddish bars of light on our gentle, tranquil neighbourhood. A fresh wind had come up, swirling the dead heaps of dry fallen leaves over the precisely mown lawns, between the gaps in the rotting garden sheds, and into the artificial ponds. Everything seemed to be making preparations for the big death, for the deep sleep from which there would, I hoped, be a new awakening.

Now we were strolling along the winding network of walls that separated the numerous gardens from one another and that from a bird's-eye view must have looked like a maze. Bluebeard was hobbling laboriously along in front of me, like one of those absurd toy-shop contraptions that do nothing but perform funny-looking motions. His tailless rear was in full view, and I could witness for myself the splendour of his virility swinging perkily back and forth between his thighs. It was almost a miracle that his family jewels had not been included in his voluminous collection of disfigurements.

The longer I trotted along behind this proud invalid and had to contemplate the damage done to him, the more insistent became the question of who or what had done it. Accidents, particularly car accidents, are the most frequent cause of death for my kind. A false reaction, a faulty calculation while crossing the street, or a sudden fright followed by mindless flight across a road and in no time your intestines are stamped into a tyre tread. Very few survive their spectacular first-hand encounter with a Mercedes-Benz or Golf. And, as for those who do, do they look like this?

I had often had the opportunity of witnessing such accidents and their consequences. As a rule, the victims can be divided up into three categories. Ninety-nine per cent die on the spot, to bequeath posterity nothing more than an unsavoury, scarcely recognisable self-portrait on asphalt. The second category of collision candidates only have very close calls, but are initiated into the mysteries of concussion for the better part of a week until they recuperate with completely changed views on progress and technology. The worst fate befalls the third category. They have to submit to the torture of depressing disfigurements, or of even more depressing psychological traumas, usually leading to a premature death. In all these cases the only winners are vets and dog lovers – the latter because they once again have an opportunity to make cynical remarks on the intelligence of my kind.

But what perverse car accident could have ended with a punctured eyeball, a cleanly amputated tail, and a mutilated right front paw? An accident as involved as that could only have been dreamed up by an exceedingly cunning scriptwriter. But my own imagination had wings, and naturally I couldn't help but think of another explanation (though I wished I hadn't) – that Bluebeard's disfigurements weren't caused by a car accident but by a sadist, a thoroughly insane tin-opener. Since sadists rarely possess surgical skills, they tend to torture the victims of their insanity in a crudely unprofessional manner.

As much as I tried to concentrate on finding a logical explanation for Bluebeard's condition, I couldn't arrive at any plausible conclusion. Of course, I could have simply asked him about it, but I had gradually learned to appreciate the obstinate ways of my companion and I didn't think he would tell me what had really happened. I knew that it would be a long time before I would be initiated into his medical history.

In the meantime, we had gone a long way from the house, which had now disappeared behind walls and trees. We had reached the centre of the square and were thus on foreign soil, which I admit did frighten me a little, since I could well picture how my amiable brothers and sisters would deal with intruders on their patch. Like an escaped convict, I kept glancing left and right, expecting at any moment to see one of my kind going psychotic at the sight of my humble self. Despite my fear, I memorised the topography of the neighbourhood because I had to assume that it would be my home from now on.

While my eyes shifted back and forth in my state of increasing paranoia, I was able to take a good look through the back windows of the old houses. Time and again it was the same familiar story. . . and the same familiar feelings welled up at the sight of warm, golden windows illuminated by the setting sun, bright rectangles in the dusk, radiating trust, security, confidence, love. A whole impossibly perfect world. You really could imagine the entire family assembled around a massive oak table having supper, the children chattering away all at once, the father occasionally making an off-colour joke, at which his wife would admonish him not to make remarks like that when the children were around. And you, you were there too, waiting under the table for someone in the family, or maybe all of them, to hand you a choice titbit. It was Christmas behind these windows flushed with the glow of sunset, forever Christmas!

Naturally that nasty, wrinkled, little old man who always makes himself heard in my mind when I get too sentimental then told me the truth – that no such thing as Christmas had ever existed. Sitting around behind those windows were the same old ordinary, flaky people with their flaky opinions and their flaky lives. It was the same familiar story: some boring marriage crisis, someone fooling around with someone else, some recent, successfully concluded divorce, some abused child, some tumour whose surprising appearance out of nowhere some old fatherly GP would confirm when the lab test results came back, some hopeless loser with alcohol problems, some eternally lonely people, some miserably pathetic suicide attempt that failed as usual, someone weeping and bawling about life's missed opportunities, some hysterical laughter at the bad jokes of a bad comedian on the telly with a smile so wide you could count his false teeth – the same familiar, stupid, meaningless, laughable things. No, it wasn't a Frank Capra film being staged behind those windows, but the same old shabby commercial urging you to go on living while not naming one single reason why.

Suddenly, behind a gable window that looked like it had been filched from a cathedral, I saw an animal. I admit that it may sound grotesque for me to use the word *animal* in referring to my kith and kin. But it took only one glance for me to see that the strange creature at the window of one of those old buildings that had been renovated beyond recognition had only the remotest relation to my kind. He was very young, nearly a baby, so that even his more dominant markings were hard to distinguish. A layman would have thought right away that he was a member of our universally liked family of Felidae, and probably the family that had given him a place to live had thought so, too. He had bright, sand-coloured fur, and tiny, flat ears. The head was perfectly round and the body thick-set. Most fascinating, however, were the eyes. Like twin suns, they glowed in the dark, as if waiting for something very special to happen. His bushy tail knocked again and again at the window-pane, but otherwise he was as motionless as a statue. Then a light went on in the room from which the animal was calmly watching us. He sprang down from the window-sill and was lost from sight.

This encounter had me so spellbound that I nearly recoiled in fright when, right in front of us on the wall, two slimebuckets appeared. These two were to give me a lot of trouble in the future.

They were typical of the nasty delinquents who typically stand around on street corners, creatures whose mission in life it is to pester innocent people day and night, take every possible opportunity to raise hell, and get into gory brawls – but only when they involve opponents weaker than themselves. The greater part of their intellect, to the extent that they can be said to have one, is concerned only with how they can best bring ruin to themselves and others. These two were rat-faced, wily looking, oriental Shorthair mutants who no doubt got their kicks by swiping meals from the bowls of others and crapping on expensive carpets. Cowardly and psychopathic at the same time, one more loutish, more repulsive than the other. The cleverer of the two was so cross-eyed that he probably saw what was going on in the world 180 times; crossed eyes are a distinctive genetic defect that says more about character than any scientific study. The other sleazeball had a silly, crooked grin that probably reflected his sense of humour.

They stood facing us on top of the wall blocking our way. And – does a bear shit in the woods? – they immediately went into battle positions. The two sleazeballs stared at us and made offensive sounds. Their ears stood up as straight as candles. Their pupils narrowed. And their tails, as thin and elongated as stove pipes, whipped tightly around their bodies.

Bluebeard stopped, yawned, looked past them, and acted as if they were an obstacle of no greater concern than a dog turd.

'Well, I'll be damned,' he said with a smile that was almost congenial, 'Herrmann and Herrmann, the two merry arsewipers at our service. What a pleasure to chance upon such great friends. Now, don't tell me you're going to rave to me all over again about the benefits of castration? I believe you, boys, you don't have to say a word. Lot less weight without balls, right?'

They looked at each other nervously from the corners of their eyes while snarling and growling ever louder. Looking down from the wall, Bluebeard let out a side-splitting guffaw.

'Kong,' he challenged. 'Why for God's sake do you still put up with these miserable wimps? They're just making you look bad. Still, maybe a couple of eunuchs are pretty good company when there's nothing on the box.'

A grim laugh rang out from a berry bush directly under the wall, a 'you really have a big mouth' kind of laugh.

'Bluebeard, you old basket case,' said an intentionally insulting voice from the bush, 'I can see you've been out with the bum-chums last night. The sweet things can't leave you in peace, can they? The little runt behind you *is* a gorgeous specimen. Is he teaching you how they do it?'

'No, but he could show you. He knows the ideal position for all three of you.'

Suddenly, a beast as big as a deep-freeze shot out of the berry bush and landed right in front of us. He was truly the largest, most awe-inspiring brother I had ever come across. One is inclined to ascribe the character traits of the engagingly silly Persians to Colourpoints,[6] but this satanic mammoth put every stereotype description to shame. The name Kong hit the nail on the head. A black head the size of an overripe watermelon grew out of his dirty-white coat, which had probably never seen a comb and, like the coats of most long-haired clowns, was hopelessly knotted. The azure-blue eyes, the tiny ears, the snub nose – indeed, every normally visible sense organ and limb – were all but invisible in a gigantic furry ball of filth and noxious stench, making it hard to discern Kong's intentions.

The two orientals humbly took a few steps back, making room for their master. Kong fixed us the while with his piercing gaze before giving out a booming laugh, which seemed to make not only the garden walls but the entire universe tremble. My brave Long John Silver, however, gave no sign of being impressed, and looked him in the face with a successful combination of impassive disdain and cool superiority.

'Has it escaped your attention that certain laws and regulations with respect to territories are in force, my crippled friend?' asked the giant.

Unmoved, Bluebeard yawned for a long, long, long time.

'Kong, don't act as if a play-pen gangster like you would let crap like territories get on your nerves. Let's cut the bullshit and get down to business. The way I see it, you're looking for a fight. OK, you can have one. But I don't think I'm the reason why you're itching for a scrap. As you will remember, up to now we have had only one difference of opinion from which you, if I recall correctly, came away with some irreparable damage to your sweet behind. It's true you were only a little runt then, and every time your owner gave you a pat you'd piss in his hand in sheer delight. But like I said, in case you have any complaints, I'm ready any time of day to cure you of them. But I suppose that you're more interested in my friend Francis than in me. If that's so, then you'd better know that I'm not going to watch an unfair fight without taking action. So think first before you do something you or your rear end may regret later, not to mention those two circus acts behind you.'

While my friend was talking, Kong got so angry it seemed as if his body doubled in size. And it looked as if a chemical trick had transformed the blue of his eyes into red, blood red. In fact, he gave the impression that he was going to explode at any moment and take all of the witnesses in this tense encounter with him. As for me, it hadn't taken long to realise that this piece of turd was the undisputed despot of the district. I had had more than enough of his kind. I had never been anywhere where there wasn't some arrogant headcase who fucked the ladies until they dropped dead, who solved the dental problems of others by brute force, thanks to the muscular strength Mother Nature had endowed him with, and who unselfishly applied his entire energy to making life even more difficult than it already was for the peaceful and law abiding. Yet for some reason, even dictators know their limits. Bluebeard was one such limit. It wasn't quite clear to me why someone like Kong, who had in excess all that his opponents lacked, would be afraid of a poor cripple like Bluebeard. But suddenly Kong chuckled roguishly, as if the whole business had only been an April Fool's prank. 'Heh, heh, heh,' he bawled, 'I'm so afraid I'm wetting my pants, my friend. The mighty force of your front stump is a world legend. Just don't worry about the two of us missing out on a little dance. When the time comes, our account will be settled, just like all accounts are settled sooner or later.'

Then he turned to me and gave me a cold stare.

'And as for you, sweetie, you can bet your right paw that we're going to have a very entertaining conversation between ourselves in the not-too-distant future, a conversation you'll remember for a long, long time. And so until then, my friends . . . ' he said, then jumped down from the wall. Both of his rat-faced lackeys followed him, and slunk away into the bushes.

Without giving them so much as a glance, Bluebeard left immediately. But I chuckled softly to myself.

'Hey!' I called after him. He stopped in his tracks and turned around.

'I'm afraid you seem to be forgetting your own principles.'

'Is that so? And how, if I may ask?'

'You told them I'm your friend.'

Then . . . I was astonished by what I saw in Peter Fonda's garage. Deep Purple lay stretched out on the wild postal clerk's carefully polished Harley-Davidson, gazing at the ceiling with wide-open eyes. He lay stiff on his back and had all four limbs extended as if he wanted to demonstrate the most extreme gymnastic position of which he was capable. My premonitions were spot on. Good old Deep Purple turned out to be the aggressive geezer of the previous day who had insisted so vehemently on the inviolability of his patch.

As soon as we approached the back of the garage, we saw a long, irregular trail of blood smears and drops left behind in the garden.

In my opinion, the last minutes of his life must have passed as follows: someone bit Deep Purple several times in the neck while he sat on the boundary wall of his territory. Then he plummeted from the wall into the garden. But he did not die immediately, and that was remarkable for his age. Once the murderer had convinced himself that his handiwork had been effective and had gone on his way, something happened that was nearly a miracle. Despite his great loss of blood, Purple apparently regained consciousness and gave some thought to his place of death. Whether this was the reason for what happened next, or whether it was only mental confusion, in any case Purple partly crept and partly staggered back to his home, to the postal clerk whom he loved (and hated) more than anyone else in the world. Arriving at the rear of the garage (which had a rickety, do-it-yourself look), he faced his most difficult obstacle, because he could only enter through a tiny opening where some bricks had fallen out, just under the corrugated iron roof. And so Deep Purple made a risky leap for the last time in his life. He jumped from a standing position nearly seven feet high, five times his body length. And he succeeded. He squeezed himself through the opening, let himself drop into the garage, pulled himself up on his legs, and limped to the Harley. Racked by pain, he climbed up on the machine and gazed drunkenly around from the newly waxed leather seat.

Meanwhile he had become cold, so cold that he thought he would never be warm again. He did not understand what had happened and why it had happened. Or did he? Had he made a mistake? Did he know the reason behind the blood-thirsty attack? Might he have known his bestial murderer?

Questions . . . questions upon questions that very likely would never be answered.

Suddenly he fell over. Like an elephant shot down in the savannah, Deep Purple collapsed on the black leather and stretched out all four limbs.

'I saw the trail of blood in the garden and followed it,' said Bluebeard.

Seen from below, the motorcycle resembled an Indian burial mound on which Purple lay like a legendary, fossilised chief. I jumped up on the saddle and looked the corpse over closely. It was puzzling how the old buzzard could have managed to come this far with a huge, gaping wound in his neck. Not only his neck, but also his entire head now looked like a wrung-out, blood-soaked dish-cloth. Apparently he had fallen several times along his path to Golgotha and rolled in his own blood, for his coat was covered with crimson stains.

But Bluebeard had once again overlooked something, namely the most important detail of this horrific still life.

I turned away from Purple and looked with reproach at my limping friend.

'He wasn't above fun and games,' I said.

'What do you mean?'

'As old as he was, he still wanted to immortalise himself.'

'Immortalise himself?'

'Well, have children.'

'What? Purple and screwing? Now I've heard everything. You might as well tell me he held an orgy here every night. It's out of the question. At his age, most people would be happy if they could read the word *erection* with two eyeglasses and a magnifying glass, let alone delight the ladies with one.'

'Come up here and see for yourself.'

'No thanks. Today is the only day in the month when I get liver. And I'm not wild about having my appetite ruined by a dead, dirty old man. Besides, it's pretty damned hard for me to waste even one tear over a bastard like him.'

Yet I could see that something was bothering him: 'You really believe that Purple was a secret one-man breeding machine? That's too much, just too much. The world is crazier than I thought.'

Why, I asked myself, should he think that? And what in fact was the mysterious connection between the murder victims – if indeed any connection existed at all? Thoughts spun wildly through my mind like electrons around a nucleus. Nevertheless, a disciplined procedure had to be followed, and all the clues had to be put in the correct sequence. The most prominent characteristic of the murders was the fact that they were sex related. Of course, I couldn't completely disregard the possibility that this was a psychotic murderer killing at random, but the psycho theory was unlikely. Psychotics don't really exist in the animal realm, and if they do, then they don't get very far; they usually enter the eternal happy hunting grounds right after childhood. On the other hand, it could have been pure coincidence that the bogeyman had so far struck out only at randy brothers. If, however, it was no coincidence, then someone either (A) had something against screwing in general, (B) was himself horny and had strange views on competitive fighting in territories, or (C) did not want a very special lady to be coveted by others.

In the end, after thinking it over, I had to admit to myself that it was so senseless there had to be a psychotic at large.

'I still think that it had to be a bastard tin-opener,' Bluebeard growled below. 'Shit yes. I mean, for what idiotic reason would one of ours make such an awful mess? You don't have a logical explanation either, do you? That disgusting shit would probably have kicked it in a month anyway, whether he could still have got it up or not.'

'Well, I'm dealing with the same mystery as you are. But let's not kid ourselves. This bloody hole we're looking at is a wound caused by a bite, not an ice-pick. Anyway, it looks like it's high time for me to find out more about our local disaster area and its godforsaken inhabitants. And you can help me in this regard, Bluebeard.'

'Oh, and will I, Inspector?'

'Sure you will, if it's as important to you as it is to me that this nightmare come to an end. So, how shall we proceed?'

'Well, I'll introduce you to someone. He knows what's going on here better than I do. Besides, he wasn't exactly born yesterday. You're not the only clever bastard in this fucked-up neighbourhood of retards, you know.'

'Right now?'

'Hell, no. I've had enough of playing detective for today. Besides which, I don't want to miss my rendezvous with that liver. First thing tomorrow morning, you can meet the Professor.'

I jumped down from the motorcycle seat, stood beside Bluebeard, and looked up once again at Deep Purple. He seemed like a sacrificial victim, butchered in honour of an evil demon on an altar consecrated with blood and lightning. Placating the spirits was what it was called. Blood still seeped down over the chrome of the bike and dripped into a pool that was already drying at the edges. Looking at Deep Purple now, I felt sorry for him. I imagined that he had given many, particularly humans, pleasure and joy – not only through what he did but also because of what he was. He should have had a better death. Probably a better life, too. But wasn't that true for all of us?

CHAPTER

—— 3 ——

IN THE NIGHT I HAD two more nightmares. Only during the second one, I was wide awake . . .

After the bizarre post-mortem examination, Bluebeard and I went our separate ways, and I returned home in a thunderstorm that had just broken out. The torrential rain and fierce lightning had scared all the locals away from the gardens so that I was spared a further confrontation with Kong and company.

On this subject, allow me to make an admission so that I may be spared the reproach of snobbery or of being a know-all: thunder and lightning scare the hell out of me, too. And not without cause. People, particularly those in the industrialised part of the world, tend to see nature in terms of the 'noble savage'; witness the attitude to the Indian, whom the white man poisoned with his gift of alcohol. They regard the manifold forces of nature as old-fashioned side-show effects that at best inspire feelings of contemplative awe. This, however, is a mistake that only certain soft-headed beings are capable of making, beings whose knowledge of nature is limited for the most part to glossy photos from *National Geographic* or to certain repeats of that imperishable television series *All Creatures Great and*

Small. But Mother Nature is in reality a bloodthirsty witch who has evil in store, and never mind technology and its marvellous accomplishments. Even today, most of those who suffer a violent death die from the terrorist attacks of nature. Every year nearly seven thousand people throughout the world – not to mention all those things that creep and fly, the so-called 'animals' – are electrocuted by lightning. My kind acts with great prudence by hiding under beds and dressers when the meteorological toughs are on the march. May the unsuspecting fool joyfully take pleasure in 'nature's unfolding drama'; I would rather run to my hiding-place under Gustav's dresser and watch in safety from there as God's thunderbolts strike the skulls of those who should know better, turning them into gigantic fried chicken nuggets.

At home, the renovation war had ended for the day. Archie had disappeared into thin air, and I caught Gustav standing in the middle of the living-room like a hypnotised rabbit, taking in the destruction the two of them had wreaked. The rooms had been completely stripped of their netherworld character, and now looked, so to speak, as if they could at last rest in peace. Aside from the walls, not much remained of the stately old pigsty. The two merciless tyrants had dispersed all the insect colonies, much as the Israelites had once been driven from Jerusalem. In the process, entirely disregarding the need for the likes of me to enjoy a bit of light entertainment now and then, they had made scores of proud little rodents homeless. The one good thing about the whole business was that the flat now looked incredibly clean. At least they had managed that.

After Gustav had fixed up something for me to eat (a clever mixture of lightly sautéed liver morsels and tinned food), he went to bed early. He had slaved the whole day away like a miner, and began snoring the minute his head hit the pillow. I followed his example and got into bed myself. At this point, there's no way I'm going to mention for the umpteenth time the scientific reason why my kind sleep away sixty-five per cent of

44

our lives and why we are therefore exceptions in this age of workaholics and early risers. Suffice it to say (and this, too, in accord with scientific studies) that though people who stay in bed may not be the most successful people on God's earth, you're less likely to meet a genius among the early birds.

Since Gustav had finally prevailed upon himself to turn up the heat, it was now warm and cosy in the bedroom, and I immediately slid off into a deep sleep.

I dreamed that I was once again in that gruesome garage. This time, however, Deep Purple was not flat on his back but fully alive, and sat upright like a human on the seat of the Harley-Davidson. A powerful fountain of blood shot up in the air in a vertical column from the huge wound in his neck, then splashed down again, covering him and the motorcycle. It was a terrifying sight, such as you might see in a horror version of a champagne ad.

A sardonic smile spread over the face of the zombie-like geezer, and he gesticulated wildly with his front legs.

'This here is my damn patch!' screamed Deep Purple. 'And I can still get it up! Take a look!'

He reached over his shoulder with one paw and pulled a kitten out of his bloody neck wound. The tiny kitten was like a miniature version of its father, and it looked around blinking with fear and helplessness. Purple growled in triumph and gave the baby a powerful shake.

'And do you want to know how I can manage this? The latest, the most innovative treatment methods, my dear fellow. Spasmolysis, angiography, electrocardiography, organ transplants, fibrinolysis, injections, infusions, transfusions, needles, bandages, compresses, and and and . . . Yes indeed: medical care is the alpha and omega of old age! Nowadays, without modern medicine nothing would work!'

Suddenly he lifted the kitten in the air, the kitten that had had such a repulsive birth, and threw it like a baseball. With a dull thump, the baby hit the corrugated tin wall, leaving behind a huge bloody smear before falling lifeless to the floor. Purple broke out in hideous laughter, and thrust his hand into the wound to conjure up a fresh kitten.

'This is the way of life, this is the way of the world, my dear friend,' the cruel father said. 'If you want to live longer and still get it up at ninety-nine, then let modern medicine take care of your body.'

He threw the second child against the wall as well. It struck it hard and burst open like a balloon filled with red paint.

As if he were sitting on a turntable, Purple now began to turn around on his rump while constantly pushing his hand into the wound, pulling out new kittens, and hurling them against the garage walls like one of those machines that throw tennis balls. As his speed increased, the volume of his savage laughter rose until it finally became a roar.

'Hahahohohehe!' he cried out. 'Get them to prescribe some pills for immortality and creams for potency! For potency! For potency! For potency!'

He turned ever more quickly until he was no more than a vibrating, contourless blur out of which these pathetic kittens shot in a never-ending stream and – bam, bam, bam – slammed against the walls.

Within seconds, blood was pouring down the sides of the garage. The pile of kitten corpses on the floor grew higher and higher, giving out the cloying smell of dead flesh in a slaughterhouse. Purple's screaming gradually mixed in with a ghostly howl similar to what I had heard in my first nightmare. This time, though, the howl didn't come from just one of my kind, but from many, very many.

It was about time for me to wake up – I didn't want these gutwrenching images to do serious damage to my nervous system. And so, choking down a scream, I was once again in the bedroom. But the dream had been so vivid that the cacophony of whimpering and howling continued to echo in my ears.

I leapt up on my legs and arched my back more than I had ever done in my life – but the howling didn't stop! Just as I was considering the possibility that I had completely flipped (in keeping with the norm in this area), I realised where the howling, which all of a sudden seemed very real, was coming from. It was as in my first nightmare. The sound came from the floor directly above me and I was surprised that the noise hadn't long ago woken Gustav.

I stood there like a pillar of salt, not able to believe my own ears. Although I tried to soothe my fears by assuming that the local men's choir was serenading a female in heat, or that the gentlemen were already assembled around her, panting and howling and growling at one another, the more rational part of my mind told me that what I was hearing was nothing other than cries of pain.

What could I do? Not to follow up on the matter meant not only capitulating to fear, but possibly missing out on an important clue as regards the murders. And who said that someone upstairs wasn't being murdered, because that's what the whole commotion sounded like.

My damned, untameable curiosity! If I had to name my own worst fault, then without a doubt it's curiosity. In this world there are the most wonderful hobbies and the most unusual pursuits to enjoy. Some make detailed collections of pornographic magazines, cataloguing them according to the size of the dildoes they feature. Others study UFOs in their free time and try constantly to contact extraterrestrial beings, until one day their wish is granted and they find themselves in a clinic being asked again and again by the staff psychiatrist to describe their miraculous encounter. Many paint, only to dump their 'art' on their friends as birthday presents in the belief that people are particularly pleased to receive something made by hand. Many donate sperm. Many, very many indeed, become connoisseurs of alcoholic beverages and cultivate their knowledge in this field day after day after day . . . Oh, there are the most entertaining hobbies in the world! But it is my sorry fate to have to stick my sensitive nose into the most perilous affairs, which invariably means I end up with someone trying to beat the hell out of me.

The howling had become louder. My legs a little shaky, I slunk out into the hall. I was aware that this reconnaissance could have disastrous consequences, not least because I had no idea of the layout upstairs. On the other hand, if I remained downstairs and had to go on listening to what was happening up there, curiosity and a bad conscience would slowly but surely drive me crazy. And so I decided, with typically unshakeable resolve, to clear up the mystery even though it might spell my doom.

Since Gustav in his inimitable debility had forgotten to lock the flat door, it was easy for me to open it by raising myself up on my hind legs and pressing down on the handle with my front paws.

It was pitch black in the entrance hall. Although my eyes require only a sixth of the brightness humans need to perceive the same details of movement and shape, it was well nigh impossible to recognise anything tangible out there. But that didn't mean I couldn't make out anything at all.[7] As my whiskers vibrated softly, a diagram appeared in my mind's eye that, although blurry, was sufficient for my purposes: it consisted of varying air currents that mapped the architecture of the stairwell above.

Slowly I climbed the stairs towards the wailing sound, which was getting more and more nerve-racking. When the staircase, after curving 180 degrees, suddenly began to brighten, the way it had in my first nightmare, the strain and fear nearly made me throw up. The only difference from my dream was that no glimmering light poured through the gap around the door, only a flickering glow, which reminded me of the glow that a welding torch emits from far away. Now and then, however, even this light was lost, and it was pitch black again.

The voices were the hardest thing to bear. Almost melodious cries of pain, obeying the laws of a cruel harmony, echoed endlessly throughout the entire building, weaving in and out of one another like the voices in a Gregorian plainchant.

The repulsive chemical odour I had noticed when Gustav and I first moved into the building was back, and gradually becoming so strong that I no longer had to rely on my 'J' organ, but could smell it with my nose alone. Mixed in with it was the musty smell of empty, rotting habitations.

Now at last I stood at the door. I inched my nose around the doorjamb and risked a look inside. From then on, nothing quite took place the way it had in my nightmare – it was worse, much worse . . . The scent of hundreds of brothers and sisters came surging out at me. They were out of sight, far to the rear of the large room, and my field of vision was restricted to the dark hallway ahead. But because the door to the room was open a hand's breadth, in addition to the overwhelming smell I could hear a continuous clattering and hopping. A powerful bass now joined in with the cries of pain, and although I could understand nothing of what it said, the voice seemed to be making an important speech in solemn tones.

My God, where was I? A meeting of Jehovah's Witnesses? I asked myself what might happen if I just marched into the room, and answered my own question: nothing at all, of course, because I would rather kiss a dog than take one step into that place. The very thought of such a daring move caused my brain to leap with scenes of unimaginable horror. My curiosity no longer mattered. I was still in full possession of my mental faculties, and wouldn't dream of entering a room in which hundreds of savage beasts had gathered together only to kill each other while a priest kept them company and preached.

I was just going to pad softly away from my peep-hole when I happened to look up at the ceiling of the hallway. Over the years during which the house had slowly decayed, decent sized holes had opened up in the ceiling, through which you could see up into the next floor. Of course it was impossible to see anything through them, since the upstairs flat was cloaked in darkness.

But I guessed that the roof of the room in which the 'party' was taking place was also damaged. So I only needed to run up there to get a box seat for the eerie show on the floor below. If my assumption proved correct, then I could watch the goings-on at leisure, even treat myself to popcorn without fear of being caught by the homicidal mob on stage.

I sneaked quickly up the stairs to the top floor. To my surprise and relief, I discovered that the flat door no longer existed. The door had rotted away from its hinges and crashed to the floor, probably with the help of a strong gust of wind. That was fine as far as I was concerned, for I could slip straight in without first having to rack my brains over technical problems of entry.

Although darkness seemed to be the sole tenant here as well, I noticed immediately that the flat was more like the one in my nightmare than the one below. Every room was tiled in white, like rooms in a mental institution. Not unexpectedly, most of the tiles were shattered and covered with filth and mould, but they nevertheless gave the rooms their distinctive atmosphere. Aside from the usual indefinable rubbish that tends to collect in uninhabited premises over the years, the entire flat was empty. As for my expectations of finding an ideal observation post, they were more than satisfied. The dilapidated floor was riddled with holes. It looked like the pitted, bomb-crater landscape of a miniature world war.

As I got further inside the flat, I began to see the flickering glow of the light from below. I entered the large room, and it looked exactly the way I imagined it would. As softly as a spirit hovering over the living, I slunk to the middle of the room where the floor was punctured by a hole about a yard across, and looked down.

What I saw below could have made a photographer into a multi-millionaire overnight with just one snapshot. It was an unbelievable sight. About two hundred brothers and sisters had pushed, shoved, and squeezed into the middle of a filthy room, around the frayed wire ends of two loose electric cables. Where they met and crossed, sparks sprayed out in a wide arc. An elderly brother with white, billowing fur, who was drooling out the holy tirade I had heard earlier, kept pressing on one of the cables with his paw so that it sprang up and down, creating intermittent electrical contact. One after the other, brothers and sisters were jumping over the wires where they touched and exploded into fiery sparks. This gave them powerful shocks that scorched their fur and made them scream at the tops of their lungs. The shocks threw them to the floor, dazed and exhausted; nevertheless, some of the really demented ones apparently hadn't had enough and wanted to submit themselves to the torture all over again. But there were other mental cases standing behind them who hadn't had their laughs for the day, and they pushed aside the ones who had just been electrocuted to get to the front themselves.

'In the name of Brother Claudandus!' proclaimed the preacher to his little lambs. 'In the name of Brother Claudandus, who sacrificed himself for our sakes and who became God! Claudandus, O holy Claudandus, hear our suffering, hear our voices, hear our prayers! Accept our sacrifices!'

'Accept our sacrifices!' the congregation cried out with one voice.

'The soul of the righteous Claudandus is in the hands of the Lord, and no suffering can touch him. In the eyes of fools, he seems dead, and his end is regarded as misfortune and his departure from us as annihilation. But he is in peace!'

'Hallelujah, Claudandus is in peace!' answered the choir passionately.

They were now in perfect ecstasy. A spastic quaking and quivering seized their bodies, and they seemed to be slipping into a trance-like state. Whimpering and trembling, the mob pushed its way forwards and vaulted the glowing wires more and more quickly, ever closer to the sparks. Now the electric shocks did not even seem to matter to those who brushed the wires. On the contrary, the concentrated charge made them even more foolhardy, even more crazed. The leader of the sect pressed his paw on the cable with increasing frequency, and the electrical flashes hissing from the contact created a macabre light.

'Even if he is suffering in the opinion of all the evil people out there, his vision is immortal. His was the honour of receiving great acts of charity after only a brief initiation because the Lord tested him and found him to be worthy. Like gold in a melting furnace, he submitted to trial and the Lord accepted him as the perfect sacrificial offering. At that time he was illumined by grace and passed like a spark to his new home in heaven. He shall judge the people and rule over the nations! The Lord shall be his king for ever! Those who have confidence in him shall then discover the truth, and those who have remained faithful shall dwell with him in love; and upon the elect shall grace and mercy be bestowed.'

A hysterical wailing and yowling went through the crowd, which, like a roller-coaster car gone out of control, was now racing to the climax of the gruesome show. More and more were injured, then pushed carelessly aside by the others. *Injured* is perhaps the wrong word, because after they had received their hard-earned charge, a beatific smile lit up their faces.

'Hallelujah!' and 'Claudandus, save us!' resounded from all sides as the master's unctuous sermon insinuated itself into their deranged minds, driving them to fever pitch.

In truth, these frenzied goings-on put *The Aristocats* in the shade. A sect that paid homage to a certain Claudandus and for his sake found spiritual elevation in high-voltage electrical shocks . . . Now I'd like to see someone say that since Jacques Cousteau and David Attenborough nature has no more secrets to reveal!

Claudandus . . . A name that couldn't be more inappropriate for a saint. What was its original meaning? My knowledge of Latin had deteriorated greatly since that dreadful time when Gustav, in a financial pinch, had tutored feeble-minded O level students from a neighbourhood crammer whose thoughts were clearly more on their first onanistic adventures than on Latin. But somewhere in some cobwebbed chamber of my mind, I finally uncovered the Latin verb *claudere*, which means 'to close'. If *claudere* was the infinitive, then *claudandus* had to be the gerundive, the passive verbal adjective that expresses something that must or should be done: *claudandus*, meaning roughly 'one that must or should be closed'.

One that must or should be closed – seen in this light, it was a strange name indeed for a saint or – if the muddled speech of the preacher meant anything at all – a martyr. And what cruel and mythical tortures suffered by this ominous Claudandus could have led to the founding of a cult like this? One thing was clear to me: anyone who could act so freakishly would not treat his neighbours, his religious opponents, or especially those who would mock his beliefs, with kid gloves. This crazed mob was capable of anything, including murder.

This observation was made more plausible by a further detail that I had only gradually taken in. Since I had begun observing the scene below me, I had been seized by a strange excitement that soon had me completely agitated. It took me a while to realise that this excitement was caused not only by the bizarre scene below, but also by the chemical smell emanating from the rooms. It was very likely that the fumes could stir up my kind and intensify their emotions; I could only guess at the effect they might have on human beings. The smell was, so to speak, the gaseous counterpart of amphetamines. You could easily imagine that someone who had got high on the aggressive ceremony and was further stimulated by these chemicals would commit acts of which he would not normally be capable.

This ingenious theory could have cleared up everything automatically had it not been for one small flaw. That Kong and his fascist sidekicks Herrmann and Herrmann were among the Claudandists did not surprise me in the least. Just as flies within a radius of hundreds of miles are attracted to a pile of shit, so too would any scene of misery unfailingly attract this calamity-loving trio. It was, so to speak, their destiny to romp in ordure. And so, as expected, they were lined up in a middle row, waiting impatiently for the chance to put their recklessness and perverse piety to the test.

The one who did not fit into this horrible scene at all was Bluebeard! He crouched in the darkest corner of the room, his head swaying to and fro to the rhythm of the song and prayer. Because of his various physical handicaps, he obviously did not want to risk being overrun or squeezed to death by the squirming mass. But you could see that the hocus-pocus had him body and soul and that he too was in a trance.

This amazing sight upset my clever hypothesis to such an extent that I found myself refusing to believe that my friend Bluebeard could be a member of this bloodthirsty cult. Or had I been completely mistaken in him? Had he actually been lying to me the entire time, playing the unsuspecting bystander? I have a phenomenal gift for psychological empathy at my disposal, and maintain with good reason that I can divine the thoughts and intentions of others by a mere fleeting glance. But you can never learn enough about a world in which people surround themselves with so much mendacity that they automatically assume the truth itself is the only real lie. So unless Bluebeard had pulled a fast one on me, there could be no direct connection between the Claudandus sect and the murders. This, I admit, I now found hard to believe.

The extravagant religious service had now reached its climax. The joyful congregation leapt and skipped about playfully, breaking out into a weird singsong. It didn't surprise me that the few fragments of the song that I was able to make out concerned blood and suffering. A few, very wild members of the mob sprang over the heads of those in front of them to get to the cables even more quickly. Their screams followed in quick succession, but their inspirational old guru had everything under control and merely added a few colourful remarks.

'O Claudandus, thou son of pain and of light! Our wounds are full of blood as once your wounds were full of blood! Hear our suffering and accept our modest sacrifice!'

I was so engrossed in the contemplation of this drama that I was no longer properly mindful of the danger, and found myself leaning further and further out over the rim of the hole. Without my noticing it, my front paws had begun to press down on the crumbling rim, and all at once it gave way. Tiny stones, splinters of wood, peeling flakes of paint and cement dust showered down on the preacher's head like an avalanche of snow. Seized by terror, I jumped backwards, but it was already too late. The leader jerked his head up and spied my swiftly retreating shadow.

'There's someone up there! We're being watched! We're being watched!' he called out to the faithful, bringing the ceremony to a standstill. Hundreds of heads flicked up at the same time to try to catch sight of me through the gaping hole in the ceiling. Suddenly there was nothing I wanted so much in the world as for this circus of the absurd to be a nightmare. But the repugnant ritual bore the title 'Reality', and contrary to expectation its leading role had been awarded to none other than Yours Truly.

Pandemonium reigned below, but I had neither the inclination nor the time to find out what they were planning against me. No doubt they would be up here in a few seconds.

I looked frantically around the room. A rotten beam had come loose at one end of the room and dropped half-way to the floor. Above it was a tiny opening in the ceiling through which I might be able to squeeze myself, and so find a way into the attic. The other much more uncertain alternative was the staircase. Trying to get up to the attic that way might be time-consuming and was certainly risky, and I didn't think I had time to give it a go.

'What are you fools waiting for? Go upstairs! Bring him back!' I heard the Lord's Anointed One shout. Then came the pounding and scrabbling of hundreds of clawed paws. They were on their way.

I instinctively chose the beam. I sprang on it, digging my claws deeply into the timber. The beam gave, squeaking, and dipped lower into the room. I knew that the slightest vibration would loosen the other end of the beam from its fastening and cause it to crash down with me aboard. And then? How on earth was I going to escape from this nightmare then?

I heard frenzied thumping on the stairway. They would soon flood into the room. With as much force as I could muster, I catapulted myself up from my hind legs and actually managed at my first attempt to poke my head and front legs through the tiny hole. At the same time, the beam swung away from under me with a groaning sound and slammed down in front of the paws of the mob that had just stormed into the room.

I squeezed through the hole and found myself in the attic. A quick glance at the scene below confirmed what I had feared. After some furious curses, the hunting party ran out of the room to find a way up the stairs to the attic.

I only had time to give my new surroundings a brief examination. The room, a maze of nooks and crannies, was crammed with the remnants of Doctor Frankenstein's laboratory, whose spirit I had always sensed was lurking in the house. The countless surgical instruments with their chillingly sharp and curved blades, the operation lamps, anaesthetic equipment, electrocardiogram apparatus, hypodermics, reagent beakers, retorts, and microscopes – not to mention a number of even more complicated machines and utensils that I could hardly identify let alone guess their function – were so dusty as to be barely recognisable. Most of them were corroded, or simply broken, and yet they had lost almost nothing of their petrifying aura. I asked myself why they had been abandoned to rust slowly away. Nowadays physicians refuse to install anything in their offices that is more than a year old and doesn't require an army of computer specialists to operate. But a few good business deals could have been made in the Third World with this junk. Its intimidating effect only half diminished, the dead laboratory gave me a sad look, as if I were a wizard who could return it to life.

I could ponder these incongruities when I wasn't being pursued by members of a sect that continuously jabbered about sacrifices and very likely made one occasionally.

God, Claudandus, or whoever is responsible for luck had pity on me. Just as I had suspected when we moved in, the roof was heavily damaged and broken open in places. I ran straight to the opposite gable wall, where the roof sloped down from the right to the floor and where there was a narrow crevice about a foot wide.

Just as I was slipping through the crack to get outside, about thirty brothers and sisters stormed into the attic. They didn't exactly look like the type to come all this way to sell me a Bible. My kind are better sprinters than long-distance runners, so only the strongest of the pack had made it this far. Yet those who were still in hot pursuit seemed all the more enthusiastic about my capture, and probably about what they intended to do with me afterwards.

Standing in the gutter and gasping for breath, I had an unobstructed view of our square. It had begun to get light. It was one of those stirring moments when the sun has already begun its magical re-creation of an orange-blue firmament but is itself still invisible. The wide rectangles of roofs and terraces spread themselves out before me, giving me reason to hope for a successful escape. Somewhere in this rambling confusion of backyards there simply had to be a little corner where I could hide from my pursuers. However, the dizzying drop warned me not to try any overly daring manoeuvres. The network of garden walls looked like an ingenious labyrinth from above, a totally unsolvable puzzle – as complicated a puzzle as the whole intricate affair in which I had now become involved for keeps, whether I liked it or not.

I ran breathlessly up the mossy roof, reached the first roof-top, and hastened on to the neighbouring building. My pursuers had decreased in number to about ten die-hards, but their boldness and determination sufficed for at least a hundred. I saw them hot on my heels, their faces grim, leaving me not one second to spare if I was going to get out of their sight and shake them off. I leapt from one roof to another at a furious pace, which was no great problem since the gutters of the houses nearly touched.

But I could feel that my reserves of strength were nearly spent. If a huge golden hand did not reach down from the heavens at the last minute and end this wretched game I was sure I was going to have a heart attack. As for the brothers running me down, the morning's sport apparently didn't bother them in the least, for the distance between them and me was decreasing visibly.

Eventually I reached the long side of the square. Luckily enough, from this point on the landscape of roof-tops became pretty elaborate, no longer conforming to the monotonous architecture of gabled roofs on our side. The chaos of miniature towers, crenellations, roof gardens, chimneys, staircase exits, and fire escapes made those good old jungle feelings flare up in me, and all I had to do was let myself be led by instinct. I was promptly successful, for my pursuers did indeed lose sight of me. But immediately, as if by telepathy, they came up with an age-old hunting trick. By fanning out, the gang could cover the breadth of the roof-tops and run me down individually in the wilderness of bricks, concrete and iron.

Wedged in between four huge chimneys, I finally collapsed from exhaustion and breathed in great gasps. I couldn't talk myself out of the dreadful feeling that the pack had me surrounded. But I lacked the strength as well as the confidence to continue my flight.

Suddenly there was a creaking sound . . . I couldn't tell exactly where it was coming from, but was that so important? They had me where they wanted me now: in a trap. And they were going to kill me, as sure as Claudandus went to heaven. Scared stiff, I slowly stepped backwards – and on to something that gave way underneath me.

The skylight that my rear paw had touched swung down, and before I could even begin to be afraid, I fell like Alice in Wonderland into an unknown darkness. As you might expect, I fell on all four paws, but this good fortune didn't make me feel much better. Where the hell was I now?

I looked around cautiously, and the more my eyes grew used to the changed light conditions, the surer I felt, because this cosy retreat was safe. The silken curtains were half drawn. Apart from the weakly glimmering glow of a log smoking in the open fireplace, it was dark in the room. The antique furniture made me think an old man with a snow-white beard and red robe would walk in at any moment, take a seat on the comfortable rocking-chair, and begin telling some fairy-tale. But instead of Saint Nick, a Russian Blue was sitting on the rocking-chair and staring at me with strangely glassy yet radiant green eyes.

She was a splendid specimen. Her fur was short, soft, silky, and rippled down her body like the coat of a beaver or seal; it was a powder-blue shade with just a tinge of silver, which made her glisten. She cocked her head slightly, first on one side then on the other, as if she couldn't exactly tell where I was.

'You're new, aren't you?' she asked in a gentle voice.

'Yes, my name is Francis. I've been living for the past week and a half a couple of houses down,' I said.

'Friend or foe?'

'Friend!' I said emphatically. 'A friend forever!'

'That's a great relief. It saves me a lot of trouble.'

Her beguiling beauty made my heart pound and blood race. I stared up at her, somewhat hypnotised. There was a disconcerting quality about her, too: her eyes, her cold eyes reminded me of a frozen sea, for they had a suggestion of something uncanny, yes, even deathlike.

She got up to jump down from the rocking-chair, but stopped before doing so, again turning her head from side to side. Only after this strange ritual did she descend, and slink up to me.

'My guests don't fall from the sky. And if they do, most of the time they're up to something nasty.'

'Not I,' I replied. 'And I didn't fall from the sky; the skylight gave way under me. I'm . . . well, I'm a fugitive, so to speak.'

'Really? From whom?'

'From some members of the Claudandus sect. Apparently, they object to being observed at their merry little ceremonies.'

'That would be typical of those idiots.'

She went slowly up to the window and looked down at the garden.

'Is it already light outside?'

'But don't you see . . .'

I stopped myself. The mystery of her eyes was sadly obvious now. I went up to her and looked down awkwardly at my paws.

'You're blind,' I said.

'I'm not blind. I just can't see.'

She turned away from the window and returned to the fireplace. I followed her. She looked dully at the glowing fire that was now breaking down into embers. Although I already knew the answer, I asked her the question anyway.

'Do you always stay in this place, or do you go out sometimes?'

'No, there's too much trouble outside with our dear brothers and sisters. All they want to do is fight. All the whole world wants to do is fight. And yet, not a single day has gone by when I haven't wished to take a look, just one look, at this evil world.'

My heart sorrowed for her. A life in darkness, a life between walls, in a cave, in a labyrinth – in an invisible labyrinth that had no exit. A life in which there was constant guessing, groping, listening, smelling, but no seeing. She never saw the sky, the snow, never saw her own eyes reflected in shimmering water. When the sun shone and flowers bloomed and herons stitched the sky, it made no difference to her: everything was black, blacker than black. Damn it, why did she have to be so beautiful? That made the injustice of it all even more senseless. There was no God! And if there were, then He had to be an unscrupulous, cold-hearted sadist.

'Sorry,' I said. It was a feeble, superfluous word, but I didn't know how to express my sadness. It was the truth.

'Why?' she replied. 'There are worse things in life. That's what they say, don't they? There's always something worse in life.'

'That's probably true. But where's the limit?'

'Maybe there isn't one. One can put up with everything – except perhaps having to live in a dog kennel.'

Both of us broke into laughter. She bore her blindness with humour; that pleased me.

'Were you always like this, I mean, like . . .'

'You mean blind?' she said, helping me out with an amused smile. 'Yes, from birth. But it's strange. I do see images, images in my head.'

'Images?'

'Yes. Naturally I have only a vague idea of what images are, but they pop up suddenly in my memories. And in my dreams. Again and again.'

'What kind of images?'

Her face took on a curious, far-away expression. She seemed to be concentrating with all her might on what she saw or believed she could see in her mind. You could almost feel the hard work she had to do to imagine something the rest of us could see.

'Everything is so blurry, so unclear. I see people, many people gathered around me. They are so big, so distinct, so bright. Are they wearing that wonderful white colour I've heard about so often? I don't know. They're talking all at once; they're laughing loudly. I'm scared stiff; I want to go back to my mother! One of them is bending down to me and smiling at me. But it's a fake smile, the smile of a liar. This man has piercing eyes. They have a strange glitter, as if they're about to skewer me like daggers. Suddenly the man has something shiny in his hand; he moves it as fast as lightning. I feel pain, and I fall asleep. But this sleep is a frighteningly deep, black, leaden sleep I don't wake up from. In the blackness of this sleep I hear people's voices. They're furious now; they're screaming at one another; they're making accusations. Something has gone wrong. I sleep on. It seems to me as if I have already spent a thousand years in this condition. Then something terrible happens. It is so terrible that it blots out my memory for ever. But no, there's one more memory. I'm suddenly running outside with the others. Yes, there are others, many others, hundreds. But I can't see any more. I'm blind. I'm so sad that I can't see anything any more. Everything is desolate and dead. I wander around for a while and then lie down somewhere. It's raining and I'm getting wet. I've lost all hope and know that I will die. But now it doesn't matter any longer whether I die. After this, the colours and contours of the images dissolve as if they've been dipped in solvent. They're disappearing for ever. And then there are no more images . . .'

She had tears in her eyes and was a little ashamed because of them. To hide them from me, she went back again to the window and turned her back to me. I remained where I was, following her thoughtfully with my eyes.

'You're harbouring the images of your childhood in yourself,' I said. 'You weren't blind from birth. There's some terrible secret in your past. Some human did something to you. That's when you became blind.'

'Shall I tell you something?' she asked, and I detected an ironic undercurrent in her voice. 'The nicest creatures I know are people. Who else would care for a useless blind reject like me?'

She laughed again, and that did some good. It did a world of good.

'Some day you should see what happens when our brothers and sisters stumble in here by accident. They act like psychopaths, like monsters, like beasts. They think the eternal struggle they're fighting out there goes on in here. And when they suddenly find out what manner of strange creature they're dealing with, they're irritated and react with even more anger and hatred. It's a weird scene. I've been sitting around here for a long time, and all that life passes me by without really affecting me. But maybe I haven't missed out on anything, what with that endless war out there, I mean.'

She became pensive again. I knew that she didn't believe what she had just told me. Yes, evil had passed her by like a fog driven away by the sun. But she had also missed the struggle, the great and wonderful struggle of life.

'May I ask you an unusual question, Miss – what was your name again?'

'Felicity,' she said quickly.

'Felicity, although I haven't been living here for long, I know that for a fairly long time peculiar things have been happening in the district. And from what you just told me, I gather you do keep track of what's going on in the neighbourhood by, let's say, acoustic means. I suppose that your hearing is better than that of all those brave fighters out there. That's why I'd like to ask you this: did you hear any odd sounds during the night last week?'

'You mean the death cries?'

My jaw dropped. I felt as if I had been struck by lightning, as if I would come apart at the seams if I moved a muscle. I had finally found my first witness. Admittedly she was only half a witness, but better than no witness at all. The world wasn't made in a day.

'Does that surprise you? You're right, my hearing is better than the others'. But it's no miracle, is it? My favourite sitting place is here at the window. So I get to know a lot about what's going on down below, more perhaps than those who are actually there.'

'Then tell me all the details. Don't leave anything out. What exactly did you hear?'

'Why are you so interested in this?' she wanted to know.

'Well, it concerns murder, doesn't it?'

'Do you really want to use such a dramatic word? I have the impression that the whole business is just an exaggerated form of rivalry.'

'What makes you say that?'

'Very simple. I know every brother and sister by his or her voice. And their voices, or rather the screeching they make when summoned by one of our local sexpots, tells me what is on their minds.[8] The cries, the death cries I've heard over recent weeks, all came from males who had already been in fights with their rivals and were on their way to meet whoever was calling them. And while they were still yelling away, someone joined them, someone they seemed to know, someone they had considerable respect for. Because even their heightened state of aggressiveness did not deter this unknown party.'

'That's my theory too. Do you know who the mysterious stranger is?'

'No.'

'Did he speak with the prospective corpses?'

'Yes, but I couldn't understand what they were talking about. But there was one thing I thought I could detect again and again: the stranger spoke with great urgency, as if he wanted to convince the one he was talking to of something. It sounded sort of momentous.'

'Convince him of something?'

'That's the way it seemed to me.'

'And later?'

'After they talked there was usually a pause . . .'

'And then the death cry.'

'Exactly. I suppose it was then that the stranger went for their necks.'

'That's right. He always went straight for the neck, the way our kind does in hunting. But it's nearly impossible for a killer to get at a rival's neck because a rival is usually about as big, strong and quick as the attacker. The only possibility is that the victims simply didn't expect an attack, and turned their backs at some point. But that means they had a fair amount of trust in the killer.'

'Perhaps a female who didn't want to be molested.'

'A peculiar way of keeping the guys at bay. No, no, the murders were all planned, planned in cold blood. In my opinion, the fanatical members of the Claudandus sect are the most likely neck-biters. Particularly that sinister preacher. He really looked like he once might have owned a shop selling satanic trinkets. Can you tell me anything about this sect?'

'Very little. I only know that they worship a martyr by the name of Claudandus who supposedly lived in this area ages ago. They say he was tormented and tortured from birth. Nobody really knows by whom, or why. In any event, one day his suffering became so great that he called out to God, begging to be saved. And behold, God heard his pleading, descended, and saved him from his suffering. His tormentor was killed, and very cruelly, it is said, while the good Claudandus immediately received divine sanctuary. Be that as it may, he hasn't been seen since. Like every legend, this one may have a grain of truth in it, but I never knew him.'

'Did you know that in Latin Claudandus means "one that must or should be closed"?'

'No, and I can't make head nor tail of that. But I think you're on the wrong trail. You can forget about the members of the sect. Those fools who worship Claudandus and castigate themselves for his sake are harmless. They're doing those insane things because of vague feelings of piety and devotion, maybe even simple boredom. They would never hurt anyone else. And go as far as murder? Well, I don't know . . .'

'You can defend Claudandus, but I'm still suspicious. None of those freaks looked harmless to me . . .'

Before I could complete my sentence, she tilted her head upwards. I looked up as well, at the spot on the ceiling towards which Felicity's blind eyes were directed, anxious, expectant.

Bluebeard had poked his head through the open skylight and was peering in guiltily.

'Why did you split? We only wanted to have a little chat with you,' he said, almost apologetically.

'In the course of which two hundred and forty volts would have helped loosen my tongue, right?' I replied, furiously.

Felicity relaxed again, and over her face, now gleaming silver in the first morning light, a bewitching, blind smile flitted. You could see her relief that no fight was going to take place. No fighters, no fight, no life.

CHAPTER

—— 4 ——

RIGHT AFTER BLUEBEARD showed up, Felicity's owner (type: impoverished aristocrat, including monocle, silk pyjamas, rosewood pipe, and signet ring) woke up and greeted us with a wide variety of primitive gestures and noises not unlike Gustav's. Since His Grace, lacking a servant, had to fetch his morning paper and fresh rolls himself, I availed myself of the opportunity to slip out when he opened the door of the flat. I had already said goodbye to Felicity, assuring her that I would visit her again.

I went up to the roof to meet Bluebeard, who had been waiting for me. It was pretty embarrassing for him to talk about what had happened, but by now his sensitivities meant precious little to me.

'On the one hand, you encouraged me to do something about the murders, but on the other hand you kept me in the dark about what was really important. I'd like to know what other nice surprises you have in store,' I rebuked him, gnashing my teeth.

'Important, important! Good God, who ever said that that was important? This Claudandus crap is nothing but a way to kill time, have a few thrills, see how chicken you are, or whatever you want to call it. I'm not joking! What's that bit of fun got to do with some nutty neck-biter?'

I wasn't far from exploding in rage. Was he acting like an idiot on purpose?

'Of course, nothing at all, you moron!' I said. 'That riff-raff has been meeting with the sole purpose of getting charged up into a state of aggressive intoxication during which who knows what sort of perverse things could happen. But that, of course, has nothing at all to do with the murders. You lied to me, Bluebeard! What's more, you withheld important information from me. And you know exactly what I mean, *my friend*. But I'm still puzzled. Why did you do it?'

'Well, uh, I thought maybe it wasn't that important.' He could hardly get the words out, he was so uncomfortable.

'Not that important? In a case as complex as this one, every detail is important, Bluebeard, every single one. Any little thing can be important under the right circumstances. So note this for the future: either you play straight with me, or we don't play at all.'

The rising sun now washed the roof-scape in a rich orange. The air was fresh and clear, and the sunlight began to blind us. While we were heading back to Gustav's, Bluebeard, limping laboriously beside me, told all. The sect had existed for years. Practically nothing was known about the circumstances of its establishment. The only thing that was certain was that Joker – the current master of ceremonies – was the first to begin disseminating the teachings of the afflicted Claudandus. Through the years, he had found more and more followers for his cause, and eventually almost everybody joined without really being able to explain why. As Felicity had already correctly surmised, it all probably arose from a yearning for religious belief, security, and a good dose of excitement. Besides the peculiar electric shock torture, which had become part of the ritual over time, Bluebeard had noticed nothing unusual during the meetings – except, of course, that the whole business was itself out of the ordinary. Bluebeard even rejected the argument that the chemical odour of the dilapidated premises heightened the aggressive tendencies of the members. He said he was always exhausted, even ready to drop off to sleep, after each meeting, but never aggressive. Nor did he have any idea who Claudandus really was.

All this did absolutely nothing to calm me down. On the contrary, all Bluebeard's answers raised new questions. The murderer had hidden himself in this swamp of secrets and half-truths like a virus in a monstrously complex organism, and was quietly and stealthily manipulating the puppet strings of death.

As we approached our roof, I glanced down again at the houses and gardens, which the sun had just illuminated with a scintillating gold. There aren't only human beings on this planet, I thought to myself. They have built all of this and fancy themselves the kings of the universe. But in every cosmos there are countless microcosms and the latter are always depressingly loathsome mirror images of the former. But why does this have to be? Why can't the world simply be divided into a good half and an evil half? The colour grey makes you feel uneasy, makes things seem complicated and hopeless, it upsets the notion of black and white. Good and evil? There is no such thing. There is a little good and a little evil, a little black and a little white. Grey is not an attractive colour, but perhaps it is the one that describes the world most accurately. The truth, the explanation for the horrible things that have happened, the murder motive and the murderer – all that is concealed behind this grey, behind this camouflage, the best camouflage since the creation of the earth.

At home, a bowl of freshly cleaned cod awaited Bluebeard and myself. Even if Gustav had a few screws loose, he was beyond reproach when it came to choosing food for his best friend. Of course, he had to be taught this in a strenuous course communicated by means of a series of unmistakably clear signals. Human beings never do hit upon the idea that others besides themselves might take pleasure in culinary delicacies. Although they elevate the ingredients and preparation of their own sustenance to the highest level of culture, and not infrequently to that of ideology, they seem unable to grasp that other creatures might also have gourmet tastes. Only one thing can help in the face of such narrow-mindedness: go hungry! Don't eat the crap, the refuse, the stinking hand-outs they put down in front of you, but go hungry, go hungry again and again.[9] It is important to be persistent and proud, like an old lag who goes on a hunger strike when prison conditions get bad. At the beginning of our relationship, through this method of civil disobedience, I was able to get the message through to Gustav that the 'titbits' he thought fit for me he could shove you-know-where. I was in no way willing to so much as sniff at them. Since Gustav's mental capacity, as I have often noted, lies somewhere between that of Koko the famous talking gorilla and the first Russian dog in space, it took a while before he recognised the error of his ways and finally began to prepare choice foods for me. But in the due course of time, I was able to get him to sauté my meals, for instance, and even to season them with herbs and spices. In the end, to sum things up, he was 'eating out of my hand'. This aside is only meant to make it clear that in reality there are no oppressed, only those who submit to oppression. Amen.

Since the capacity of Bluebeard's stomach was about four times larger than mine, he was still cramming down fish in record time when I was already well over my limit. I decided to risk an inspection of the living-room to appraise the current state of renovation.

It was impressive how much progress the two heavy labourers had made. Archie was already laying parquet while Gustav was gluing some kind of avant-garde plastic sheeting to the wall. As usual, he was sweating and his tongue was hanging out. When he saw me, he dropped everything, wobbled up to me, lifted me up high, and ran his sausagey fingers through my fur to give me, as he liked to put it, my 'daily dose of affection'.

Archie, who had slipped into the role of the perfect handyman and jack-of-all-trades, had dragged into the flat every gimcrack – and I mean really gimcrack – machine that he could find within a fifty-mile radius. One of them even looked like it could pick snot. Although Archie and I had ties of great affection, whenever he saw me he could not refrain from saying that Burmese cats were currently 'in' and that my breed was no longer fashionable. Whereupon Gustav would make some indignant remarks, and try to persuade me that I shouldn't listen to nasty Uncle Archie.

I didn't. I sprang down from my friend's lap and trotted back into the bathroom, where Bluebeard was waiting for me in front of a licked-clean bowl. In gratitude for my hospitality, he now wanted to honour his promise of the previous day and introduce me to the 'other clever bastard'.

The meeting with the other clever bastard exceeded by far all the promises that bubbled excitedly out of Bluebeard on the way. I am all too aware that many will doubt the truth of what I will now report – and with reason. If I had not seen it with my own eyes, I confess that I myself would have not believed it. But it happens to be the honest-to-God truth, and I have made up my mind not to exaggerate.

Bluebeard led me to an old building located in the farthest and most secluded corner of the district and covered on every side with creeping plants. Inside, however, this quaint house looked like the dream home of a dynamic young City whiz-kid obsessed by the desire to live like one of those inflated Hollywood execs who constantly grin out at you from the TV. A sickeningly fashionable interior designer might have done it up for his own family. The distinguishing feature of this house was empty space. The main characteristic of each and every room was either priceless carpeting or highly polished white marble.

Furniture and other household articles were sparingly distributed, as if at an exhibition.

It was unsettling. Where the hell did these people put things like sewing kits and shoe polish? Did they keep any mementoes of their childhood? Where in God's name did they hide the awful odds and ends every household accumulates over the course of the years? The only objects here looked as if they were on loan from the Museum of Modern Art.

Bluebeard and I managed to get in through the door, which was ajar and led directly from the garden to the living-room. The living-room was empty except for a heavy leather recliner and a CD player with an assortment of classical CDs. Only two pictures hung on the whitewashed walls. The first was a greatly enlarged photograph of female genitals, the second of the male anatomical counterpart. It was obvious that art connoisseurs lived here! How different was Gustav's taste. (Or should I say lack of taste?) Gustav once had the gall to rip out a reproduction of Van Gogh's *Sunflowers* from a calendar and to staple – please note, *staple* – it to the wall. Driven half mad by anger, I had shredded it to pieces. I asked myself whether the owners of this avant-garde domicile perhaps had an ugly rubber duck in the bathroom, like Gustav? Or whether they would take pride in calling a granny-crocheted tablecloth their own, assuming that they even had a granny. They probably didn't eat meat, either. And if they did, they most certainly wouldn't make the disgusting sounds Gustav did.

Bluebeard was engrossed in the larger-than-life photograph of the vagina, a speculative smile on his face.

'Very impressive,' I said. 'Are we in the house of a pimp or an art professor?'

'Shit, I don't know.' He thought it over. 'I think the guy who owns this place does something with science. Mathematics, biology, parapsychology – something like that. Anyway, he must make a lot of dough to be able to afford all this crap.'

'And where is the clever bastard who's the owner of the clever bastard we're here to visit?'

He shrugged. 'Dunno. Let's have a look for our one.'

We wandered over carpet and marble, marble and carpet and on and on until we were heartily sick of the sight of all the latest fashions from the wonderful world of ultra-ultra-modern design. We saw more than enough of African totems – sometimes the only furnishings in a room – Le Corbusier recliners and Ron Arad chairs. We overdosed on Mariscal, and gawped at two Biedermeier wardrobes whose restoration had probably cost more money than was earned during the entire working lives of the stupid farmers who had been cheated out of them for a song in the first place.

And then, at last, we found the goal of our search.

When we entered the second-floor study, I didn't notice him right away because a portrait on the wall to my right claimed my immediate attention. The huge painting depicted a broad-shouldered, rather stout man in his mid-forties with a large head, a high brow, gold-rimmed eyeglasses framing friendly yet penetrating blue eyes. His look suggested intelligence and curiosity, and there was a hint of roguishness around the corners of his firm mouth. He wore the civilian clothing of an ecclesiastic: a black frock and trousers stuck into high, sturdy boots. He stood amid indefinable plants whose branches and leaves enveloped him in such a way that it seemed as if he himself had grown out of all this greenery. Below, in the right-hand corner of the painting, was written in fine, swinging handwriting: *Gregor Johann Mendel*. Perhaps the master of the house was a religious person; or maybe the painting portrayed a relative, perhaps his father.

My gaze wandered away from the painting and came to a stop at a computer on a glass slab desk: our friend sat at its colour monitor. At first I thought he had fallen asleep. But then I saw how he moved his right forepaw to operate the keyboard with graceful speed. It was simply unbelievable. This guy could have brought the world to a standstill! I had heard the weirdest tall tales about our folk, but this scene was simply absurd. It went against nature. Even worse, it went against Desmond Morris's *Catwatching*!

While I was still holding my breath in surprise, he turned away from the monitor and winked at us.

'A most cordial welcome to you, my dear friends!' was his enthusiastic greeting. 'I was just beginning to wonder where you were. Bluebeard told me . . . '

He noticed my astonished gaze, and shook his head, looking pleased.

'Oh, you just happened to catch me playing my little game here. Well, the achievements of micro-electronics have brought upon the world the vilest of all vile curses: thou shalt play until it be thy ruination! So, in future, don't let any proud computer owner tell you that he needs these miraculous machines for purely rational purposes. Most of the time people play games on them. I'm no exception.'

He was a Brown Havana, a member of a breed that ran circles around all other breeds in terms of intelligence. The head is somewhat longer than wide, the nose has a marked 'stop' between the eyes. Because of the characteristic form of his muzzle and oversized, forward-pointing ears, I could not compare him with any brother or sister I had ever seen. His velvet smooth coat – a strong, warm, chocolate brown that in dim light could pass for black – absorbed the rays of the autumn sun streaming through the huge floor-to-ceiling window behind the desk. Yes, he was truly a beautiful sight, and yet . . . Like almost all the brothers and sisters in the neighbourhood, something about him didn't seem quite right. I couldn't exactly figure out what it was, but somehow he gave the impression that he was put together like a child's puzzle in which the pieces didn't interlock properly. Perhaps it was his maturity that put this image in my mind – he was already on the threshold of old age.

Or perhaps someone had done something terrible to him at an early age, just as they had done to Felicity . . .

'OK, this guy's name's Francis, and the smart aleck over there's Pascal,' Bluebeard said in introduction.

Pascal sprang down from the desk and came up to us, and I was able to catch a glimpse of what was on the monitor. But I couldn't make out anything except for hieroglyphs of a text interwoven with colourful threads of graphics.

'It is a pleasure and an honour to make your acquaintance,' said Pascal with unnerving courtesy, halting in front of us. 'May I offer you both a little something to eat? I have braised kidney with crab here.'

'Thank you, but we've already eaten,' I replied. His inflated politeness was gradually setting me on edge.

'Well, um, I wouldn't say no to a little snack. Somehow I just didn't feel that hungry this morning, plus the stuff I did eat really didn't go down that well, if you know what I mean.' Bluebeard stared down at the floor with his one unharmed eye, embarrassed, then gave me a sidelong look by way of a plea for understanding.

'But of course, my dear Bluebeard. Lack of appetite is a serious matter. It would, perhaps, be advisable if you underwent a medical examination. You can never be too cautious about such complaints, minor though they may be.'

'Oh, no, no,' Bluebeard played it down. 'It was just what they call indigestion. I'll feel a whole lot better after a few mouthfuls.'

'Excellent. The kidney is in the kitchen, which is this way.'

On hearing these magic words, Bluebeard began limping ahead in the direction of the kitchen, but I quickly blocked the computer expert's way.

'Excuse me, Pascal, but I never would have dreamed that one of our kind could operate such a machine. Could you, perhaps, demonstrate it to me?'

An enthusiastic smile spread over his face. The old boy was charm and hospitality in person.

'Why certainly, Francis, I'd love to. If you'd like, I could even teach you how to use it. By the way, Bluebeard has told me a great deal about you. Only good things, of course. I find your efforts towards ending the murders in the district simply exemplary. In my modest way, I too have been trying to outwit this cruel butcher. If we join forces, we could put an end to his game in no time. Now, here's how the system works . . .'

We sprang on the desk and sat down in front of the monitor, which was on top of the central processing unit. The master of the house hadn't pinched pennies here either. It was the very latest in IBM hardware. Apparently the text on the screen was a research paper, because after reading the first line my concentration evaporated as quickly as perfume escaping a bottle.

'My esteemed master naturally does not suspect that I play with his equipment in his absence. But he's out all day long and, believe me, it can get wretchedly boring here. At my age, you don't feel much like roaming around out there any more.'

Yet another who dreaded being 'out there'. Only hermits lived in this neighbourhood. But that was understandable when you considered that 'out there' was the territory of a deranged throat-slasher.

'This is really unbelievable, Pascal. How on earth did you learn to operate it?'

'Very simple. The programming manuals of my companion are always lying around somewhere or other in the study. I just take a look at them and teach myself what I need. I borrow the diskettes from him. And, behind his back, I even managed to manipulate the system so that I could install hidden files on the hard disk.'

'Not so fast,' I protested. 'If you still want to keep your audience, you're going to have to speak more slowly. Programming manuals, diskettes, hard disk – all Greek to me.'

He gave me an abashed smile. 'Give old Pascal enough time and he'll bend your ear all day long, mainly with a lot of rubbish. I suppose it's just age. You want to talk away all that loneliness. But don't worry, Francis. I'll teach you everything. It's really very simple, because it's just a matter of logic. And I can tell just by looking at you that you're a born logician.'

'I wish my logical genius would give me some help clearing up these murders. Despite the various hints and clues I've been able to collect up to now, I know as much now as I did at the beginning.'

'Which brings us back to the topic of our discussion.'

Pascal pressed one of the function keys at the top of the keyboard. The monitor darkened from top to bottom until it was completely black. Then a list appeared in the blackness, consisting of a large number of roman numerals and titles. At the top was the heading: FELIDAE.

'Do you know what this word means?' asked Pascal.

'Naturally,' I replied. 'It's the scientific term for our family, which is divided into *Panthera*, *Acinonyx*, *Neofelis*, *Lynx*, and *Leopardus*. Zoologists still dispute the classificatory criteria, but all these genera are officially assigned to the main family of origin, the Felidae.'

Pascal had a distant look, as if he had been removed to a primeval time, shrouded in mystery.

'Felidae . . .' he whispered almost yearningly. 'Evolution has brought forth an astonishing number of living creatures. More than a million kinds of animal live on the earth today, but none of them compels as much respect and admiration as the Felidae. Although it includes only about forty subspecies, absolutely the most fascinating creatures alive belong to this group. It may sound like a cliché, but they are indeed a miracle of nature!'

'But what does this list mean, Pascal? Are you using the computer for conducting genealogical research? And what does all this have to do with the murders?'

He smiled impishly.

'Patience, my young friend, just have a little patience. When speaking with an old man, you need two qualities above all: absolute immunity to bad breath, and patience!'

By tapping a key, he made each item on the list light up in sequence until he reached the heading COMMUNITY, then he pressed a further key. The list disappeared, and suddenly a voluminous register of names turned up; beneath each was roughly half a page of text.

'This is a detailed listing of the members of our community, the inhabitants of our district,' explained Pascal. 'Every one of our kind is registered according to his or her name, age, sex, race, markings, family, owner, personality traits, distinguishing features, state of health, and so on and so forth. In particular, the various ties among individuals are documented, and significant interrelationships can be traced down, if desired, by a complicated search and classification system.

'Oh, while I'm on the subject, I should say that I have yet to list you . . . But altogether about two hundred brothers and sisters are included. I made the list when I began teaching myself the computer so that I could try out the functions of the data management program using challenging material. Just for fun, more or less. Since then, however, it has acquired an entirely new meaning.'

He pressed a key again, and in the top right corner a small blinking question mark appeared. Beside it, Pascal entered the word MURDER. The processing unit made whining sounds as it moved the list up and down in accelerated motion, finally stopping at the name ATLAS. This and the attached data were framed in black; the name itself was underlined in blood red and marked with a thick black cross.

'Atlas was the first to fall into the snare of our bogeyman. He was a regular Casanova: young, without a care in the world, nothing on his mind but an insatiable hunger for life and love. Unlikely that he would ever have made serious enemies. He was uncastrated, so must have had some run-ins with the big bosses in the district. Like the other uncastrated, he also had a cavalier attitude as far as territorial claims were concerned.'

'Did you know that all the victims at the time of their . . .'

'Yes, they were all sexually aroused at the time of their murder, that is, chasing some randy female. That's probably the only thing they had in common, if you disregard the fact that they were all male and that cross-connections existed between their families. But let's leave that to one side for the time being.'

Again he pressed one of his magical keys, and again a name marked with a cross appeared.

'Second victim: Tomtom. A neurotic beast, suffered continually from delusions of persecution. Extremely shy and not very fit for life. Sooner or later he would have had a nasty end anyway. Corpse number three: a nameless brother. Probably a homeless stray who changed neighbourhoods daily. Very likely lived from hand-outs and rubbish. Pure coincidence that his libido happened to flare up in our district. The fourth corpse was Sascha. He was hardly out of childhood. It's almost certain that he had reached sexual maturity just a few weeks before the fatal neck bite. Special characteristic: too young to die. The fifth and last in the group is Deep Purple. Bluebeard informed me that he has already told you about him. I would not have thought that this Mr Prim and Proper concealed a secret libertine.'

'I have an idea,' I said. 'Tell the computer to find out the breeds of the murder victims.'

'Not a bad idea,' agreed Pascal with pleasure. Now he was in his element. The joy of having found an equally enthusiastic game partner was written prominently on his face, although he must already have known the answers because he himself had entered the data. His paws whooshed with blinding speed over the keyboard.

After a few seconds, the computer presented us with the results, which were illuminated in a yellow window at the top of the screen:

Name	Race
ATLAS:	European Shorthair
TOMTOM:	European Shorthair
FELIDAE X:	European Shorthair
SASCHA:	European Shorthair
DEEP PURPLE:	European Shorthair

'None of the five are particularly distinguished representatives of Felidae,' commented Pascal.

'Nevertheless, one further feature in common,' I replied.

'That, my dear friend, proves nothing at all, because the European Shorthair is one of the most widely distributed breeds in the entire world. If you'll permit the expression, the European Shorthair is one of our standard models. I estimate that seventy per cent of the district belong to this breed.'

He was right. Yet my instincts still told me that I must be on to something.

'It's strange nevertheless. All the victims are male, aroused, and European Shorthairs.'

'No, not all.' His face darkened suddenly. All levity vanished from his sparkling eyes. 'Because I haven't yet had time to enter the sixth victim.'

'What sixth victim?'

I didn't understand what he was saying. Had Bluebeard concealed something from me again? Without bothering to reply, Pascal again pressed a few keys. The computer searched a while before spitting out a list of brothers and sisters whose names began with F.

A terrible thought began to take shape in my head. But I would rather have died than have thought it through. No, the idea was simply absurd, it stood logic on its head.

I was suddenly horrified. Pascal stopped the list, which was scrolling upwards, at the name FELICITY and began to underline it in red with the help of the function keys.

'Felicity?' I cried out, on the point of hysteria.

Pascal, without betraying the least emotion, continued his work, solemnly.

'Yes, Felicity as well, unfortunately.'

'No, no, Pascal. That's impossible. You're getting something mixed up. Just an hour ago I spoke with her. She seemed very much alive to me then.'

'I was told the news just before you and Bluebeard arrived.'

'Who told you?'

'Agathe. She's a harmless stray and gets around a lot.'

'Why didn't you tell me about it right away?'

'I didn't want to begin our first meeting with such terrible news.'

'But why? And how?'

Suddenly it dawned on me. The open skylight . . . Her owner had left the flat with me to do his morning chores. She was alone after that.

All at once the tears filled my eyes. What was the reason? Why? Why kill this poor creature, who had already been so badly abused?

I sprang down from the desk and ran out of the house. Outside I tried to convince myself that what Pascal had said was not true. He had meant another Felicity. Yes, that had to be it. I had the power to turn back the course of events if I could see that Felicity was still alive.

I ran heedlessly along the garden walls. I looked desperately for a way to climb up to the roofs. It seemed to me that everything around me was whirling past like pages from a calendar torn off and thrown into the air. There – a fire escape! I rushed up it, and then, completely out of breath, once again found myself in the roof-scape. No pausing now – I had to see her, just had to see her. She could not be dead; this thought now had a schizophrenic hold on my conscious mind.

Finally I reached the skylight, which was still open. My heart beating wildly, I stuck my head through the frame and looked down.

It was like a scene in a horror film. The old aristocrat sat on a rocking-chair crying his eyes out. At his feet was Felicity, her head almost completely severed from her body. The murderer had struck with particularly drastic brutality this time. Not only had he applied his fatal neck bite, which alone would have served his purpose, but he had also jabbed and torn at her neck long after she had died. So much blood had poured out of her body on to the carpet that it seemed as if Felicity were swimming in the crimson fluid. This inhuman thing must have been just about to rip off her head when he suddenly heard the steps of the old man and, after an extraordinary jump, fled out through the skylight. Felicity's blind eyes were open very wide, as if, even in the face of death, she had wished for nothing more deeply than to see.

So much hate, so much fighting, so much evil in the world. She had had good reason to be on constant guard against what was 'out there'. For 'out there' were the others, the murderers. Despite my desolation, I was convinced that the theory I had tried out on Pascal was right. Felicity's murder differed from the other five only in that she was a witness. She was killed because she may have wanted to divulge some essential information to me.

A chill of fear abruptly shivered down my spine. I must have been shadowed by someone the whole time. The murderer was anything but a raging, drooling madman. He was unusually intelligent, and absolutely didn't want anyone to meddle in his plans.

I looked at Felicity, saw the silvery gleam of her coat, now soiled with splattered blood, saw the shimmering green eyes in which I could read her longing for sight. I saw all this damned injustice, and I swore revenge: whoever did this would die the way Felicity had.

CHAPTER

—— 5 ——

Tʜᴇ ɴɪɢʜᴛᴍᴀʀᴇs ᴀssᴜᴍᴇᴅ an undertone of increasing cruelty.

In a catatonic emotional state, absolutely numb to external stimuli and filled with indescribable grief, I made my way home like a sleepwalker. The fury that had flared up briefly in my heart was now changing into resignation and depression. A peculiar weariness had seized me, and I thought it best to rest for a few hours.

To the accompaniment of Richard Strauss's *Four Last Songs*, I entered the bedroom, located a cosy cushion on which to sleep, and slipped into a sinister dream. The place where I suddenly found myself looked like the stage setting for a post-apocalypse film: it was obvious that the world had been wiped out by a nuclear holocaust or bacteriological war – but why? Only the wretched vestiges of civilisation, if a civilisation it had ever been, were still in evidence. It took a while before I realised that this expanse of ruins had once been our district. Of the charmingly renovated houses, only hollow shells remained. They had been demolished, gutted, and bombed. Huge holes gaped in the façades, behind which terrible secrets seemed to dwell. Strangest of all, however, were the plants. Stubborn green vegetation had covered the entire district like an inexorable carpet of slime, smothering everything, forcing itself into the smallest cracks the way a creeping plant does in real life. When I looked around more carefully, I discovered that the vegetation consisted of pea plants of gigantic dimensions. It was insane, but then dreams are not exactly rational. Evidently humanity was no longer making even a guest appearance in the great, evolutionary drama, and had yielded the stage to pea plants. The scene reminded me somehow of *Sleeping Beauty*, the only difference being that there weren't any more human beings to fall under the soporific spell.

Once I had had my fill of this hallucinatory scene, I trotted aimlessly along the garden walls, which in this doomed world seemed like the remnants of a Buddhist temple. I stopped again and again, looking around attentively in the hope of finding a clue that would explain the destruction. All in vain. Aside from noticing that the pea plants had even eaten their way into the houses, I discovered nothing.

The green nightmare became thicker and thicker, more and more tangled. I was just starting to get desperate when I saw a tiny opening in a thicket, through which shone a blinding light. I ran up to it quickly, poked my head in, and then squeezed my entire body through. What I saw filled me with dread.

Before me was a wide clearing bathed in brilliant light, strewn with the corpses of members of my kind. Obviously, not only the human race had met with destruction. Mountains of corpses were piled carelessly on top of one another, like refuse on a rubbish dump on which a shower of blood had fallen. Millions of wide-open eyes stared pensively at the red fluid running down from millions of lacerated necks. Some of the corpses had already putrefied; their coats had holes in them large enough for their insides to be visible. And yet they continued to bleed as if supplied by a hidden pump.

Although this sight made my eyes well up with tears, through a veil of misery I recognised familiar faces lying dead on the nearest heap of corpses. Not only Felicity, Sascha, and Deep Purple, but also Bluebeard, Kong, Herrmann and Herrmann, Pascal, and friends from my former neighbourhood were guests at this mute party; their dead eyes stared as expectantly as if they were listening to a speech of welcome from their host. Even Atlas, Tomtom and the unknown brother, whom I thought I recognised although I had never seen him before, were here at this gruesome cemetery. Human beings had remained faithful to their old and venerable customs, and had brought disaster not only on themselves but on everyone else as well.

Yet the silence did not last long. Suddenly, the earth vibrated as if an underground train were rushing along a few inches under my paws. A distorted roaring sound could be heard, as if the nuclear bomb that had destroyed this world was about to rise again out of the earth and mushroom skyward in reverse motion. The corpses began wriggling wildly as if reacting to a rapidly shifting magnet hidden in the earth. The roaring reached the pain threshold, the dead jumped like hooked fish being landed, the sky turned a dark crimson, and a powerful wind blew up.

Then, with an ear-splitting boom, *he* shot up out of the middle of the lifeless bodies, perhaps ninety feet high, gargantuan, eyes glinting ominously behind eyeglasses that reflected the reddening sky, black frock flapping indolently in the wind, hair swirling like blazing flames. He laughed, but his laugh was more of a scream, the caricature of a laugh. It was Gregor Johann Mendel, the man in the portrait, who had now become a colossus.

'The solution to the mystery is really very simple, because it's just a matter of logic, Francis,' he barked down at me scornfully. 'And I can tell just by looking at you that you're a born logician.'

Grinning balefully, he looked around at the corpses below him.

'*Panthera, Acinonyx, Neofelis, Lynx, Leopardus*: Felidae! More than a million kinds of animal live on the earth today, but none of them compel as much respect and admiration as good old Felidae! It may sound like a cliché, but they are indeed a miracle of nature! But be careful, Francis! Don't underestimate *Homo sapiens*!'

Only now did I notice that he had concealed his right hand behind his back. Still grinning repulsively, he now brought forward this hand to reveal an oversized cross of the kind that is used to control puppets. But there were no strings attached to the many pieces of wood of which the cross was constructed.

The giant Mendel swung the thing in his hand self-importantly, as if he were performing a marvellous magic trick.

'Don't despair, my friend. Only at first glance is death a matter of finality. Bear in mind how He called Lazarus to come forth. You should include the Claudandus case in your reflections. I shall live again and again, although I have long been dead. Watch!'

He whipped the cross downwards. Suddenly, thousands upon thousands of black strings grew from the wooden guides and fanned out. Their ends snared the limbs of the dead bodies like fishing hooks.

Mendel jerked the control upwards, shouting happily: 'And up, up, up, up . . . '

The mouths of the reanimated dead emitted a grisly bloodcurdling howl that sounded like a burial march played backwards and soon became a black vortex of sound. The hairs on my back stood on end like wire bristles. I was afraid I would lose my mind if I had to witness this insane performance any longer, but there was no escape.

The dead rose from the sleep of death, rising to their feet with jerky movements, and then lined up in rank and file. The puppeteer twirled the control like a virtuoso, skilfully manipulating its strings. Accompanied by a chorus of yowls, legions of zombies began a robotic stamping dance, during which they were thrown back and forth by the strings or forced to make jolting leaps and pirouettes. I saw Felicity twitch her head up and down mechanically to the rhythm of the music, and Blue-beard attempt to imitate ballet poses, his various disfigurements causing grotesque effects. Despite their swinging movements and the furious tempo of the dance, their faces revealed their repugnance and their protest at this forced resurrection.

Mendel had worked himself into a frenzy and was pulling at the control like a madman, back and forth, up and down; then he himself began to dance a wild jig. The army of dead Felidae obeyed his cruel commands, exceeding themselves in their daring contortions and ecstatic stomping.

'And up, up, up, up!' the colossus bawled like a lunatic. 'Plant hybrid experiments! Plant hybrid experiments! More hybrid experiments! The essence of the matter is hidden in the pea! Plant hybrid experiments! Plant hybrid experiments . . .'

While he repeated this again and again, like a parrot gone berserk, and continued his perverse dance, he grew larger and larger until he was the size of a tower block. The undead, however, could no longer endure the strain of the wild dance and gradually fell apart. Detached limbs, decomposing heads, indefinable organs flew around in a vast eruption that slowly thickened into a stinking black cloud, from the middle of which Gregor Johann Mendel, a demented leer on his face, rose like a tornado . . .

When I opened my eyes, Mendel stood in front of me with an odd smile. I was about to scream when I recognised the man before me. It was not the dancing colossus, but Gustav. He kneeled down beside me on the floor and caressed me softly. My whole body was shaking as badly as if I had spent all that time in a freezer.

Darkness had fallen. The first winds of a gale whistled around the house. The window shutters, whose latches had all fallen off, slammed uncontrollably against the outside walls. Gustav had lit four candles, and their flickering light added to the unnerving atmosphere. He vanished briefly from the room and returned a few minutes later with a portable television in one hand, his army cot in the other. That was when I knew what day it was. It was time for that sacred event of the week, Gustav's Saturday late-night movie. All the horrible events of the past few days, and particularly of the present day, had robbed me of my sense of time.

Gustav came and went again and again, lugging blankets, diverse cushions, and his Saturday evening ice-cream sundae – the last quarter of which I was allowed to lick up – all in keeping with time-honoured tradition. Before departing for dreamland in the middle of the film, he expected me to take part in what had become a cherished, if not compulsive, ritual over the years. Since I, however, had just come from dreamland, I didn't feel much like spending the evening in the usual way. Nevertheless, I obliged him until he conked out in the middle of *Rebecca*, which I had already seen more times than I cared to count. Then I turned my back on that flickering blue screen and sneaked out of the room to do what I always do when I want to clear my head and urgently need diversion from stress: hunt rats.[10]

And now a few words of enlightenment for animal rights advocates. For many, the sight of one of my kind with one of these plague-bags – excuse me, with one of these rodents – between our teeth is a heartrending sight. They feel pity for these pus-buckets – excuse me, rodents – and start to lament the cruel creed of kill or be killed. As if that weren't enough, some even keep these louse-lumps – excuse me, rodents – as house pets. You can't reproach these people, for how are they supposed to know what megalomaniacs their 'house companions' really are? But once you know the facts, it's obvious that rats are out for world supremacy! And there are more and more signs that suggest they will reach this goal in the near future. Bias? Grotesque exaggeration? Paranoid fantasies only to be expected of my kind? Well, here are some sober statistics: it takes only a hundred rats to devour one and a half tons of grain annually. Damage caused by rats worldwide is estimated at over thirty billion pounds per year. Some more figures? At present, about one hundred and twenty million rats make their home in Great Britain. There are ten rats for every inhabitant of New York City; that means there are ninety million rats for the nine million inhabitants of that city alone. I will spare everyone a lecture on bubonic plague and the other charming infectious diseases with which our cute little friends have blessed the world. The human race has sought ways to eradicate these mischief-makers since time immemorial. But even miracle weapons like Warfarin, an ingenious chemical that causes internal bleeding, have failed in the end because rat populations rapidly build up a resistance to it. But woe betide those of us who make an earnest attempt to put an end to the ambitions of *Rattus rattus* to world supremacy. If people overcame their maudlin sentimentality and gave us a free hand, then we would make short work of this blight. Heaven knows, I am no supporter of the Rambo mentality, but in life we often face problems that leave only one way out: ready, aim, fire!

Frankly, I lacked the nerve to go on another expedition upstairs. So this time I decided to go down to the cellar, as cellars are well known as the traditional terrain of these vermin.

When I got to the cellar door by way of the hall, I discovered to my chagrin that it was locked. Its upper half, however, had two long glass windows. One of the panes was shattered and had a hole right in the middle through which I could catapult myself – with a leap carefully calculated to avoid injuring myself on the protruding splinters. But what awaited me on the other side? No doubt a very steep wooden staircase, meaning that after gliding through the hole I would fall for about nine feet. I also had to assume that the stairs would be rotten, so I would slip and slide down the entire flight, thump by thump.

I didn't care. I was really thirsty for the hunt. Taking my time, I aimed and jumped.

I had hardly passed through the hole in one piece when my worst fears promptly came true. The wooden stairs dropped down even more steeply than I had imagined. How I would have liked to turn back; but it was too late, too late . . .

I fell three or four yards, then smacked down hard on a lower step. Hellish pains shot up from my front paws to my whiskers, which vibrated in sympathy like tuning forks. Of course I had tried to absorb the shock of landing, but the narrow step severely limited any ballistic adjustments. I got up carefully and stretched my body until the pain started to go away. Then I began to listen intently.

If my ears didn't deceive me, my friends down here were having an early Christmas. Scratchings, slurpings and squeakings came from every corner of the cellar, and warmed the cockles of my heart. Might I have the good fortune of making the acquaintance of a really fat, self-satisfied, impudently smiling rat? Such good fortune was looking distinctly possible.

I switched over to silent mode. That meant that my movements were so soft and slow that they resembled those of a ballet dancer in slow motion. Since my eyes had now grown used to the changed light conditions, I could make out every detail of my surroundings. The stairs led to a narrow, stuffy room that was jammed full of odds and ends of medical equipment and instruments – a definite case of *déjà vu*. But since that first dream I had become so used to the traces of Dr Frankenstein that at first I didn't pay much attention to the stuff. The door of this room was open a fraction, revealing a mazy cellar, and I approached this opening with the same gingerly tread I would have used if I had been instructed to defuse a bomb. Only after I had moved into position beside the doorjamb did I risk a look inside.

Paradise! A biblical paradise! In one glance I detected at least four rats, among whom one was a particularly well-nourished specimen. A positive pasha of a rat, he was playing the role of archangel enthroned on high, casting down pleased if somewhat bored looks at his inferiors.

Unlike the others, this huge, gloomy room was chock-a-block

with paper. Mountains of files, computer printouts, books, forms, and bundles of correspondence created an impressive Grand Canyon landscape, complete with gulleys, craters, rocky terraces and rifts of paper. Above, below, and in between were our friends. Always industrious, always sociable, always game for a laugh . . . and waiting patiently for day X when they would seize power.

Despite this fine prospect, a wave of sadness and depression overcame me. For a moment, my thoughts drifted away and returned to my nightmare, to Felicity, and to all the others who had been snatched away so cruelly. I lived in a bloody madhouse, and here I was engaging in bloody shenanigans just to distract myself from the atrocities hemming me in on all sides. I was acting according to the motto: if insanity laughs at you, laugh back! Caught by this reflection, I didn't know whether to laugh or cry.

But immediately I was gripped by a cold fury. I wasn't going to drag myself down with negative thoughts. Every new day should have a positive beginning! That was a good motto, too. The hunt was on, and I felt instinct taking hold of my entire being. I was getting angrier and angrier at these rats, sitting there like remote-controlled automatons with their dull brains thinking only of procreation and of finding something to gnaw on. I wanted to wipe them off the map and teach them what hell was. Now!

Like an arrow of steel I shot up the highest paper pile and rammed my fangs into the neck of the pasha. The guy was so surprised and shocked that he immediately took a shit on the pile. But I had only wounded him; my good old neck bite had not had the chance to sink in. He wriggled and howled between my teeth while his pals ran around below, squeaking excitedly and looking for a hiding-place. I had to look out, too, because that stinking beast had teeth every bit as sharp as my own. I shook him loose and worked him over with a couple of powerful swipes from my claws. Smeared with blood, he reeled away like a stuck pig, searched in panic for a way out, and ended up plunging from the paper pile.

After landing he seemed to recover his strength, and picked up speed. I made a giant leap and let myself drop right down on his back. He opened his mouth to let out a penetrating shriek. I bit into him with all my might. The pasha's neck cracked loudly, and his scream ended abruptly. Then his eyes closed, as if he were weary, as if he were about to fall asleep, slowly, very slowly, and then he exhaled the last breath of his meaningless rat's life.

That was all. No trace of his companions. They had left him to his fate. To save their own skins, they had left him to the fangs of the behemoth. Cowardly pack! United, they could have ripped me to shreds. This realisation made fury and disgust froth up in me again. I clamped the dead lump between my chops, straddled him on the floor, and scratched and tore his body with all four paws. The more fervently I worked him over, the more I felt my aggression recede.

Finally, left panting with exhaustion, I understood all at once that the cause of this unrestrained outburst of rage was not this foul rat but the nightmarish days I had gone through. The pasha had merely been a convenient whipping boy.

I let my prey go and looked off into space sadly. I was about ready to burst into tears, but for today there were no more tears to cry. The dead rat lay in front of me like a piece of meat ready for the frying-pan. His blood ran down over a thick, brown-speckled book that served as his funeral bier. Deep in thought, I absent-mindedly tried to decipher the handwritten title. Dirt and moisture had badly stained the cover. At the top, large block letters spelled out 'JO NAL', and under them, 'PRO E S R JUL US PRETERIUS'. The spaces between the letters had been obliterated by a motley mess of rat shit and some indefinable slimy substance that must have dripped down from the ceiling.

Curious? Of course I was. It was my old, incorrigible vice – or should I call it an affliction? I guess I would march down into hell without batting an eyelash to find out what the weather was like down there. And so my twisted, riddle-addicted mind once again began putting two and two together, while my paws automatically shoved the dead rat aside.

JO NAL . . .

One look in the book, of course, would have made the title obvious. But twisted minds don't work that way. They don't like easy solutions to riddles. Then, in a flash of inspiration, I had the answer. Idiot, why didn't you get it right away?

JO NAL was JOURNAL.

Then, step by step:

PRO E S R was PROFESSOR.

JUL US was JULIUS.

The journal of Professor Julius Preterius. I had him at last: my mysterious Dr Frankenstein. The miserable sinner had kept a diary. But to what purpose? And why was this confidential document among all this rubbish?

My paw trembling, I turned the cover of the book. The first yellowed pages were crammed with the sort of doodles that humans draw when they're bored or excited and don't have anything particular in mind – when they're telephoning, for instance. The remarkable thing about these doodles, however, was that each and every one showed brothers and sisters in poses that were sometimes funny, sometimes grotesque. The whole thing looked like some bizarre preparatory sketches for a painting of my kind at its silliest. I turned to the next page, and Professor Julius Preterius's secret entries began. Outside, rain began to sheet down. Through a vent in the wall facing me lightning flashed, and no doubt the gardens beyond were lit up as if by an exploding strobe. But this time neither the lightning nor the thunder frightened me.

I read on and on. And shuddered. Sheer terror at the guilt that had burdened this man overwhelmed me. Guilt, dread, and insanity. Or as good old Nietzsche said so well: 'And when you look long into the abyss, the abyss also looks into you . . .'

Chapter

— 6 —

15 January 1980

I am happy! I am the happiest man on God's earth! For a month I have had the feeling of being under the influence of drugs. But drug euphoria is not 'tangible', that is, the euphoric mood induced by stimulants always has a touch of the unreal. But this state . . . I could rip out entire forests, I could embrace and kiss anyone passing by in the street. Rosalie thinks I look at least ten years younger, which (and I can say this without false modesty) is in fact no exaggeration.

I have to marshal my thoughts, must set down the coming events in this journal for posterity. Although I have enough to do with two laboratory notebooks and the correspondence with Switzerland, here I would like to give an account of the project from my private, quite unscientific point of view as well. I confess that I am vain. For a month, I have had every reason to be!

My dream has come true. In retrospect, the years at the Institute seem like a bad dream. Professor Knorr's humiliating laughter, which greeted every one of my creative ideas with such *scorn, like a spiteful flourish, is now once and for all a thing of the past. I worked for ten years at that stultifying Institute, which is famous only for serving the best cafeteria food in Europe. And the thanks for it was: 'You will see, my dear colleague, that what you have set your mind on belongs in the realm of fantasy.'*

They can all go to hell! I don't even hate them; they are nothing more than paltry bureaucrats who spend their intellectual energy the whole livelong day on fiddling their expense accounts. Count me out, dear colleagues. Adieu!

Even PHARMAROX has employed them, these bureaucrats. But then unlike in their governmental sinecures, they have to come up with some good ideas now and then if they don't want to end up on the street one fine day along with their expensive office furniture. Mr Geibel and Dr Morf have 'donated' the lab to me and granted me funding for a research project for one year. They want to see results by then; otherwise their generosity will end.

I thank Almighty God.

24 January 1980

The lab is a dream! It has been set up in an old three-storey building and is equipped with the most modern examples of laboratory and medical technology. I still can't believe my good fortune. Besides my monthly salary of ten thousand Swiss francs and this experimenter's paradise, if I am successful I will receive a bonus of one and a half million francs and three per cent share of the profits, not to mention income from the patent rights. I'd like to see someone say now that the Swiss are greedy misers!

Sometimes I ask myself how things would look for me now if I hadn't knocked in person on the door of PHARMAROX last winter and asked to speak with Geibel. The old porter in the cathedral-like entrance hall must have thought me insane, but he did bring himself to make the call. Luckily, Geibel had read my article in Scientific American *and wanted to see me. The rest, as they say, is history. But what would have happened if everything had turned out differently? I am now fifty-one years old, and not one black hair can be found on my balding scalp. From my childhood on, I wanted to give my life meaning. If I die, I would like to leave something of myself behind in the world, and not simply go out like a tiny flame in a sea of tiny flames. What I leave behind need not be spectacular, but it should be meaningful. But the annoying peddling, the endless correspondence with pharmaceutical firms all around the world, the Sisyphean labour of convincing business boards has pretty much worn out my nerves and strength. To be honest, PHARMAROX was my last resort in the search for a financier.*

But why waste time worrying about a black day that never dawned? My life is no longer a study in black, not even in grey. While writing down these lines, I look out of the window of my second-floor office right at the sun. It is shining clearly and brightly, as if it wanted to congratulate me on taking up residence here.

To my annoyance, I have to keep in touch with the Institute. Knorr and his associates exert a not inconsiderable influence on the veterinary authorities responsible for animal-experiment permits. According to my information, some of that bunch even have positions on the boards. Is the nightmare ever going to end?

1 February 1980

The team is finally complete. Ziebold and Gray, the Australian molecular biologists, joined us today, and we fooled around a little with a magnum of champagne. You have to motivate your staff, otherwise you can forget the whole business right away. This I know from my own miserable experiences.

Apropos of being miserable: it was, of course, wishful thinking to suppose that PHARMAROX would allow me to tinker around here without supervision. They have infiltrated my operation with a certain Dr Gabriel, who is officially supposed to act as staff physician but who in reality is a rotten little spy. He knows it; I know it; everyone knows it. I will have to resign myself to being under permanent surveillance.

I 'kidnapped' Ziebold from the Institute. At first glance he seems to have chosen the wrong profession. His fashionable clothing, changed daily, and his foppish behaviour seem more appropriate for a male model than a scientist. But when he works an uncanny transformation overtakes him, and he concentrates like one possessed. Then brilliant ideas simply bubble out of him. A young, imaginative careerist, bold as brass, who would not be without his hundred-dollar aftershave even in the middle of the Gobi Desert – this is what the next generation of researchers may be like.

On the other hand, I dislike Gray completely. Unfortunately I cannot do without him, since he is reputed to be a genius in his field. He already thinks he knows everything better than I, and criticises my ideas with such rhetorical subtlety that I myself may soon be persuaded that they are absurd. When will scientists realise that imagination is of the greatest importance in this calling? But I'm not complaining. I thank God for this unparalleled opportunity.

In twelve days, we want to begin mixing the substances. If the first animal experiment succeeds, then I'd like to fly to Rome with Rosalie and live for a whole week on nothing but Chianti Classico. It will be a magnificent celebration!

2 March 1980

The soup is ready!

That's what we humorously call the mixture in the lab: the soup. Actually it consists of seventy-six experimental preparations, each with differing constituents, but the differences are so slight that essentially it's one and the same substance. In a very noisy meeting, we accepted Gray's proposal to prepare bacterial cultures that accelerate the production of coagulating enzymes, and then to integrate them into the soup. As things stand now, we will have to make thousands of experiments. I myself am ready to listen to the wildest ideas of my staff, although I will not deviate from my initial idea of finding a solution primarily along chemical lines. No matter how you look at it, the principal substance must remain autopolymerising plastic, for only its particular molecular structure will bind two objects quickly and firmly. Living cells are no exception.

The idea of the soup occurred to me ten years ago when I hurt my hand rather badly while cutting out newspaper articles for my private archives. Still somewhat absorbed in the work, I absent-mindedly took note of the cut in my palm and then saw paper glue in front of me on the table. I had a sudden flash of inspiration. It would be so practical, I thought to myself, if I could quickly glue together the slightly open wound instead of first treating it with antiseptic cream and bandages and then having to put up with a painful healing process.

Excited by this insight, one wave of inspiration followed another, while the blood dripped merrily from the wound on the desk, soaking the newspaper in red. I thought of the tissue glue, the so-called two-component fibrin glue that is already in use for smaller injuries and for those operations where sewing is impossible, as with certain internal organs like the spleen, and with those organs whose cellular composition is not up to the stress. Fibrin glue, however, has never been able to deliver what it promised. It is compatible with tissue and capable of being absorbed well by the organism, but it does not work with gaping and mechanically induced wounds. The upshot is that it can only be used in conjunction with the classical method of sewing wounds. And so it is hardly surprising that surgeons do not like this fibrin glue, but remain sold on good old sewing, which also gives them the opportunity to show off their skills.

This will change, because I have a radical solution in mind. Although it is foreseeable that I will receive no Nobel Prize for my soup, it will nevertheless revolutionise medicine. And what does the Nobel Prize mean to me anyway? It wasn't awarded to the inventor of the light bulb either, although that invention has caused greater upheavals in this century than the splitting of the atom. The small, invisible revolutions are the ones that count!

My intention is to eliminate the sewing method completely. It is complicated, time consuming, and can only be carried out by experts. I will even go a step further and maintain that my 'instant glue' will one day be in every first-aid cabinet. An open wound will simply be glued together on the spot. That will have life-and-death significance, particularly in traffic accidents and military conflicts.

The following is to be achieved: primary wound healing is more or less done by nature alone. Problems begin only during secondary wound healing. In most cases, the wound edges do not meet exactly. Often, the wound remains open, a piece of tissue is lacking, or the tissue is so heavily damaged that it dies. Bacteria quickly penetrate torn tissue. The wound must therefore be given assistance, which means joining the wound edges by sewing, stapling, clamping – or gluing. Ideally my soup will take care of all that.

Of course, my tissue glue will not be capable of doing what the skilled hands of surgeons can accomplish. Nevertheless, in the case of the injured soldier at the front or the bleeding child in a traffic accident, even orderlies will be able to give first aid by this means.

In the event that the preparation does indeed glue wounds instantaneously, it remains necessary to refine the following:

1. It must be antiseptic or 'intercept' bacteria at the preliminary stages, when they penetrate the wound.
2. Because of its polymerising property, it will instantly

*join the edges of a wound. However, it should never make
the wound airtight. Oxygen deficiency induces the spread
of infection.*

3. The immune system should not, or should not prematurely, reject the preparation.

*4. The soup must, so to speak, inhabit the human body
like a spirit, evaporating into air after use. Two to three
weeks seem to me to be a realistic period of time.*

*5. One must be able to handle the substance in an
uncomplicated manner – practically like a genie in a tube.*

*If we can achieve this, then we will indeed have done humanity a
glorious service.*

*I have been pursued by misfortune as far as the recognition
and realisation of my dreams are concerned. But why shouldn't
I be lucky some day too?*

17 March 1980

*Everything is coming along splendidly – a little too splendidly.
Just a little more research on extravasal blood clotting and then
we can begin the animal experiments. Rosalie says I'm overworked and should get some rest, at least at the weekends. The
good woman simply can't imagine that once work becomes an
obsession it has nothing in common with the traditional concept
of a job.*

*It is now one a.m., and I'm still sitting here in my nice new
office, which has been livened up by Rosalie's pansies. The
others left long ago. The only light on in the building is the
antique reading lamp on my desk. I have allowed myself a
couple of glasses of red wine, and am slowly getting into a
philosophical mood. My thoughts drift to Robert and Lydia and
to those happy Sundays when they were carefree children. I still*

love them from the bottom of my heart, although now they only honour us with their company during the Christmas festivities, which they have managed to make into a boring game with their bored expressions. A silly and depressing game. We have become total strangers; aside from a few trivialities, we have nothing to say to one another. Even my surprising career breakthrough does not seem to interest them. Lies, empty phrases, and coldness characterise the relationship between my children and myself. Is this the way of the world? Is everyone condemned to the same fate? Do we all wish for children and then find that we have brought strangers into the world?

My only remaining joys are my work and Rosalie. Or does Rosalie also figure in that chapter called 'The Deceptions That Life Has Contrived'? Isn't it closer to the truth that she is only a fond habit, one I can't drop because then I'd have to admit, shamefaced, that she was really nothing but a habit and that for years I have made much ado about nothing? I hope not.

I have never had passionate relations with women. I have neither understood them nor have they particularly interested me, not even as a young man. I married the first woman who struck up a friendship with me. I never did find the entrance to that realm of life described by the poets as the one worth living for. What, then, have I done with my life?

I must stop this demoralising moping around. It'll get me nowhere. It is late. The animals will be delivered tomorrow morning, and I have to be there when they arrive. I requested permission to perform experiments on chimpanzees, but, just as I expected, my application was not approved. Their flimsy argument was that primates may only be used in the last phase of the project. Ignoramuses! Something truly epoch-making is in the works here, and they're too blind to recognise it.

But I have to keep calm. Really, I should at least be happy not to have to experiment on mice; their thin skin renders them a waste of time for my purposes.

18 March 1980

The animals have arrived! An incessant mewing resounds throughout the building, and the lab technicians are beside themselves with delight at the droll behaviour of these lively creatures. We have fed and caressed them together. They'll have a good life with us here: I guarantee it.

27 March 1980

The first experiment failed. We made small incisions in the heads of five animals without anaesthetic and treated the edges of the wounds with the soup. But instead of sticking together, the mixture burned the skin away completely, and ate its way like acid through the skull to the brain. The animals had to be put to sleep immediately.

So, it was a setback. I hadn't expected anything else at such an early stage, but, on the other hand, I also hadn't reckoned with the frighteningly aggressive nature of the substance. Something basic is out of kilter. We have to work even harder. Rome has been cancelled.

2 April 1980/1:20 a.m.

I'm hopelessly drunk and really astonished that I'm still capable of putting my thoughts down on paper. Last week's failure was a crueller blow to my self-confidence than I was at first willing to admit to myself. It's really peculiar. We used a mixture which should have had an excellent chance of succeeding. No one could have foreseen the terrible consequences. Even Gray, who regards everything with scepticism, was shaken by the effects.

The virtuous Dr Gabriel leaked a message to his accomplices before I could write my report and send it off to Switzerland.

Then Geibel called personally to get the details of the débâcle. This scaremongering is scandalous and can only harm team morale.

After the autopsy of the animals, we are assuming that the failure of the experiment may be attributed to an excessively high concentration of malic acid. The scalp, the skull, and the brains of the subjects look like plastic that's been melted by heat. Diluting the solution may be next month's answer.

I have to work twice as hard now. Rosalie will have to get used to seeing me only rarely.

11 April 1980

An irony of fate: although we now house thirty animals here, this morning a rather dignified fellow found a new home with us. While parking my car in front of the lab, I saw him running back and forth at the door, energetically scratching at it again and again. Courageous fellow. He looks like he's homeless, although his muscular body shows that he has a first-class constitution. The lab technicians are convinced that he's a stray. So we took in the cheeky devil and appointed him our mascot. He has the run of the building with everyone spoiling him and giving him treats to eat. It would interest me to find out what he thinks about the other members of his species in the cages.

25 April 1980

A new experiment, a new flop. Three animals had their bellies shaved and cut open with a scalpel. Then the edges of the wounds were coated with the soup and the wounds closed with clamps. Five hours later, we discovered to our disappointment that the cementing effect hadn't properly taken place. In my opinion, decreasing the acidic component caused the failure.

Obviously, the acid exercises a catalytic effect on the mixture. I must admit that the other substances do not harmonise with one another very well. In order to achieve a breakthrough, many more experiments are going to be necessary, and consequently we will need more animals than we originally calculated. But most of all, we need more time. The whole business is annoying, especially because once we have solved this problem, we still have to concern ourselves with whether or not the immune system will tolerate the preparation; there may be a time-delayed rejection. This will be an uphill battle.

Soon I will write my report and send it off to Switzerland. It's devastating to have to report bad news, but that's the way things are. I have, however, the strong suspicion that Dr Gabriel has already informed PHARMAROX long ago. Incidentally, this fine gentleman makes no effort whatsoever to conceal his true role in the project. As if that were not enough, that repulsive Knorr from the Institute has given word that he will visit us. Under the cloak of wanting to maintain friendly contact, his real intention is to secure evidence of my failures.

While I write all this down, I am very near to tears. God, give me the strength to free myself from this dilemma. The stray I recently picked up, now sitting on my desk, is watching me with a reverent look. He is probably the only one who understands my troubles. The others have adopted an air of indifference towards my project. They are at the very top in their fields and can find work at a firm or institution anywhere they please. They probably regard me as an idiot because I'm devoting my time to an idea as childish as this. Not without reason, perhaps.

7 May 1980

With great fanfare, spring has made its appearance in the garden behind our building, awakening a dizzy riot of life. With the dazzling sunshine and the festival of scents all around, I should be shouting for joy. Yet I may very well be the unhappiest man on earth. This morning we conducted a new experiment on ten animals. The result was our worst defeat so far. Long incisions were made in various parts of the subjects' bodies, creating large, gaping wounds. After we had coated the incision areas with the soup, we pressed the edges of the wounds together with forceps. It was horrifying. At first, the edges actually did stick together, but within seconds the mixture was eating its way into the tissue, fraying it and turning it to pulp. The wounds got larger and larger until finally they became an unrecognisable mess of blood and purulent discharges. When the reaction was over, all ten animals were dead.

I simply do not understand what happened. It contradicts all logic. Although we have learned how to deal with the acidity problem, living cells still cannot tolerate the preparation. I am so overcome by shame, anger, and self-doubt that my whole body is shaking. Now more than ever I would like to step up the pace of the experiments, but I have no idea how to justify that to the team . . .

11:25 p.m.

Since the others left the building, I have been consoling myself with a bottle of red wine. The whole time my thoughts keep circling around this seemingly insoluble problem. But my ruminations haven't provided me with any particularly good answers, because I find no mistakes in the concept. That's why, in just a moment, I'm going to start a new experiment. Although I am not accountable to anyone, I must keep this experiment a secret because, to be honest, I myself see no justifiable reason for it. The one who'll have to have faith in it, I'm afraid, is the nameless stray.

2:30 p.m.

A miracle has happened! It worked on the very first try!

That is perhaps a little exaggerated, but you could certainly call the experiment a success, if only a rudimentary one.

While I was carrying out the operation, I suddenly asked myself what I was doing in the operating room in the middle of the night. I felt like a criminal, and everything I had done seemed senseless and manic to me. I had not counted on success right from the beginning. My behaviour was like that of a defiant child, desperately rebelling against his omnipotent father although he knows he doesn't have the slightest chance against him. And then this happened . . .

After I had shaved the stray, injected a muscle relaxant, and tied him down on the operating table with his paws extended, I made an incision of about six inches in his belly. He cried out and growled miserably, even trying to bite me. Before blood could actually start to flow out of the wound, I treated it with the mixture. I pressed the edges of the wound together with my thumb and index finger, and then, in the twinkling of an eye, the wonder occurred: they stuck together for a moment. I was so amazed that I thought I was hallucinating on all that good red wine, which, I must admit, had clouded my senses a bit. But at this success I sobered up right away. A thousand questions shot through my head, but now that I had achieved something I had wanted for so long, they seemed trivial. Why did the same preparation work that had failed sixteen hours earlier? Was it a matter of the dosage? Had my staff done slipshod work? I sat down on a chair, smoked a cigarette, and watched the patient, who seemed surprised himself at his sudden healing. For the next hour and a half, I cleaned up the operating room and struggled to come down from seventh heaven. Then I examined the wound again. The edges had separated a little from one another, which was of little consequence since we are only in the initial stage of development. To be safe, I sewed the incision together and put the patient into a cage. He looked at me perplexed, as if wanting to know what the whole business was supposed to mean. I chuckled softly, and then was about to leave the room when it suddenly occurred to me that the patient didn't even have a name. After thinking for a moment, I decided to use the classical method of naming, and baptised my helper and friend 'Claudandus'.

10 May 1980

They took it with nonchalant equanimity, not because I had abused Claudandus for the test but because I had done it behind their backs. As if I were an unimportant lab assistant who had to ask permission just to clean a test-tube! They still don't take me seriously. That's the real trouble. There must be something about my face, about my behaviour, about my entire personality that makes people doubt my authority (assuming I ever had it). But that doesn't matter to me now, because all that counts is the soup.

Claudandus has made an excellent recovery from the operation and sleeps most of the time. It remains to be seen whether his immune system will reject the glue after the expected period of time. I have sprayed his entire belly with a substance that tastes awful so that the animal will not lick his wound or bite through his stitches. In a few weeks, we will repeat the experiment on several animals, proceeding exactly as I did on that miraculous night.

Triumph follows on triumph. The much-feared visit of that cretin Knorr took place without a hitch, and he was denied the satisfaction he so much desired. After all, we had Claudandus to show for our work.

1 June 1980

I am on the brink of losing my mind. The breakthrough that I assumed had long ago taken place – how arrogant of me – was apparently false. The experiments on all five animals have failed. Not only did the mixture show no effect on them but, inexplicably, it obstructed natural blood clotting so that the animals bled to death most miserably.

I have a nasty suspicion. We are waiting on tenterhooks for Claudandus's abdominal wound to heal. Then we will have to 'take him apart again'.

14 June 1980

It is just as I thought. Claudandus is a mutant. We do not know what makes him different from other animals, but some factor in his genetic make-up enables his organism to assimilate the soup without any difficulties.

Today we got busy on the flanks of the animal, where we made incisions of varying length and depth. Some superficial incisions were also made in his internal organs. After treatment with the mixture, the edges of the wounds stuck together so well we were even able to do without safety stitches. Then the same experiment was repeated on another animal, but it was a complete failure. We did not even bother to patch together the injured animal, but put him to sleep on the spot.

It is lucky that Gray is with us, for from now on our battered research train will chug off in the direction of genetics. We will have to carry out an infinite number of studies on Claudandus to discover his secret. Experiments with other animals will naturally continue to be carried out. Considering how uncertain success has become, I am seriously concerned that PHARMAROX may be planning to distance or even dissociate itself from the project. What will happen to us then? I will never return to the Institute!

2 July 1980

Busy night and day analysing Claudandus's genetic make-up, in so far as is possible with our modest equipment. The animal is not to be envied, for it is being subjected to unimaginable suffering. Tissue samples must be taken continually, injections and pain-causing substances given, and operations on its internal organs made. It is a heartbreaking sight. Since we have already used half of the time allotted to us, we will have to continue to work under great pressure. It's a macabre routine: slitting open nearly a dozen animals daily and stitching them back together again, often mutilating them or even having to put them to sleep. Moreover, I have been quarrelling more often with Rosalie about my drinking. She simply refuses to understand that I am nearly at breaking point because of stress and depression and that I need a way to let off steam, at least at night.

I have never loved alcohol, not even in my spare time. My affinity for red wine actually has an epicurean origin. In recent months, however, alcohol has stimulated all my senses, enabling me to think more clearly as well as providing the relaxation I so bitterly need. Rosalie understands nothing of this. But has she ever understood anything at all? I mean the significance of my work, my dreams, the meaning I have tried to give my life? Apparently two people can live together for an eternity without knowing and understanding each other. This insight is bitter and sad, like everything else here.

17 July 1980

*We aren't making any progress. Yet that doesn't seem to be the
real problem; rather, my staff are losing interest in the project,
and even seem reluctant to go ahead with it. Young people,
particularly ambitious ones, seem to possess an unerring sixth
sense which warns them to take their bets off the wrong horse
before it loses. Although they try not to show what they're
thinking by industriously going about their daily work, dutifully
laughing at my jokes, and pretending that every insignificant
advance amounts to a breakthrough, one would have to be very
insensitive not to notice that the paralysing darts of resignation
have long since stung them. How can young people be so short-
winded and short-sighted? Don't they know that great things
are accomplished only by people of great courage and dedica-
tion? This sad matter does have one cheerful aspect. The more I
work with these animals and learn about them, the more they
fascinate me. No matter how the project ends, I plan to give up
research after this and probably not work any more at all.
Breeding these beasts, on a strictly scientific basis, would be a
nice and even profitable hobby. To be honest, I have already
begun doing so in secret.*

14 August 1980

*Ill tidings three times in one day. Now it's official: this morning,
a letter from PHARMAROX landed on my desk in which
Geibel informs me that funding for the project will be reduced
by one third. The concrete consequences of this senseless cut?
Dismissal of nearly all the lab technicians and one biological
assistant, a reduction in salaries, and drastic economisation on
experimental animals and diverse odds and ends, the lack of
which will make the work even harder for us than it already is.
These penny-pinchers are doing exactly the opposite of what*

*they should be doing. In these demoralising hours, just when we
aren't making any progress and need more financial incentive,
they cut the budget. To top it off, Gray has given notice. I
assume he doesn't want his name associated with a flop, which,
admittedly, is a sign of intelligence.*

*Compared to the above, the third piece of catastrophic news
was relatively harmless. The veterinary board has approved
fewer animal experiments than we applied for. To keep the
present number of permits, the commission wants detailed
information on the experiments, which in plain language means
that they, too, want to see results. Well, what's there to say to
that? It's as if the project were being financed not by PHARM-
AROX, but by these smartarses. Of course I know who's
behind all this meddling: Knorr and his philistines. Since they
see no other way of sabotaging my work, they're resorting to
dirty tricks.*

*It is now two a.m. The entire building is sweltering in heat.
I'm drunk again, and all my feelings seem numb. Just now I was
in the animal room to see my patients and give them water. They
all have big, ugly scars, clearly visible on their shaved bodies. It
is regrettable that some of them have had to be mutilated, but
we had no choice. The one in the worst state is Claudandus,
whose genetic code we still haven't been able to crack. Countless experiments have gradually given him the appearance of a
monster. He was sleeping, but even in sleep he moaned in pain.
If a wonder does indeed happen, I will perpetuate his memory. I
will call the preparation CLAUDANDUS.*

23 August 1980

*I did it today. When I left the lab at three in the morning and
staggered back to the car, I was somewhat disoriented, being
under the influence of a considerable dose of grape juice. Still,
they caught my attention. One of these strange creatures was*

sitting in front of the door of almost every house, keeping watch over its territory. Since they are primarily nocturnal, they are compelled to go out at midnight. Then the world belongs to them. It has to be seen to be believed. They more or less take over the city. I suddenly had the absurd suspicion that they feel superior to humanity and are only waiting for the opportune moment to subjugate us. It reminds me of the story of the carnivorous plant that someone brought back home as a seedling and cared for until one fine day, tall and strong, it devoured the entire family.

I was strolling wearily down the street when I saw two good-looking specimens sitting on a garden wall. Their faces had a philosophical expression, as if they were meditating on the endlessness of the universe. The thought amused me, but at the same time I remembered our lack of experimental animals and our constant trouble with the veterinary authorities. In doing what I then did, I was conscious of no guilt. With scarcely a moment's thought, I clamped the two philosophers under my arms, rushed back to the lab, and locked them up in cages. They glared at me nastily, obviously no longer meditating on the endlessness of the universe.

And now I ask the imaginary judge in my mind: am I a criminal just because I seized two living beings for an experiment on whose success many lives, including animal lives, may depend? Am I a dirty rotten scoundrel because I take risks for science? But the judge in my mind is silent; he has no reply. And that is much worse than if he were to condemn me. But it is not the silence of the judge that makes the blood in my veins freeze in terror, but that of the victims.

15 September 1980

The rats are abandoning the sinking ship. Today, Ziebold departed. He never gave a plausible reason for leaving. During

*the sad interview we held in my office, the man spoke the whole
time like a book of riddles. Gradually, however, I have become a
world master at solving riddles and know now how to interpret
signs and half-truths correctly. Everyone here is conspiring
against me; they are all waiting for my complete and utter ruin.
The failure was probably planned right from the beginning; why
else would Ziebold have so readily left the Institute to sign up
with me? He never said anything about feeling unhappy here
before. He accepted my very first offer to join the project – in my
naïvety I took his commitment for granted. But I have learned a
thing or two since then. Today I know that my project was
sabotaged right from the beginning. It's rather strange that up
to now the only one to have achieved any success has been I.
Yes, that must be it. They want to ruin me.*

*My telephone has probably been tapped. But I will not make
myself conspicuous in any way. I will eke out a solution here,
and work right to the bitter end. As far as I'm concerned, they
can all leave. I can do without them.*

3:20 p.m.

*I have the suspicion that even Rosalie is in cahoots with them.
Why else would she make life hell for me day after day with her
reproaches? Surely only to weaken my intellectual powers and
keep me from my work. This is why I won't go home any more.
The situation is unpleasant enough as it is. Moreover, I have more
than enough to do every night 'organising' experimental animals.*

29 September 1980

*A free-for-all worthy of Hollywood took place in the lab today.
Knorr, Gabriel, and I all suffered black eyes and bruises. No one
has ever called me violent, but in the face of the kind of*

impudence I have to put up with here, even Gandhi would see red.

While making my routine rounds this morning, I surprised Dr Gabriel while he was showing the experimental arrangements in the lab to that imbecile Knorr, who had turned up unannounced. I assume Gabriel was initiating him into our secrets; in any case, he was waiting on him hand and foot, as if not I but he were the head of the lab. When I saw the two of them whispering to each other confidentially, I suddenly blew up. I threw myself at them, lashing out wildly. The spies tried to defend themselves, but I found the strength of a madman in myself and was giving them a thorough thrashing when we were separated by the lab assistants, who had come rushing to the scene.

That'll teach them a lesson. I'm sick and tired of the unending sabotage. And I'm firmly resolved to defend the lab – by tooth and nail if necessary!

17 October 1980

I no longer respond to the harassing letters and calls from Switzerland. Funds have long ago been cut to the level of bare maintenance, and besides me only a biological assistant and two technicians remain in the building. The most insolent news came this morning. Knorr is supposed to take my place next year. My suspicion is now fully and unquestionably confirmed: the project has fallen prey to hateful intrigues and secret agreements with the Institute. My task was to do initial research for PHARMAROX, nothing more. Credit for any success was to have gone to that disgusting, double-dealing Knorr. But they didn't count on my putting up a fight. When they come I will greet them with bullets. As far as I'm concerned, they can install as many bugs as they want, anywhere they want, and they can have their spies drive up and down the street in black limousines to see if they can't find out what I'm up to. I'm ready for them.

I have dismissed all the people who were still here so that I can work all alone next week in peace and quiet. I don't need their damned money and their damned personnel. I don't need anyone!

If only I knew what these strange formulae that sometimes glow on the walls are supposed to mean.

November

It's great to work alone! You can turn up the radio, drink as much as you want, do what you please. Undisturbed by sabotage, I am making progress much more rapidly, although not for a moment may I forget that I am under the closest observation. Why else would they have put the lab at my disposal? Naturally, every day another letter arrives in which they demand that I leave the building; however, they will not immediately summon the police. Why not? Why not? I am well up to their sinister plans: they want to let the head-case experiment until he finds what he's seeking — and what they are seeking.

Meanwhile, I have been setting about procuring new animals with undiminished enthusiasm. They are the only ones who know how to appreciate my work. How brave and self-sacrificing they are in putting their little bodies at my disposal, how grateful they are for the little food they receive, and how worthless their own lives must seem to them in comparison to the inestimably great service being done to science.

I get through about seven animals daily. Since the mixture still does not show any adhesive qualities, I have to operate practically all day long. I make incisions in every part of their bodies: in the neck, in the anus, in the intestines, in the muscles, in the eyes — everywhere. Thanks to my ingenious breeding programme, some of the females have given birth to kittens, ensuring a plentiful supply of subjects. I work, of course, most intensively on Claudandus, although he continues to conceal his secret from me.

Really I should take a break now and clean up the lab. There is a terrible stench of blood and animal cadavers.

November

Rosalie, oh my poor Rosalie, don't worry about me, you virtuous woman. You have just been standing at the door and ringing the bell for a very long time. I didn't open the door for you, although I was watching you from behind the blind. Your face was full of worry; I could see it clearly. Your husband, who loves you more than anything, will return to you after he has completed his work, and then everything will be the way it was.

The way it was? I can no longer remember how it was. In fact, it's hard for me to formulate a clear thought, even to determine whether it's day or night.

Oh, Rosalie! Did you know that blood possesses a magical power of attraction and that the body of an animal is almost identical to that of a person? One should not work as intensively and as long with blood and bleeding bodies as I have. You start to get funny ideas. Then you can no longer get to sleep, and if you do, you have these terrible nightmares in which the bleeding bodies return from the dead, proffer their gaping wounds reproachfully, and scream: Glue them together! Glue them together! But you are not in a position to glue together all the wounds of this world, because your glue fails, fails again and again. But then the little, wound-covered bodies cry out again and again: Glue! Glue! Put us together again! Then you wake up, screaming and drenched in sweat, but reality cannot offer you any consolation because all these slit-open bodies lie next to you and because you are completely soaked in their blood.

There are infinite versions of hell, Rosalie, and all of them begin before you die. Ask Claudandus, he can confirm this for you. I often sit in front of his cage and watch him for hours, sometimes all day long. He has changed a great deal since he started to suffer, not only physically. He glares at me with so much knowledge and hate in his eyes, it's as if he were human. Yes, there is something human in his clouded eyes. I believe that he has lost his innocence. Mad, but sometimes I have the feeling that he wants to talk with me. But what does he want to say to me? Does he want to pour out his sorrows? Does he want to beg for mercy? No, no, I cannot take that into consideration. I am a scientist, an animal capable of knowing itself.

Rosalie, my darling wife, it is certain that we will find a way back to the way it was, believe me. And then it will be much more beautiful for us. I will receive the Nobel Prize and make constant television appearances. Complete strangers will congratulate me in the street, healed patients will shower me with gratitude. Thank you, Professor Preterius, thank you, thank you for CLAUDANDUS, this glue that has saved each and every one of our lives. Even the animals will thank me. Thank you, Professor Preterius, you slit us open and then you glued us back together. For this we are most grateful to you. Thank you! Thank you! Thank you! Thank you! Thank you! Thank you!

November

    Dear Claudandus, come and be my guest,
    Show me what you have beneath your breast.
    Gaping wound and festering abscess,
    Slitting you open is effortless.
    But still I'd like to know, kind sir,
    What lies beneath your fur?

Professor Julius Preterius
The discoverer of CLAUDANDUS, the revolutionary glue for
tissue adhesion
Awarded the Nobel Prize for biology in 1981
incredibilis vis ingenii

Black, Black December

It doesn't stick together! It will never stick together!

Even the spirits, the transparent, glowing creatures that buzz around me during my many operations call these words out to me incessantly. Go away! Away you bastards! I cry out, yet they circle again and again around the operating table, laughing at me with their whining voices. They also dwell within the mixture, and this is why it remains ineffective. However, I will steadfastly continue to experiment and not allow myself to be stopped by anything or anybody.

Since I have become too weak to go out at night to capture new animals on which to experiment, I am now completely dependent on what I breed. But that works out splendidly. I have a dream of a unique race, a race that has never existed before. A super race! An ingeniously simple solution, breathtaking in its originality! Is Claudandus still capable of producing offspring?

Year of Our Lord, Anno 1980

Hacked-up intestines, gouged-out eyes, chopped-off tails!

Professor, can a head that has been cleanly cut off be rejoined to the trunk?

We'll give it a try, dear students.

Is it possible to cement a sawed-off paw back to the stump so that the poor creature will not have to hobble later, Professor Preterius?

We'll give it a try, honoured members of the Nobel Prize committee.

Professor, do you believe that your mixture could glue together an animal that has been injured in a head-on collision — one perhaps staged for the purpose?

I haven't the faintest idea, my dear television audience. But we'll give it a try.

Away with you, you phantoms! Leave me in peace, you devils! I didn't mean to do anything wrong!

He spoke today! Yes, Claudandus spoke with me. Fascinating, isn't it? An animal that can talk. And this is my discovery! I will surely receive the Nobel Prize for this.

But what did he say? What could it have been? I can no longer remember. He spoke so softly and seriously, and somehow sternly. That animal has no sense of humour whatsoever. Didn't he say that I should let him out of the cage and prepare to fight him? Is that what he said?

Oh! Everything is swimming before my eyes. The lab is gradually dissolving into rosy little clouds. I must save Claudandus!

CHAPTER

7

'What you've put on record, Professor, is extremely impressive, but just what does this slasher movie have to do with those brothers and sisters of mine who have woken up recently with a wound in their necks of such awesome size that even your miracle glue couldn't have saved them?'

'But it's quite elementary, my dear Francis. As you may remember, in the remaining months of my memorable stay at the laboratory, I applied myself intensively to perfecting your species. In that time I succeeded in breeding an extraordinary "super race", only its hunting instincts got a little mixed up. Right now the offspring of that breed are prowling around your neighbourhood, and at regular intervals, unbalanced as they are, they snap at any neck that presents itself to them. What do you think? A terribly exciting solution, isn't it?'

'Professor, what you've just said is nonsense! You really are straight out of some hackneyed horror film – witness the abject failure of your research project. I find your "super race" theory simply ridiculous. First, a very long period of time and many generations of animals are required to breed a special, not to mention extraordinary, breed. But the most limited of your resources was time. Second, your journal hinted at your wish to breed an omnipotent species, not a murderous one. Third, the process of breeding a race of killers (assuming in fact that such a race was created) quite obviously ended when the laboratory was shut down and the animals set free. So keep your fairy-tales to yourself, and come to us with facts.'

'OK, I lied a little. But now I'm finally going to tell you the truth. So prick up your furry little ears and pay attention: I confess! I'm the murderer! As you know, the horrifying events at the end of 1980 were only very vaguely referred to in my journal. And that does give rise to speculation, doesn't it? Admittedly, towards the end of my research I was acting pretty crazy. The perpetual brooding about the soup, about its nature, and particularly about Claudandus's genetic make-up completely undermined my rationality. You should, however, turn your attention to what really triggered off my psychotic breakdown, namely my much too intensive study of your species. I was infatuated with you little beasts. Anyway, to cut a long story short, after this, the biggest fiasco of my life, I ended up in neither a padded cell nor a coffin. On the contrary, I am enjoying the best of schizophrenic health and slink around in the district like the phantom of the opera, killing one felid after another. Why? Well, because I'm insane, utterly insane, understand? And dangerous! In all of my exploits I camouflage myself most artfully, stick closely to animal habits, and dispatch my victims by their own characteristic killing method: by a lethal bite in the neck. Isn't that a stroke of genius?'

'I'm afraid, Professor, that you're even more cracked than you think, for apparently you've lost all control over your imagination. You can hardly expect me to buy this phantom-of-the-opera nonsense. Look, it's child's play to expose your lies. It's silly, not to mention illogical, to claim that after you went off your rocker you actually began living a phantom existence in order to mess around with the necks of brothers and sisters. Where have you been hiding all this time? Where have you been getting your food? At least eight years have gone by. Weren't you ever ill? You aren't some small animal that nobody would notice when you went out, presumably on all fours, on your nocturnal hunts for unsuspecting Felidae. And since to all appearances you've lost your marbles, you wouldn't even be capable of the most basic hunting manoeuvres, which are complicated and require stamina.

'I have another theory. You were performing experiments in your Frankenstein laboratory that the veterinary authorities refused to issue permits for. I have seen the evidence of these prohibited experiments running around loose in the district. A dear friend of mine named Felicity told me (if only by way of describing a dream) that in the last, reclusive phase of your mad research there was a mutiny in your laboratory that led to the liberation of your guinea pigs. The fact is that the victims of those inhum . . . no, *inanimal* experiments are still alive and among us. But the PHARMAROX big shots were ready to go to any length to prevent an animal-cruelty scandal associated with them from becoming public. At first they wanted to replace you with your arch-enemy Knorr, but then research in this area was completely stopped. When the people at the top woke up, they realised, if a little late, what a mess you had made in those months when nobody was keeping an eye on you, and the laboratory was shut down at short notice, the sign outside hurriedly taken down, and the "Tissue Cement Project" abandoned to sink into oblivion. But some traces of your work remained, and they were causing these gentlemen a great deal of worry. They saw no way of covering them up without attracting attention, because they were free and at large, wandering through the district gardens, or perhaps even in hiding. What would happen if other people were to discover these freaks? Would they become suspicious and link these miserable, mutilated beasts with the mysterious laboratory in their neighbourhood? Of course they would! Consequently, every animal that had broken out of the laboratory had to be eliminated. This explanation certainly sounds more plausible to me.'

'Hahaaa! Your wild imagination exceeds even my own disturbed mind, my dear Francis. So you really believe that, rather than me, certain animal assassins commissioned by PHARMAROX are running around killing off your friends? Presumably on all fours? Very amusing. Really, very amusing. You walked right into your own trap. Allow me to demonstrate just how untenable is your flimsy hypothesis. First, there is the time factor, which again defies your logic. After eight years, have these ominous hit men still not been successful in liquidating all the crippled experimental animals? Do you seriously believe that a firm like PHARMAROX would need eight years to finish off those pinheads? Second, if the killers had really been planning to wipe out the flesh-and-blood evidence of an illegal experiment, then why is the whole neighbourhood littered with their corpses in full view of anyone out for a stroll? And third, Sherlock, the sixty-four-thousand-dollar question: were the murdered, except for Felicity, mutilated in any way? No? Ha, ha, ha, ha, ha! Think before you speak, says the educated humanist! Hahaaa! Hahaaa! Hahaaa!'

This was the dialogue that ran through my mind after I had finished reading Professor Julius Preterius's journal and was desperately trying to connect it with the murders. Was that such a strange thing to do? When you considered it objectively, no links seemed to exist between the present murders and that gruesome laboratory in 1980. But I felt deep down that somehow there was a connection. For one thing, the horrors described in the journal were of such unimaginable dimensions that they must have started a chain reaction of evil that would have further influence in the future. Evil is like a cell endlessly dividing itself; once it comes into being, it will beget even more evil. It's the relentless quantum mechanics of the universe. For another, you would have to have had the sensitivity of an amoeba not to notice that the mysterious series of murders involved only my kind. Both murderers and murdered belonged to my species; no elephants had a role in the affair. So there had to be some particular element that was specific to us, something that concerned Felidae alone. And this 'something' would probably lead to the solution I had been searching for for so long. I felt it; I knew it.

These penetrating insights aside, perhaps it would have been fitting to have had a minute's silence in honour of all the tormented and dead whose memory only Preterius's musty old journal, in a grotesque way, kept alive. But I couldn't. I chose to play the terribly clever sleuth rather than ponder the meaning of that hell on earth which, though it had taken place in the past, was by no means a thing of the past. Nothing gets lost in this world; everything lives on. But I should have wasted a thought or two on Claudandus, on that wretched creature who probably died when the drama came to an end. Tears should have filled my eyes at his immeasurably sad fate, at what had been made of his life, and at what living beings do to other living beings once they have attained a certain body size, a certain brain capacity, and a certain degree of self-awareness. I should have been bent over with sorrow at the memory not only of the victims, but also of the victimiser, because, well, because all aspects of the affair demonstrated to me the everlasting desperation of the world and the imperfection of those who live in it. In short, I should have just understood it, and contributed my little bit of sadness.

Instead, I only felt hatred, an indescribably immense hatred, for Preterius and for the execrable members of his race. Preterius, though, had vanished, and was in any case much too miserable and much too fantastic a figure to be worth hating with all my heart. And even the other human beings, those who went about their own human business, pursued their absurd activities, who acted as if they were clever, informed, contemporary, compassionate, funny, talented, who acted as if they were really human and really humane, were too anonymous and too insignificant to warrant my precious hate. I therefore focused – not very consciously – my entire charge of hate on the perpetrator of the vile murders. He was nearer to hand and nearer to being seized, and with a little thinking I might very well have a chance to put him where he belonged.

There were three ways to solve the mystery, but they all had stumbling blocks the size of the Empire State Building. I mentally reviewed every line of the journal, and every significant and insignificant event of the past few days, considering them forwards, backwards and sideways, forcing my brain cells to establish connections. But it was no use. Right then I couldn't come up with any further possible solutions. But maybe solutions had become superfluous, because I suddenly started to get the feeling that I was being watched. I didn't know exactly how much time I had spent reading the journal and thinking about it, but I was absolutely sure that the eyes that now had me under observation could only have turned up a few minutes ago.

Was my time up? Was I about to be number seven, about to meet the killer?

He sprang, no, he shot at me like a rogue guided missile. He had been lurking behind a broken ventilation panel in the wall that separated the basement from the low-lying garden. A bloodcurdling shriek rent the air. My insidious assailant plunged through the air, his shark's mouth very likely wide, wide open.

Before fear could paralyse me, I reacted. Swift as a dart, I catapulted myself to the side as if I had been thrown on to a trampoline, then bounced up in the air again.

Kong's face smacked down on the rat, splattering the gleaming white fur on his chest with scarlet. But Kong did full honour to his reputation, for the embarrassing mishap seemed to diminish neither his pride nor his devilish aggression. No sooner had he hit the floor than he rose up again like a demon from hell, glaring at me with the cold finality of a cobra staring down a rabbit. And he laughed his earsplitting roar of a laugh.

'Didn't I promise you that the two of us would have a little chat one day?' he joked, while the rat's blood dripped down from his chest on to the journal.

'I have a dim recollection of it,' I said. 'What did you want to talk to me about? The art of noiseless stalking? I guess I could give you a tip or two about that.' Well, I could be a comedian too.

'That's really funny.' He had the gentle smile of a hangman. We began circling around each other, very slowly.

'Yeah, seems you're a really funny guy. Or maybe I should say fancy guy? I took one look at you and knew you thought you were something special. You're an arrogant fancy pants, aren't you? Is that what they say, fancy pants? You know this high-falutin chit-chat better than me. I tend to go for the crude stuff.'

'I would have thought so,' I said. He started to close the invisible circle, his stare becoming more and more mesmerising. We were both waiting for the other to pounce. But he was also watching for the moment when I might show the slightest hint of weakness, by turning my gaze from him. Then, as quick as lightning, he would pounce on me and puncture my neck with his fangs. But instead of weakness I showed him my dazzling 'conceited fop' smile, an ingenious combination of condescending irony and implicit threat. I had to keep this beefcake on slippery ground – that was the only effective tactic.

'Well, well,' I continued, taunting, 'so you're the one who's been doing the dirty work around here, right? Of course someone has to sacrifice themselves for a good cause and tidy up the community. Otherwise, who knows, the world might come to an end. Order is your middle name. You're right at the top, and under you in the proper order are all those who respect your wishes, submit themselves to your control, and accept you as king, excuse me, as King Kong. And if a newcomer, especially a "fancy pants" like myself, should enter your kingdom, then first of all the rules of the game have to be explained to him, right? And since you can't help but be unselfish, naturally you're the one who has to take care of this bothersome task. With your pedagogic talent, almost everyone gets the message pretty damn quick about what the house regulations are like: that is – how did you put it? – oh yes, *crude*. But even that doesn't satisfy you. You want the new boys to commit your ten commandments to memory right from the start. That's why the first and most important lesson goes: if you don't toe the line, it is going to be extremely painful for you, so painful in fact that you may never be your old self again. Have I understood the status quo correctly?'

He bellowed enthusiastically. Wherever he went, whatever he did, he always had a quaint sense of humour – a true gentleman.

'Yeah, yeah, you got it, brother! Not often do I meet someone with so much understanding for my concerns. You're a clever little shit, aren't you? That's why I'm so looking forward to tasting your blood.'

A violent thunderstorm had brewed up outside. The lightning and thunder seemed portentous and supplied the appropriate background music to our uncomfortable conversation. Kong slowed the tempo of his circling bit by bit, coming dangerously close to me. The grin had vanished from his face, revealing the primitive mug of a street tough. Now I didn't feel much like joking, either.

'Kong,' I said sternly. 'Don't you think we should stop this stupid game and deal with serious business?'

'OK. Like what, for example?'

'This place is being terrorised by appalling violence. Terrible things are happening. Day after day our brothers and sisters are being killed, murdered in cold blood. A monster's roaming the neighbourhood on a wild killing spree. Don't you want to help me find this psycho?'

'You don't have to look for him any more. I can tell you who it is.'

'Oh? Who is it then?'

'Me! The killer's right in front of you!'

'And what's the reason for your attacks?'

'Let's just say that some people don't know their place – just like you for instance.'

He was even more primitive than I had thought. A Neanderthal *par excellence*.

'Don't be angry with me, Kong, but I don't buy it. I mean, you're tough, but I just don't think you're capable of murder. Your motive doesn't sound very convincing, you know.'

'You'll see soon enough how convincing I can be.'

'Well, my friend, if it really has to be, then it really has to be. But I'd like to call your attention to the fact that this time around you won't get any protection from those two clowns of yours. One on one with me – do you think you can take it?'

'Wrong!' He burst out laughing and looked up triumphantly at the ventilation panel. As if on signal, Herrmann and Herrmann squeezed their ratty, rain-soaked faces through the opening, grinning at me slyly. I should have known that a general would not start a war without an army.

'Is that fair?' I asked. It wasn't so much a question as a philosophical flight of fancy.

'No,' he sniggered. Obviously he had no appreciation of philosophy.

Above, the two raven-black orientals exchanged mocking glances and broke out in scornful laughter. Then, one after the other, they pushed themselves through the opening, dropped into the cellar, and surrounded me. I now found myself in the centre of a triangle formed by the Herrmann brothers and the inscrutably smiling Kong. Why they wanted to try out their fighting prowess on me had become irrelevant. It was a long-overdue ritual that had to be celebrated for its own sake. The only odd thing was that they wanted to force me to my knees right in my own territory. It was pretty obvious that they had never taken a look at one of those expensive, glossy, learned tomes about our species, or they would have realised how grave this violation was.

A savage cellar battle took place as follows:

The Bermuda Triangle broke up abruptly when I jumped an astonishing five feet to the summit of a computer printout mountain. They were in no position to coordinate their attack strategy, being full of pent-up rage, and by the time they had all soared up after me, I was already hopping up to the next highest summit. The Marx Brothers slammed into one another on the peak of the paper mountain behind me, which was naturally too small for them, scrambled in panic to prevent themselves from falling, then finding no support, tumbled down head over heels.

Once again, Kong was the first to pull himself up. He looked quickly around to orientate himself, then jumped up to my peak. But while he was still in mid-flight I let myself drop to the floor, where Herrmann and Herrmann, their eyes wide with fury, madness, and stupidity, were lying in wait for me.

'He's mine!' roared Kong, who had just scaled the paper mountain. But Herrmann and Herrmann had become so enslaved to the adrenalin in their veins that they could no longer control themselves. The cross-eyed Herrmann even seemed to be frothing at the mouth.

We all sprang at the same time. As the duo lifted off and flew at me, I hurled myself into the air right at them. I managed to fly between the goons about two feet above ground, with stiffened front legs and claws extended. While Herrmann and Herrmann whistled past me, I brushed silkily past them, cutting deep grooves into each of their furry sides.

But I had not reckoned on Kong's unfailing aim. As I felt the floor under my paws again, he leapt down, landed squarely on my back, and immediately tried to sink his fangs into my neck. Yanking back reflexively, I shook him off, shot between the orientals, who were licking their wounds in surprise, and rushed to the wall where the vent was located about eight feet from the floor.

Eight feet was quite a height, but I couldn't afford the slightest hesitation. My attackers, having recovered from their shock, rushed in pursuit, their faces disfigured by fury. With little reflection, I bounded up on the nearest paper mountain and from there blindly to the vent. There was no alternative but to ram my entire body right through the tiny opening.

Pain shot like hot lava through my body as I failed to make anything like a smooth landing. My head caught the sides of the vent, giving me a hefty blow and scouring my left cheek and lips. My front paws found a temporary hold. Trembling, I swung from the hatch while the bloodthirsty mob below sprang up again and again, trying to snap at the lower half of my body as if it were a meaty morsel left dangling as a reward for the best highjumper.

Slowly, using all my strength and concentrating on nothing but what would happen to me if I plopped down, I drew myself up bit by bit until I was finally in the opening. A last look down assured me that this bad film was far from over. As soon as Kong and his underlings realised I was escaping, they vaulted up on the paper piles and made enthusiastic preparations to get after me.

I left the vent and ran headlong into the garden. A regular flood awaited me. Everything the sky had to offer seemed to be pouring down that evening. What came pounding down and soaked me to the bone within seconds could hardly be called rain – it had to be the Atlantic Ocean itself. The raindrops had turned into daggers that jabbed painfully at every inch of my body. The rain was falling so heavily that you couldn't see more than a yard ahead. And, as if to announce Judgement Day, lightning seared and thunder boomed over and over again.

I ran straight ahead to the garden wall and mounted it with a leap and a scramble. At the top, gasping for air, I shook the raindrops from my fur and looked back at the vent. They'd made it! First Kong, then Herrmann and Herrmann slipped through the opening and rushed towards me. The watery end of the world didn't seem to impress them in the least.

While the Niagara Falls showered down, flooding large areas

of the garden, I ran aimlessly and heedlessly along the walls, farther and farther away, turning where the pattern of walls dictated, to the left and right, trying all the while to persuade myself that I had shaken off my pursuers. But again and again they loomed out of the curtain of rain, hot on my heels, their bounding silhouettes betraying no tiredness at all.

Finally I had to stop in my tracks to take stock. Continuing to flee without a plan made no sense, for sooner or later I would hit the back wall of a house and have to wait in fear and trembling until the trio caught up with me. On the other hand, it would be sly, if not a stroke of genius, to jump into some garden and take a quick look around for an open cellar window or ramshackle garden shed. It just had to be possible to find a place to hide, and quickly.

Although the rain limited my range of vision, the garden below, which was large, seemed suited to such an endeavour. It was rambling in shape, wildly overgrown with trees and bushes, and strewn with plastic garden furniture. The artificial pond in the middle was overflowing with water, thus enlarging the habitat for its stock of toy fish. The weathered old building above the garden was cloaked in gloom and had an ominous look.

The only snag was that from my vantage point on the wall I couldn't see a safe spot to land – everything was hidden in the shade of the trees and the wall. But this was a risk I just had to take.

From that moment on, events developed in a manner so surreal that in retrospect they seem like yet another nightmare. I was immediately dragged into a maelstrom of terror that made everything that had previously occurred seem no more than a timid overture to the main event.

Without giving any more thought to where I would end up, I sprang down from the wall, landing, to my relief, in high grass. I wanted nothing so much as to vanish as soon as possible, but suddenly a powerful sheet of lightning that seemed to last an eternity illuminated the garden. When I recognised what I had nearly stumbled over, I froze on the spot.

She lay directly at my paws, her azure-blue eyes gazing dreamily off at the furious discharges in the night sky. She was a snow-white Balinese with a characteristic brownish sheen on her face, ears, paws, and tail. Her long coat, the most prominent feature to distinguish her from a Siamese, was soaked with rainwater, and her silky hairs had stuck together in ugly knots so that her fine-boned body now looked like a crumpled garment from the washing machine. The face in her long, wedge-shaped head gave no hint of the monstrosity she had confronted a short while ago, but had an expression of now being far removed from this cruel world. No blood flowed from the huge wound in her neck or the scratches on her legs; if a few drops still did squeeze out they would immediately be washed away by the pouring rain. What was most heartbreaking, however, was her advanced stage of pregnancy. The outlines of her tiny offspring stood out against her moist belly.

All my speculations about the murders were now proved wrong, the way a painstakingly built house of cards collapses because of a single misplaced support. The corpse was not male, but female. At the time of her murder she had not been in heat, but pregnant. She was no 'standard', no member of the gigantic family of European Shorthairs, but was of fine extraction. The only recognisable common feature between this and the other murders was their horrible absurdity. Only a lunatic, a psychopath running amok, could be reckoned capable of such an atrocity. It was impossible to find a 'rational' murder motive in the face of this arbitrary butchering.

The bright glow of the lightning went out, and deep darkness once again enveloped the Balinese. Nevertheless, since I now knew where she lay, I could make out her form. Without the harrowing aura she had had in the harsh glare of the lightning, she had become a shadowy creature. I was so petrified that I couldn't even twitch an ear. While I stared down at the corpse, unable to look away, as if it were a long-awaited manifestation of the divine, the rain beat down on me to its heart's content. It felt like needles piercing my insides through the pores of my skin. My body was seized by a violent trembling that might well have been the first symptom of pneumonia.

'Well, well, what do you know? The little runt ran out of breath. Probably been stuffing himself with too much junk food.' A panting Kong stood on the wall and looked down at me, grinning triumphantly. Herrmann and Herrmann joined him quickly from behind and imitated his silly grin. They didn't seem to have noticed my find.

'Yes,' I said sadly. 'I'm out of breath. But apparently I'm not the only one.'

'What are you babbling about?'

Kong jumped down from the wall and landed right beside me. Both of his lackeys followed. Continuing to smile, he scrutinised me a while from the side. And then his gaze fell on the corpse and straightaway his expression of scorn turned into pure shock. His eyes seemed about to pop out, and his mouth opened in a silent scream. Even Herrmann and Herrmann were clearly upset, something I would never have expected from them.

'Solitaire!' came at long last from Kong, and he began to howl with all his might. 'Oh Solitaire! Solitaire! What have they done to you? My dear, sweet, beautiful Solitaire! My God, what have they done to you? Oh Solitaire!'

He wailed and sobbed and sniffed at the corpse, he hopped around madly like a rain-dancer, he tore up pawfuls of grass from the lawn. Like all the stirrings of his heart, Kong's grief was of gigantic dimensions. The enormous beast wore himself out with mourning, until finally he threw himself down on Solitaire's lifeless body and licked her rain-drenched coat, whimpering pitifully.

'Who was she?' I asked the cross-eyed Herrmann at my side. He turned his thuggish features away from the entwined couple and looked at me so downheartedly and distractedly that you'd never have thought I'd tattooed a little souvenir in his flank just a few minutes ago.

'Solitaire was the boss's main bit of fluff. And what she was carrying was probably his, too,' he answered curtly.

It was something new, seeing this trio of out-and-out toughs so desolate. They were such a team that each seemed to be sharing the thoughts and sentiments of the others. Herrmann and Herrmann had even begun to howl in solidarity with their master.

But Kong was gradually regaining his composure, and the incorrigible skunk that was in him now returned with even more drastic venom. He puffed himself up mightily in his now familiar, awe-inspiring manner and exploded.

'I'll kill him!' he yelled, so loud that he drowned out the thunder god's symphony. 'I'll make a hamburger out of him and boil his guts in a microwave! I'll bite out his throat and swig his blood! I'll rip out his balls and make him eat them. I'll, I'll . . .' He was shouting so much that he could hardly get any air, and coughed up snot and some clumps of undigested food. Then he continued to roar, disregarding the disgusting interruption.

'What scum did this? Who? Was it you?'

He gave me a half-insane look, but then shook his head in disbelief. That was a load off my mind.

'No, it couldn't have been you. You couldn't have done it. You're too feeble to have done this. Besides, you didn't have the time. But who was it then? Who? Oh . . .'

All at once his massive rage fell away from him. Deeply grieved, he once again regarded his beloved. His emotional life seemed to consist of floods of feeling that surged up only to recede as abruptly as they had come. Poor Kong – I really pitied him now – was like a little child who can't control his behaviour and lurches from one fit to the next. Herrmann and Herrmann approached cautiously to console him in his hour of need. In the end, the three companions held their heads together and sobbed softly over Solitaire's corpse.

Suddenly there was a rustling sound as if something were writhing in the branches of the shrubbery. We all heard it at the same time and pricked up our ears. Although the storm provided a continual background of noise that made it hard to hear more subdued sounds, the rustling was clearly audible. Someone was very close.

An electric charge seemed to pulse through Kong, and he raised his head up high. His nose twitched in staccato rhythm. Herrmann and Herrmann followed his example, also beginning to sniff intensively. Our gazes shifted little by little towards a tree about four steps away. All at once something hopped out of the leafless shrub at the base of the tree and waddled clumsily behind the trunk of the nearest tree to hide itself from us, which was pretty dumb because we were all staring squarely in that direction. Nevertheless, the entire stunt took place so quickly and suddenly that, while we saw that the stranger was one of our kind by his unmistakable silhouette, beyond that we couldn't even identify the colour of his coat, let alone recognise him. And so he continued to hide behind the thin trunk, apparently convinced that he had evaded us with this diversionary tactic.

It was just like Kong that his first move was to announce his intentions.

'God help you!' he bellowed out. 'God help you! If you have ever felt pain, then that pain will seem like an itch compared with what now awaits you! I will rip off your head and shit down your neck! I will tear out your heart and play ping-pong with it! I will . . . '

The preliminary announcement of these future pleasures had its effect: the stranger took to his heels and ran in his strangely waddling gait towards the opposite wall. Kong and his retinue immediately shot after him, while several bolts of lightning split the sky as if to dramatise the scene.

I wanted to call after them not to act too hastily, that maybe the stranger – like us – had only stumbled across the corpse as a chance witness, that we should first submit him to an interrogation, and that everyone is innocent until proven guilty. At the same time, I realised how ridiculous these appeals would be. It would be like telling a stampeding herd of horses to pay attention to traffic signs. So I had no other course of action but to try and track both hunters and prey and prevent the worst from happening.

From a distance, the waddler looked like a neglected, grey-haired Persian; or if not that, then a mongrel with Persian blood. He was astonishingly nimble. Running non-stop to the end of the yard, he seemed to flow up the garden wall like a jet smoothly taking off. Once up, he risked a hasty, strangely detached look back at his pursuers, who were loping up to the wall as if they were storming the Alamo. A gigantic bolt of lightning, followed by an earsplitting bang, again lit up the scene, and I could see his face for the first time. He didn't seem to understand what the hunt was all about, and knit his brow nervously. He was obviously taken aback, yet made no effort at all to yell out anything in his defence or plead for mercy. Evidently he felt no fear, but only profound irritation. His facial expression showed mainly distraction, and this, along with his strange behaviour, made him seem a very odd character indeed.

He jumped down from the wall into the neighbouring garden and vanished from our sight. When Kong, Herrmann and Herrmann and, after a few seconds, my humble self finally reached the wall, we were just in time to see that our suspect had already climbed the wall facing us and was coolly preparing to spring down into the next garden. So we had to do it all over again, crossing the garden and mounting the wall in the wake of His Oddness.

He was gone! Disappeared into thin air, departed for the Yellow-Submarine-Land from which he might well have come. What we now set eyes on was only a mirror image of the previous scene: once again a garden, once again walls meeting at right angles, once again a tangled landscape of bare trees, dead flower beds, garden furniture tossed about, indefinable garage junk, and the obligatory forlorn-looking barbecue.

Kong churned it over, and as with all the thinking processes in his simple head, you could see the intellectual effort writ large on his face. He would have made a terrific teacher for deaf-mutes. He turned to me.

'Any idea where the bastard's hiding out, fancy pants?'

He was asking me for my opinion! What an honour! What a blessing! The guy had wholly forgotten that only a few minutes ago he had wanted to put me on a hook, quarter me, and run me through a meat grinder.

'No,' I confessed. 'With this foul weather and awful gloom, I don't even know where my own house is any more.'

'He moved on right enough, boss,' suggested the Herrmann with the eternal grin. 'It's sure as shit that he's already over the next wall. There's just three gardens left and that's it. Right where the square ends is where we nab him!'

Kong conjured up an enthusiastic smile. Simple solutions fascinated him.

'Yeah, yeah, yeah,' he panted. 'OK, boys, let's go!'

The three musketeers scooted down the wall, rushed across the garden, mounted the next wall, and were then lost to sight. As for me, I was fed up with nocturnal games of hare and hounds, dead bodies in the rain, and alleged murderers. Maybe it was my duty to stick around so that when they captured that oddball they wouldn't lynch him on the spot, but my night's exertions had left me so knackered already that I was beginning to stagger. No matter how guilty I felt, I was going to have to pass on this one.

All at once the Persian popped up. I could hardly believe my eyes, but I saw him squeeze himself through a hole caused by rust in an old washtub that was upside down in the grass, offering a perfect hiding-place in an emergency. He paused to catch his breath. The excitement seemed to have knackered him too, but that was certainly better than being served up for Kong's breakfast. He had had a damned narrow escape.

Since he was sitting with his back to me, he didn't notice that I was still there. From the safety of his hiding-place he would have seen his pursuers loping onwards, and because he had probably forgotten to count in the confusion of the chase, he no doubt thought he had shaken us all off. Without looking around, he got up clumsily and waddled as cool as a cucumber diagonally across the garden to where two walls came to a corner half hidden with ivy, long-bladed grass, and a clump of shrubs. He slipped into this impenetrable vegetation and vanished.

OK, so I was exhausted, but . . . Well, you know me well enough by now. I leapt down from the wall and approached the thicket cautiously. Lo and behold, there in the undergrowth, ideally camouflaged by the ivy, was a nondescript opening, like the mouth of a pipe or tunnel. From its mouth resounded the echo of scratching and scuffling noises. Presumably, the tunnel went down to the sewers or to some other underground installation.

I gave it little thought. The way things looked, I faced two possible deaths. If I didn't follow his trail, then I would probably burst with curiosity right then and there, and if I did follow his trail, the mass murderer would buy me a one-way ticket to the hereafter. I soon decided to die the second way. The first seemed a much greater torture.

After I had forced myself through the opening, I discovered that the secret passage was square, extremely narrow, and apparently carved out of basalt. The inner walls were crusted with dirt, moss, and the indefinable deposits of time. Whatever purpose the passage served or might once have served, it looked as if it had lain hidden under the earth for centuries. It was very stuffy down there, and I made only creeping progress, striving with all my might to fight off fits of claustrophobia. Nothing more could be heard of the mysterious Persian. Obviously he had already reached the other end. The ominous tunnel led downwards, but I had to struggle to make any head-way. After a while, however, the passage began to slope down so precipit-ously that, although I desperately tried to brake my descent, I was soon sliding down at high speed. This torture lasted a pretty long time, and continual contact with the sides of the tunnel was no doubt making me look like a chimney sweep and stink to high heaven. And then I didn't feel anything under my paws any more and was into free fall.[11]

I crashed down into a tiny, tub-like chamber which looked like the inside of a Moorish dome chiselled out of stone and turned upside down. It was murky in this place, but a little light shone through a vent to my right and enabled me to orientate myself.

Once again trapped, I had no alternative but to prepare myself for further excitement, though my yearning for adven-ture was now greatly diminished. It was certain that I would soon happen upon the butcher himself, who of course knew his way around this labyrinth much better than I. First he would ask me what time it was and then he would eat me alive in one big gulp. Like any intelligent living being endowed with an imagina-tion, I had often speculated on the manner of my departure from this life and had revelled in the most romantic visions. I had not realised that the final act in every life always unfolds shabbily, if not in abject poverty. So this was how clever bastard Francis would breathe his last: missing under the earth, in a cold dark cavern, in the stinking jaws of a Persian half-breed also known as 'The Waddler'. Yes, many would grieve and Gustav more than any. He would cry his eyes out after my sudden departure, that is, disappearance, and would spend the following weeks in bed in misery. But the pain would gradually recede; the wounds of loss would heal. And (who knows?) perhaps within a mere two or three months someone else would be eating from my bowl, letting himself be scratched behind the ears by 'my best friend', and farting in sheer pleasure. What had that honourable zombie Deep Purple said in my charmingly eerie dream? This is the way of life, this is the way of the world!

What a dumb beast I was! What was I doing here anyway? With that question, something unprecedented happened: I found myself yielding to resignation. Whether out of weariness or incipient senility, I was not sure. But it was obvious that all the upsetting events I had gone through were beginning to change me into someone else. I had to admit this to myself, much though it appalled me. The only remedy for this insidious sickness was a hearty, 'Keep your chin up! Pull yourself together! Show some courage!'

My heart pounding in fear, I passed through the vent and into a dark corridor that seemed to confirm what I suspected this place to be. Apparently I had landed in an underground system of tombs, in a sealed catacomb. To be honest, I was not greatly astonished, because the only thing I share intellectually with Gustav is an enthusiasm for archaeology. How often have I sat for days at a time poring over fine reproductive volumes and historic studies of relics, kingdoms, and cultures that have long ago died out? It was no surprise to me, therefore, that I should stumble across such an amazing find. Research on catacombs, for example, which were forgotten and only rediscovered in the sixteenth century, has still by no means been concluded. Not only Christian but also Gnostic and Jewish catacombs have been unearthed; in Rome the catacombs have a total length of nearly one hundred miles.

As far as my own discovery was concerned, I ventured to guess that on the surface, where the backyards and gardens were now laid out, there had been either a church or a monastery at some earlier time, very likely in the Middle Ages. For reasons unknown, the buildings above ground must have been razed, leaving the lower complex untouched. The tunnel that led down here would have been built to supply this underground realm with fresh air.

The walls of the stone corridor were decorated with early

Christian paintings of saints, now covered with a patina of dirt and almost unrecognisable. It led me to further passages, and after a while I had the impression of having stumbled into a maze. Many burial niches containing the crumbled remains of human skeletons had been set into the walls, though the contents of some were obscured by weighty stone slabs inscribed with biblical verses. Now and then, walls that had fallen in and single, large stone fragments blocked the path, and I had to climb over them. Often entire sections of the ceiling had collapsed, and I had to hunt for a gap before going on. Presumably earthquakes or bombing during the Second World War had caused this devastation. All in all I thought that my find, with its rather unexceptional treasures, would scarcely have raised a murmur in the world of professional archaeologists. I was probably correct in reckoning that this mysterious construction had once been the seat of a small and insignificant religious order.

Nevertheless, the catacombs did not fail to have a certain effect. Enraptured, I wandered through the stone labyrinth, counting on being attacked at any moment by the sinister Persian. Rainwater seeped through cracks in the wall; the sound of the drops hitting the floor and echoing through the corridors could have competed with the most eccentric music imaginable. Paralysed by fear yet gripped by fascination, I roamed through the dead subterranean kingdom for some time, until I thought I knew its layout by heart.

Suddenly I arrived at a round chamber with a groined ceiling. I looked around and nearly lost my mind. Embedded in the continuous wall of the vault that formed the domed interior were countless small niches that at one time might have held candles or sacred paraphernalia, but were now being perversely misused. Resting in each niche were the skeletons of brothers and sisters, many still in full possession of their skins, which had dried out or had even been tanned, and which despite or because of the air conditions stubbornly refused to decompose into dust.

In their niches the dead sat upright on their rears, like human beings, staring at me from empty eye sockets. Each was decorated with dried flowers that were now in the final stage of desiccation. The most degenerate and repulsive sight was the altar. It stood in the middle of the room, a mighty stone block with an artlessly chiselled cross on its front; heaped upon it, next to some candelabras dripping with centuries-old tallow, was a towering hill of bones. A skull capped this gruesome work of art, which also had flowers strewn decoratively around it. The stone floor was littered with the pieces of this nonhuman, skeletal puzzle – bits the deranged high priest responsible for all of this had probably found no use for. Some distance away from the idolatrous altar, scattered haphazardly, lay a pile of leather-bound volumes, many of them open and all of them largely decomposed. Numerous mammals had gnawed the pages and bindings, ruining them beyond redemption. I supposed that they had once belonged to the monastery library but had been moved to this room. An extensive network of spiders' webs covered the entire nightmarish vault, and quite possibly a colony of mice led an idyllic life here.

Gaping in awe, I was drawn further into the vault. I tried to estimate how many brothers and sisters had found their final resting place, or rather their gruesome end, here. I caught an odour of decay. Not all these wretched creatures had entered the merciful stage of dry skin and bones. A few were still suffering the last discomfort of putrefaction, which meant that right now legions of worms and other delightful living things were at work on them. Although many smells, mainly of fecal matter, pervaded the vault, this morbid aroma assailed my nose with particular pungency.

I thought of Kong, and how quickly his barbaric instincts had recognised the true murderer. I, on the other hand, had wanted to be clever and had approached the matter in my roundabout, analytical, and ultimately totally ineffective way. I had wanted to imitate human beings – a childish enterprise – and had entertained the most ingenious theories, not realising that the real solution to the murders was illogical. The murderer was a mentally unbalanced Persian who ambushed his victims, killed them, and then threw them down into the engine-room of his cult. Motive: it was a part of either a ritual or an insane obsession.

One mystery remained unsolved. Why hadn't he brought the six brothers and sisters who had died just before Solitaire to the catacombs? Luckily, I didn't need to rack my brains over details as subtle as these, because my encounter with 'The Waddler', probably soon to take place, would spare me any further intellectual effort. The most sensible course of action now was to enjoy the stunning view.

I walked along the wall, looking up at the calcified brothers and sisters, who gave me suspicious looks from their kingdom of dried flowers. It was astonishing how well preserved some of them were. If you gave them only a fleeting glance then you could almost believe that, although extremely emaciated, they were still living, and simply looked like the ones you sometimes encounter in countries where animals are mistreated. Only now and then an insect would creep out of a crack in the skin and destroy the illusion.

A brother in one of the darker niches impressed me the most. I interrupted my walk just to have a good close look at him. Although his body was in shadow, I clearly saw that he possessed all the physiognomic characteristics of the living and that even his shaggy coat was still intact. His eyes were closed, and he seemed to be sleeping quietly. You would have been tempted to believe he was breathing if you hadn't known for sure that he . . .

Suddenly his eyes flicked open! And almost at the same time I realised that he wasn't a member of the mystical army of the dead, but good old Waddler, who had apparently devised a very special surprise for the scene of my execution. My heart stopped; fear made my teeth chatter. It would be short work for a beast so deft to spring down on me and give my neck the now traditional treatment. But oddly the Waddler was trembling too, and his large, wildly rolling eyes blinked nervously.

'Do no harm to the Guardian of the Dead,' he said with a worn-out, croaking voice. The shaking that rippled through his body gradually became a violent shuddering. At the same time he rolled his eyes again, rather comically, which fitted his queer appearance. I had correctly identified him up in the garden: he was indeed a Persian, but down and out, mud-spattered, his coat all knotted up. A closer examination showed that his coat was not grey but blue, though of a shade that only trained eyes could have recognised. His body odour, which wafted down to me periodically, almost made me faint. In a flight of gallows humour, it flashed through my mind that this might well be his way of anaesthetising his victims.

'Do no harm to the Guardian of the Dead,' he repeated.

I noticed that he didn't heed me when he spoke, but stared stubbornly ahead.

'Verily, verily: the Guardian of the Dead has sinned, desecrated the Temple, and broken the Holy Rule. This last may prove to be the worst sin, and he shall have to atone for it most bitterly. But if there shall no longer be a Guardian of the Dead, who then shall bring flowers to the dead? Who then shall decorate the House with such splendour? Who then shall remember those long past? Who shall pray for them, who shall receive them? I swear by the Prophet, by the Almighty Ruler of the Dead, that I shall never leave the Temple, and never desire to meddle in things which are the province of Yahweh alone . . .'

And so on and so forth. Obviously he had been poking his nose much too deeply into these ancient monastic tomes, with lasting effect on his manner of speech. I asked myself when he would end his solemn oration and attack me.

'When are you going to get around to murdering me, brother?' I at last interrupted him, more out of curiosity than fear.

'Murder? Kill? Oh, of murder there is no end in this vale of suffering. Yahweh, Satan rides through the land on his flaming steer, and forces your flock to war with itself. The sinners know not the path of peace; there is no justice in the ways of the sinners. They make their paths crooked, and whomsoever follows them knows not of peace. Thus is righteousness far from us, and justice reaches us not. We hope for light, and behold, it remains dark. We go astray at midday as at dusk, we live in darkness as do the dead . . . '

'Stop, stop, stop,' I cried out, unnerved. 'Do you always hold a morning mass like this before going after somebody's throat?'

Felicity had noticed that the murderer addressed his victims in momentous tones before striking. Whether this lecture could be described as 'momentous' I did not dare to guess.

In any event, the Persian broke off his sermon and looked down at me for the first time. Since he did not seem inclined to answer my question, which he probably had not understood anyway, I posed the next one right away.

'What's your name, friend?'

A suggestion of happiness flitted across his ugly face.

'They call me Jesaja, the good Guardian of the Dead,' he replied proudly.

'Ah, so you are the one who's been up to all this mischief? I mean, all these skeletons? Did you kill them and lug them down here?'

The rolling of his eyes stopped abruptly, and he favoured me with a fanatical glare.

'Oh no, stranger, the dead come to me. They are sent by the Prophet.'

I slowly relaxed while the fear drained out of me. Yes, if you took a close look at this character, he really didn't seem like a killer – more like a run-of-the-mill eccentric. Perhaps someone was using him as an expedient scapegoat, as a tool. I had to find out whether Jesaja knew this mysterious someone and how the whole crazy business had begun.

'You don't need to be afraid of me, Jesaja. My name is Francis. I'd just like you to tell me a few things. It would be nice if you could concentrate a little bit on remembering them. First question: where do you come from and how on earth did you ever end up in this terrible place?'

This last remark seemed to have been ill-judged, for his face showed he was offended. Yet he was willing to give the information.

'The Guardian of the Dead has inhabited the Temple for endless ages; he is a child of the darkness. For should he see the light, then he shall be blinded, and shall have to depart from the realm of the living. Yet once there also existed the Land of Dreams where the Guardian of the Dead was born. Anger and agony ruled it; there was no laughter there. But the Prophet was also at work in the Land of Dreams, the Prophet who brought us salvation at last. For thus he spoke: Lord, thou who art mightier than all, listen to the voices of the despairing, and save us from the cruelty of evil-doers! Free us from our fear! Rise, Yahweh! Bring us salvation, O Lord!'

'How did you escape from the Land of Dreams, Jesaja?'

'God heard the pleading of the Prophet, and He shattered the cheeks of all his enemies, and smashed the teeth of evil-doers. And when the bright day exploded, the Land of Dreams also exploded, and the suffering came together to flee headlong in all directions!'

'What happened to the Prophet?'

'He ascended unto heaven.'

'Did you see him?'

'No. No one laid eyes on the miracle. Those who knew the Lord died in the Land of Dreams. All that remains to us, the Children of the Blessed, are many strange visions.'

'What did you do after the bright day exploded?'

'I wandered as if inebriate through the Land, with many pains racking my body. Day and night merged into one another, and in the end they became one. Then, hunger and thirst tired me and made me fall senseless, and as I stood at the crossroads between this and the other world, I met Father Joker.'

'Joker?'

'Verily, verily: our good, dearly beloved Father Joker. He has called this Temple his home for long ages, and he carried me here and provided me with all manner of good food and drink. In the years following our meeting, he taught me how to hunt, and he taught me how to find fresh water in the underworld. Furthermore, he taught me how to read so that I was able to study the Holy Scripture and at last could become a virtuous man of God. The time came, however, when Father Joker was full of sadness, for he had to leave me to proclaim and spread the word of the Prophet. All should know what the Risen had done, and evermore lead pious lives, he said. Thus he made his departure, and I alone remained behind in the Temple.'

'This is all really very informative, Jesaja. Could you perhaps also tell me how dearest Father Joker explained this fine collection of bones?'

'Oh, no, no. When Father Joker and I lived together, the dead did not yet dwell among us. The Temple was a place of meditation and of prayer to Yahweh. Until one day, long ages after Father Joker had departed, I heard a rumbling in one of the meandering tunnels that connect the World of Night with the World of Day. I ran swiftly to the tunnel, arriving at its mouth just in time to see a dead sister come flying out. "Oh my God, what does this mean, by the raven-black coat of the Prophet?" I cried out in my ignorance. Like one possessed I ranted and raved over the dead sister, and called out to Yahweh for help and counsel. Was it possible that the Prince of Darkness himself was playing a joke on me? Or had a horrible war broken out above? It was all one to me, for I felt only mortal fear. But suddenly I heard the voice of the Lord, of our blessed Prophet, who spoke to me gently.'

'What? You heard a voice from the tunnel?'

'Not just a voice – His voice!'

'And what did His voice say?'

'It said that I had been chosen to take up the duties of the Guardian of the Dead. But I spoke into the hole: "Lord, you are omnipotent, and I am but a miserable fool before your immeasurable wisdom. I know that your plans are inscrutable, but please tell me where this dead sister came from, and why she is splattered with blood." Then the Lord spoke, and now His voice was filled with wrath and poison: "Do dutifully your service as Guardian of the Dead and do not concern yourself with the things of heaven! For if your little head should brood too much it will swell up to the size of a pumpkin and then burst! And if you should ever dare to go up to the World of Day, I will consume you in fire!"'

'So you obeyed him and took delivery of the corpses that were being thrown down at regular intervals.'

'Yes, that is so. To the full extent of my powers I made a home for the dead in my Temple. I decorated them with the flowers that grew in the canals, and I prayed for the salvation of their souls. The Lord praised me for obeying His will so conscientiously, and often gave me His blessing. Again and again He had wise advice for me, and even sent down a fat rat now and then. But now, all at once, everything has changed.'

'Oh?'

I suspected something.

'The Lord no longer sends the dead to the Realm of the Dead nor has He spoken with me recently. He has forgotten me.'

'And because of this deficiency you went up there tonight. You wanted to look out for the dead personally and, if you should find any, bring them to the Temple, which you certainly almost succeeded in doing.'

'It may be true that I committed a grave sin, for the sacred prohibition says that I am never under any circumstances to go up to the Realm of Day. But if the Guardian of the Dead has no more dead to welcome, then what purpose shall he serve? Alas,

149

the Lord has abandoned me, and has turned away from his loyal servant.'

Yes, but why? I was tempted to ask, but at the very last second I decided not to, because I thought I already knew the answer. He would explain it by saying that he had prayed too little or hadn't done enough penance or hadn't carried out his duties perfectly, or whatever other naïve speculations his archaic view of the universe could produce.

All at once this evil story had become much worse, its scope now seeming to extend into hell itself. There were now not seven but hundreds of victims to mourn for. If all this were true, the grisly deeds of the murderer had been going on for many, many years, very likely as far back as the closing of the laboratory. Once again, the mad professor I had in my mind began to babble, reminding me of his various theories concerning the murder motive. But I shut him up. While Jesaja continued, with biblical eloquence, to tell me about his divine calling, I mentally reviewed all the important facts I had been able to gather so far.

First of all, the venerable Joker was presumably the only one in the area who could fully remember the insane events of 1980 and their horrifying consequences. It was likely that he himself had not been a guinea pig but an outsider who could nevertheless obtain comprehensive information on what had occurred. He had spent his life in the catacombs before then, and was probably nothing but a stray, but perhaps during a stroll he had been alerted to the existence of the laboratory by his brothers' and sisters' calls for help, had seen the gruesome happenings through a laboratory window, and from then on had minutely observed the entire tragedy as it unfolded. He had witnessed how only a few, maybe even none, of the grown animals had survived, and that only the younger ones had managed to escape death – if narrowly and with ghastly mutilations. One murky question remained: what happened during the last days of the laboratory that led to the liberation of the experimental animals? Did they receive outside help, maybe from Joker? Whatever may have occurred, afterwards Joker vanished into the underworld again, popping up only at rare intervals – for example, to save Jesaja from starvation and to bring him up as his sorcerer's apprentice – but otherwise devoting himself to the life of a hermit.

But then something extremely odd happened. Joker decided to found a religion, the Claudandus cult, a hotchpotch of martyrological mysticism, flagellation rites, and resurrection hocus-pocus. He bade farewell to his hermit ways as well and went out into the big wide world, disseminating his doctrine with great fervour and converting all his brothers and sisters to Claudandism. Why the switch? There was no doubt that Joker was a religious creature through and through. But what sort of interest did he suddenly acquire in inspiring the entire Felidae world with the Claudandus teachings? In this regard, it was of paramount importance to remember that Joker, unlike Jesaja, had never broken off contact with the world above ground. Had he become acquainted with someone up there who had persuaded him to take this decisive step? Who was this someone? The Prophet himself?

Second: who was the Prophet? According to the legend passed down by Joker, Claudandus was a perfect saint who had called upon God because of his unbearable suffering, had had his prayers answered, and ascended into heaven. Yet, according to Preterius's notes, Claudandus was in reality a pathetic laboratory animal. Nobody knew what his actual fate had been, though it might be logically supposed that he died miserably as the result of his injuries. (And by the way, what actually happened to Professor Julius Preterius?) If you took Jesaja's account as a starting point, then the Prophet was the murderer – or rather it was a brother in the guise of the Prophet who was bumping off his brothers and sisters, for as yet unknown motives. However you looked at it, the only one who really knew about the real, or phony, Prophet was our dearly beloved Father Joker.

Third (and I thank a brilliant flash of inspiration for the following): the murder of Solitaire and the six preceding it did in fact have something in common – if you considered Felicity a special case because she was a witness whom it was absolutely necessary for the murderer to silence. Both the male victims and the Balinese had been busy doing the same thing, namely, producing offspring. Whether this was also true for the society of skeletons surrounding me I obviously couldn't verify, but I had to assume so for the time being. Accordingly, one possible murder motive was that the killer detested children, and so killed those of his brothers and sisters who were about to beget or were pregnant. He might even – and the idea made me shudder –have murdered infants! But which offspring were undesirable? Which race was to be eliminated to its very last member? European Shorthair? Russian Blue? Balinese? Or did the bogeyman have a murderous aversion to all Felidae?

Fourth: Mister X had known how to hide his repellent deeds splendidly for years by shoving the corpses down into the catacombs. He had even found a sucker to lug them into safe hiding, thus shielding them from all too inquisitive eyes. (A) How had he hit upon this neat solution for getting rid of the corpses? Through Joker? Perhaps. (B) Why had he so abruptly discontinued a practice that he had been fond of and that was so ingeniously practical? Had he come to regard himself of late as so unassailable that he no longer needed to take any precautionary measures? Perhaps.

Fifth: what goal was the Claudandus cult or Claudandus doctrine pursuing? This question sounded somewhat silly at first. You could just as well ask why something like religion exists at all, one of the answers being, surely, that every thinking being possesses religious sentiments and somehow has to express them. Yet in this particular case it seemed to me that religion was serving a certain purpose, like a preliminary toughening-up process, a preparation for something very special, for something beyond imagining. But, by the raven-black coat of the Prophet, what?

Questions, questions, questions, and no answers. But at least some damn clever guesses! After I had interrogated Jesaja a little while longer, a leaden weariness crept over me. I had had enough of playing detective for the night. So I asked the Guardian of the Dead to get me out of the stinking labyrinth as soon as he could, which he dutifully did. He took me to a different tunnel from the one I came down so that I popped up very near to our own garden. The exit this time turned out to be a disused water conduit, crudely carved out of stone, which ended, strangely enough, in the hollow trunk of an ancient tree. Jesaja told me that there were many more secret passages like this one, but that only he knew their locations.

'Just a few final questions,' I said before leaving the tree through a large knot-hole. 'Jesaja, have you noticed anything in particular about the dead you've received all these years? I mean, for example, had any been in heat?'

'They were indeed, brother. And some strangely mutilated brothers and sisters also came down to the Temple, and I sinned by asking myself sometimes whether Yahweh might have forgotten them.'

'And pregnant females? Were some of the dead also pregnant at the time of their death?'

Now his rolling eyes filled with tears. I wanted to embrace and console him.

'Many,' he whimpered. 'Oh, many, brother!'

I said a warm goodbye to him and departed. On the way, feelings of guilt tormented me, since I had not come out with the truth but had left him with his belief in the evil Prophet intact. On the other hand, I was afraid that he would be unable to adjust himself to the hard realities up here. He was so naïve, so innocent, so full of belief in his god's holy work that I simply could not bring myself to rob him of his illusions. The truth that was valid for me did not necessarily have to be valid for others.

The reality that surrounded me did not necessarily encompass the entire world. Jesaja needed the catacombs, the Temple, and the dead. It was his calling, his life's work. And the dead needed Jesaja, the good Guardian of the Dead. For who else would bring them flowers?

CHAPTER

—— 8 ——

I SPENT THE rest of the night sleeping, or, to be precise, dreaming. It wasn't actually the rest of the night, because when I finally climbed through the bathroom window into our flat, morning had already dawned outside. I was so hungry that I could have eaten a horse. But since Gustav was always whinge-ing about how he liked to get a really good night's rest 'at least on Sunday' (which is absolute nonsense, because the man sleeps late practically every day), I didn't dare call his attention to my need. So I whisked off into the bedroom and settled down on the soft wool blanket girding that tub of lard, who was snoring fearfully loud. The storm had passed. I sank rapidly into a deep, leaden sleep.

To my relief, this time I was spared any nightmares. Instead, a kind of vision:

Once again I was within a shapeless, radiant whiteness in which neither space nor time nor reality existed. But unlike the dream in which the faceless man strangled me with a diamond collar, there was no threatening plot in this one. Now and then in this strange place, thick clouds of mist floated past, covering the whiteness here and there with pale grey shadows.

I wandered euphorically through this nothingness, and the further I went, the more a nearly unendurable, and yet pleasant, tension built up inside me. Occasionally the mist enveloped me and made me lose my bearings. But since there was nothing anyway that might serve as a point of reference, that didn't really bother me.

The tremendous tension I felt fell away abruptly when I thought I saw in the distance what had both caused and was now relieving it. I had not known the aim of my restless wandering, nor whom I had been hoping to meet, but when I saw *him*, I realised suddenly that my growing sense of expectation had been geared towards this one encounter. Naturally, he was a fiction – that much was obvious even in my dream. For I neither knew him nor could I form a clear idea of his outer appearance. Nevertheless, in that moment I was filled with a certainty such as I had never known in my entire life: I had finally found him!

His coat was indescribably fine, indeed downright majestic in its silkiness, and of such a radiant, otherworldly whiteness that it hurt the eyes just to see it. Because he was sitting with his back to me, he disappeared into the white background now and then – like a ghost flickering in and out of existence. He was stately and bewitchingly beautiful; in short, he was such a splendid creature that the producers of television commercials would have killed for him. Little clouds of mist hovered around him, as if he were a holy mountain.

When I came to a stop a few yards away from him, a veil of mist lifted to reveal beyond him a huge cage of glittering chrome, a faithful and detailed enlargement of an animal cage such as those used in experimental laboratories. In it, as if possessed by a thousand malignant spirits, Professor Julius Preterius ranted and raved and giggled like mad. He was strapped into a straitjacket, and around his neck hung a gleaming bronze sign with the inscription:

PROFESSOR JULIUS PRETERIUS
AWARDED THE NOBEL PRIZE FOR
BEST SCHIZOPHRENIA IN 1981

I had never seen him before, but I recognised the good old professor with the same certainty I had felt in the presence of the master of ceremonies in charge of the whole eerie show. In the background, further banks of fog had parted to reveal a vast army of brothers and sisters, who grinned at me strangely. In the very first row were Bluebeard, Felicity, Kong, Herrmann and Herrmann, Joker, Deep Purple, Solitaire, Sascha and Jesaja.

What then happened I saw as if in slow motion.

Very gradually, the white murderer turned his head towards me. I looked directly into the golden-yellow furnace of his eyes.

'At last I have found you,' I said. In my excitement and joy, I was on the brink of tears.

'Naturally,' he said with an unfathomable sadness in his voice. 'Naturally, dear Francis. It was foreseeable that you would find me sooner or later, for you are even more intelligent than I. At some time or other, yes, at some time or other this had to come to pass. Congratulations, my friend, I am the one you've been looking for all this time: I am the murderer, I am the Prophet, I am Julius Preterius, I am Gregor Johann Mendel, I am the eternal riddle, I am the man and the beast – and I am Felidae. All of these I am in one person, and more, much more.'

Once again, clouds of mist enveloped him, pierced only by glowing eyes that shone like precious stones. The professor, meanwhile, was kicking up an increasingly noisy racket in his cage, giggling crazily, babbling incoherent gibberish. Finally, he hammered his head against the bars, cutting his face and dousing the cell with blood. Then he turned his blood-smeared face in my direction and cried out:

'It reminds me of the story of the carnivorous plant that someone brought back home as a seedling and cared for until one fine day, tall and strong, it devoured the entire family.'

He lapsed into his insane giggling. The veil of mist lifted to present the white murderer anew in all his splendour. He rose slowly from his seat, turned towards me, and looked at me as if from the remotest depths of the universe.

'Everything that ever was and ever will be no longer has any meaning, Francis,' he said, and his sad voice echoed into infinity. 'The only thing that's important is that you now change sides and come to us, come with us.'

I was completely confused. I did not understand what he meant with this enigmatic talk. I had come to take him captive and to stop his murderous activities once and for all, but instead of pouncing on him, I was suddenly perplexed. I felt compassion for him. Following a weird hunch, I finally asked him:

'Like the Bremen City Musicians?'

He nodded gravely.

'Precisely. Like the Bremen City Musicians: "Come with me," says the ass to the rooster, "You'll find something better than death everywhere!"'

The huge army of my brothers and sisters in the background affirmed in unison:

'Come with us, Francis! You'll find something better than death everywhere!'

The murderer turned away from me and floated over to the others. Then he became a tiny figure in the crowd and looked back once again.

'Come with us, Francis,' he insisted. 'Come with us on a long, wonderful trip.'

Now they all turned their backs on me and wandered off casually into the thickening mist.

'Where are you going?' I called after them.

'To Africa! To Africa! To Africa!' they called out with one voice, until they gradually disappeared in the fog.

'And what will we find there?' I still wanted to know.

'Everything we lost, Francis, everything we lost . . .' I heard them murmuring. But they were now lost to sight; they had already become one with the magical mist.

An unbearable sadness crept over me, because I had not followed them, because I had been afraid to set out on the long journey, because I was now completely alone. Africa! It sounded so alluring, so mysterious, so exciting. Everything you ever dreamed about was there, my unerring instincts whispered to me. Africa! The lost paradise, El Dorado, the Promised Land where once, long ago, everything had its beginning. Yet Africa was unimaginably far away, and I was only a comfort-loving, four-legged animal used to thinking in terms of short distances. The nocturnal songs of the gods were unknown to me; so too the hot wind of the savannah. Never had I slept under a canopy of stars, never had I set foot in the sacred jungle. Africa! But where was Africa? Wherever else, not in me, not in my yearnings, not in my heart. It was somewhere else, very far from me, irrevocably far from me.

And yet:

'Take me with you,' I wept quietly to myself. 'Take me with you, my brothers and sisters . . . '

When I woke up my eyes were full of tears. Bright sunlight streamed into the room through the window above the balcony door, and reflected off the tools scattered everywhere. But it was the light of a cold sun. I knew that the thunderstorm last night had been the curtain call of autumn. Very soon, probably even before the day was over, it would begin to snow. You could almost smell the snow. Winter was encroaching on the world.

Gustav was still sleeping, a simple-minded smile occasionally flitting over his face. Presumably he was dreaming of chocolate, or of the annual refund his private health insurance company paid him. While I tried to interpret my peculiar dream in my half-awake, half-dozing state, I took a cursory look around the room. In the confusion of the last few days I hadn't noticed how much progress Gustav and Archie were making with the renovation. Even the bedroom had been painted a pleasant shade of bright blue. But to my amazement, on one wall I noticed life-sized sketches of samurai – they looked like oriental quill pen drawings which have yet to be coloured in. Stylistic touches of this calibre were doubtless Archie's doing, and I couldn't help asking myself what Gustav's barbaric tastes made of such elegance. But no matter, our little chamber of horrors might well become a cosy home in the end – if only it weren't for . . . Yes, there was still this murdering monster, those skeletons in the temple . . . and then there was Yours Truly, whose duty it had become to shed light on the darkness.

It was funny, but that morning I didn't feel depressed even though the dream had been so sad. The wintry sun, the long sleep after all my exertions, and the homely Sunday mood had a positive influence on my state of mid. But things were going to get even better.

Suddenly a voice outside summoned me, a voice that the venerable author of *One Thousand and One Nights* would have summed up as 'sweet'. It differed from any other female voice I had heard in my life, though in a way I can't quite explain. Something mysterious, dark, and exotic was concealed in it, as well as a certain something you would find it hard to resist. She sang her song so melodiously and so passionately that I nearly fainted with pleasure. Slowly I rose, curved my back, and flehmed fervently. Full of encoded messages of love, her scent brought my blood to the boil, and gave back to me the yearning for physical pleasures I thought I had lost. I felt my entire ego melt like wax in a furnace; I was animated by only one desire: to unite myself with this scent. The intense urge to answer with my own song finally became uncontrollable.

I jumped down from snoring Gustav's heaving belly, ran to the bathroom, and leapt up on the window-sill.

It was an encounter with a queen! It was a vision of Cleopatra! She rolled, turned, and rubbed herself with divine suppleness on the terrace floor, all the while singing her alluring siren's song. At first I thought I had never seen one of her breed before, but then I remembered the brother who had appeared briefly at the window when Bluebeard had taken me to see Deep Purple's corpse. I hadn't been able to assign him to any race I knew either, and had been more than a little surprised. Without a doubt, the coquette who was offering herself so seductively on my territory also came from this unknown family.

Her sand-coloured coat, which fused into bright chestnut on her belly, reflected so much sunlight that you might have thought she was wearing a robe of gold. But what was most bewitching were her eyes: huge, warm yellow, hypnotising gems befitting only a lady of rank. They were all the more striking because her head was small, and her figure somewhat thickset. She whipped her bushy tail from side to side, continually half-revealing herself, as if her amorous entreaties had not sufficed to drive me crazy. But I was ablaze, and already had become her submissive slave.

Before I realised it, a hoarse cry escaped from my throat and merged with her bewitching song. To make my presence felt, I dropped to the balcony and gave the world a considerable dose of my environmentally safe, all-purpose scent. All of these odours mingled in the air, creating the enchanted atmosphere that dazed and intoxicated us.

She twisted and turned even more wildly, looking as if she could hardly wait for it. Nevertheless, caution was advised. Although her behaviour allowed for no doubt about her desire, it would be erroneous to assume automatically that she had chosen me of all candidates for fun and games. On the contrary, she had probably picked out this place as a meeting point for all her neighbourhood admirers. So I had to hurry, for as far as this sphere of life is concerned, the males of my kind possess early warning radar systems. I had a certain advantage from the start, because competitors from neighbouring territories would have inhibitions about penetrating my turf, but resisting a temptation as sweet and challenging as she would no doubt be too much for them, and in the end they could well risk everything.

In order to score a quick success, I made use of a tried-and-trusted strategy. The moment she looked away briefly, I dived down from the balcony to the terrace and stood there petrified. She noticed that, as if by magic, I had got a little closer to her, and she spat. But at the same time she rolled over lewdly, looking all the while in another direction. I seized the chance to narrow the distance between us a bit more. As soon as she turned around towards me, I once more stood rooted to the spot, looking around at my surroundings like a nonchalant fool. I knew she would attack me if she saw me actually approaching her, but a motionless body gave her no immediate reason to do so. Love, for my kind, is a very complicated matter, though to be honest I wouldn't have it any other way.

Things went on like this, in stop-and-go mode, for quite some time, until finally I was standing right behind her. I gave a meek, low-voiced trill. She hissed and continued to act aggressively, but the evidence was clear: she wanted to be sniffed at. Still she snarled, threatening me with extended claws. I calmly let her go on like this until she was out of breath, and then, at last, she sent out the signal that was my salvation. I took a quick look around. No competitors anywhere.

She stretched provocatively, right in front of me, shuffled nervously on her front paws, and cried out. I circled her once, sniffed at her body, flehmed voluptuously, and mounted her. At once she swept aside her tail to present me with her treasure. I pounced, seizing the nape of her neck with my teeth so that she could no longer budge and would stiffen in anticipation of impregnation.[12] She flattened her upper body and lifted up her rear. That was the final go ahead! I embraced my queen and went to it.

At the peak of our union, in my mind's eye I saw stars explode and universes come into being, saw my beloved surrounded by a glowing halo racing through the cosmos and floating towards me, saw ourselves perform an ethereal dance of lust, saw ourselves create billions upon billions of Felidae who in turn populated billions upon billions of galaxies and then copulated with one another to create further members of my kind, thus passing on and on the sacred creed, eternally and endlessly, never giving up until we could all become one with the unknown power that had created us. I felt that this union was completely different from every one that had preceded it in my life. At the moment of ejaculation, she let out a ringing scream, and we exploded away from one another. My vision vanished as quickly as it had come, leaving behind a faint afterglow.

Immediately she turned around and attacked me. She hit out at me hysterically, her claws spread, and screamed loudly. I retreated in a rush to a corner, cleaned myself, and watched her lust slowly cool. Now she was rolling fiercely on the floor and purring.

'Who are you? What race are you?' I finally burst out, my curiosity having got the better of me.

She smiled coldly and knowledgeably, her pupils narrowing to slits because of the harsh sunlight; only the profound yellow of the iris was visible.

'Race! What an insular and antiquated concept. Does it really matter what race I belong to?' she snarled. Then she rolled over and began cleaning her other side.

'No,' I replied. 'Nothing at all is important. I merely wanted to know with whom I'm speaking.'

'I'm not a member of any race, if that answers your question. Your lover is just the way she is, Francis.'

'You mean that your race is new?'

'Not new, but old! Or, to put it better, old and new – and different! Figure it out for yourself.'

'How did you know my name?'

'A little bird told me.'

'And what is your name?'

'I don't have a name,' she said with a mischievous giggle. 'No, that's a lie of course. But my real name wouldn't mean much to you because you're not in a position to understand its meaning.'

'What game is this? Twenty questions?'

'Exactly, my lover. But don't rack your brains over it. Some day everything will become clear all by itself. And trust me, everything will have a happy ending.'

She stretched herself sensuously and excited me anew. The whole game began again from the beginning. Her charming singsong was as bewitching as it was the first time, and I forgot the many questions I still wanted to ask her.

We dedicated the entire morning to love and lust, getting each other worked up into greater and greater raptures. Although the competition left me in peace during these pleasurable hours, strangely enough no second passed without the troubled feeling that we were being observed during our erotic gymnastics. There was no reason for this suspicion, because whenever I stole a paranoid glance around me, there was no one to be seen. In retrospect, my erotic adventure with that strange beauty seems like yet another dream – an exceedingly beautiful, but also rather bizarre dream.

When evil-looking clouds shooed away the sun at noon, she left me to vanish in the maze of back gardens. I was so drained and tired that I could no longer summon the strength to follow her. She, on the other hand, had just commenced her 'wedding party', and would be celebrating through many days and nights to come. The fact that in that condition the fangs of the omnipresent murderer might find her neck did not occur to me then, and so I didn't alert her to the danger. The reason I was so frivolous about it remains a mystery to me. Perhaps, as I justified to myself later, she didn't look like a typical victim.

I dragged myself back to the flat, and my first move was to ram my belly full with a hearty portion of fish, while Gustav looked on disapprovingly. He had just got out of bed and made my breakfast, so my escapade must have escaped his notice. Yet his expression was as sour as a lemon, and clearly betrayed his revulsion at the penetrating aroma exuding from every cell of my body. Finally, shaking his head in disgust, he blathered something about 'taking a bath' and 'usually keeps himself compulsively clean', then marched grumbling to his high-nutrition, home-made muesli with wheatgerm – one of the innovations (Archie again) in his life I most detested, and believed would quickly pass. We wouldn't have to put up with Archie today, thank God, because Gustav took a break from work on Sundays – as he frequently did on other days, too. After my meal, I went straight to the bedroom and within seconds had drifted off on my cushion into dreamless sleep.

'Do I at least know the sweetheart?'

Bluebeard must have been watching over my bed for some time already, because when I opened my eyes, there he was, stretched out on the floor, yawning. Gustav had probably let him into the flat, and he must have dropped off. I could make only a poor estimate of how long I had slept, but supposed that it was now late afternoon. I glanced at the window and saw that the predicted snowfall had arrived. Behind the window-panes shimmered a dense curtain of hazelnut-sized snowflakes falling from a steel-grey sky. Bluebeard slid restlessly back and forth, nervously licking his right back paw.

'I hope you know her,' I said, 'because she could bring us a little bit closer to solving this case.'

He assumed a sulky expression, then looked at me reproachfully with his uninjured eye.

'Case? Solution? You telling me you're still interested in that game? Judging by the way you stink, which is bad enough to make a vicar curse, you've been giving your attention to the more pleasant things in life.'

I couldn't really figure out whether he was serious, or whether his remark represented some form of concealed envy. Whatever gave him the idea that I was some kind of monk? Besides, he didn't exactly smell like perfumed soap himself.

'My, but we are in a bad mood today, aren't we? Could you

perhaps let me know what these asinine accusations are supposed to mean?'

'You've got a nerve to ask! Yesterday Felicity got wasted, and last night it was Solitaire. The whole district is in an unholy flap, and there are the craziest rumours going round about how you, Kong, and Herrmann and Herrmann let the killer get away even though he was within spitting distance. If you ask me, we're not just up shit creek without a paddle, we're sinking in it up to our necks! But instead of putting your superbrain in gear and getting us out of the damned hole we're in, you stage a couple of orgies and catch forty winks all in your own good time. Let me tell you, that's not the clever bastard I used to know.'

So, now he had got it off his chest. Of course, he couldn't know about what I had found out after Kong & Co. had taken leave of me, nor how close I had come to the solution, how there were only a few knots left for me to untie to flush out the butcher. (Or so I thought, anyway.) He had no idea, either, of the existence of that macabre journal. I was going to have to spoon-feed him with that part of the story since it was tragically connected with his own crippled existence. Anyway, he had made a big mistake about me.

'Bluebeard, I'm sorry if you have the impression that I'm sitting around doing nothing, or amusing myself with the ladies. I promise you that you're totally wrong. Last night I found out things that nobody in the district has ever had the slightest idea about. Terrible things, and yet things that could improve our chances of finding the killer. I'll tell you all about my experiences later, because at the moment I don't completely understand their implications myself. In any case, if you don't mind, I'd like to ask you a couple of questions now. First and most important: where is Joker, right at this moment?'

He seemed half-convinced now of my zeal and goodwill, for his indignation gradually gave way to a reserved attentiveness. Nevertheless, a trace of wait-and-see scepticism remained in his face, and he hummed and hawed at length before saying anything.

'Joker? Probably sitting around at home getting ready for Bible class. What else would he be doing in weather like this?'

'Where's his home?'

'His owner has a store where they sell porcelain and fine crystal some distance from here, beyond the square. The place is a warehouse, shop and flat all at the same time. I suppose Joker is somewhere around there.'

'OK. I'm going to pay a call on Pascal very shortly. While I'm doing that, you'll march over to Joker's and inform him that Pascal and I would like to talk to him about the murderer. If he gets obstinate, which is to be expected, indicate to him quietly but firmly that we may unfortunately have to let Kong know that a certain local preacher killed his beloved Solitaire. We'll all meet at Pascal's.'

'No shit! Joker?'

'It's only a suspicion, very likely unfounded. Be that as it may, you've got to scare the living daylights out of him. OK?'

'OK.'

'Second question: this morning I made the acquaintance of a lady whose race is totally unknown to me. Her behaviour, too, gave rise to diverse speculations. Her fur is sand-coloured, and her eyes are a glowing yellow . . .'

'I know that crowd.'

'Are there a lot around?'

'Hell, yes. Seems to be a breed that's really in right now. Soon the whole neighbourhood is going to be full of the arrogant snots. Every year these stupid tin-openers get even stupider ideas on how to better our kind. This time, though, with this breed, they're pissing in the wind.'

'What's wrong with them?'

'They're not like us. I mean, it's as if somehow, in the whole damned breeding process, they just never learned how to behave. They're wilder, more dangerous, like they think they're superior to the rest of us.'

'Like predators?'

'Not really. Otherwise the tin-openers would be getting nervous about having them at home. Sometimes I think they're only playing at being perfect house pets to get fed and have a warm roof over their heads while they hatch their dirty plans. Conceited bastards. I don't know exactly what they're up to, but whatever it is, they don't want anything to do with us, and they make me puke. What else do you want to know?'

'That's enough for the time being. We should go to work and get it over and done with before darkness falls.'

Because of the cold, Gustav had made an exception, for once, and shut every single door and window. So we sought him out in the living-room and let him know by vociferous mewing that we wanted to go outside. I noted that the renovation of the room had been completed, except for some plaster work on the ceiling. For want of a study, my friend had already lugged a monumental desk into the room, and had spread out his magnificent art books and archaeological treatise. For years he had cherished the dream project of publishing an encyclopaedic volume on the Egyptian goddess Bast. He worked on it like mad, every free minute. Unfortunately he only crept towards his goal inch by inch, as he had to interrupt his studies continually to write these ghastly hack epics to support us. And now that the new flat was making additional demands on our budget he had stooped so low as to supply teen mags with 'really exciting' how-I-got-my-first-period-and-pimples dramas. The very worst production he had ever put down on paper was a sleazy four-page piece of rubbish with the sensational title: MY PRINCIPAL RAPED ME SIX TIMES IN HIS OFFICE (subtitle: 'He Forced Himself upon Me Six Times! The Loathsome Act Took Place Six Times!' To carry the portrayal of this injustice to an extreme, I might have added 'And then I gave birth to sextuplets!'). But no matter how much he prostituted himself for good old Mammon, his heart never ceased beating for the mysteries of ancient Egypt. The cult of the goddess Bast, to a great extent unresearched, was to be the subject of his fourth book, and so he had ordered all the latest studies made by Egyptologists and curators. He would sit for countless days and nights over monographs, facsimile inscriptions, and photographs of wall paintings. Writing this book was a particular pleasure for him, since the religion relating to the goddess Bast – the symbol of maternity, fertility, and other feminine virtues – was closely connected to the worship of my kind; excavations have revealed that the goddess was often depicted in the form of Felidae.

And so, during this brief pause in the DIY, Gustav was once again sitting at his desk and sweating over his hieroglyphs when Bluebeard and I entered the living-room to inform him at full volume of our desire to leave the house. At first he shook his head resolutely, mumbling a few scare stories about my kind in his well-known baby-talk – for example, how they often perished in blizzards. Eventually, however, he relented and opened the bathroom window.

When we were outside, I drummed into Bluebeard's head again and again the necessity of getting tough if Joker refused to talk with us. Then we went our separate ways, and I waded on through knee-deep snow and over the walls towards Pascal's dwelling.

While breathing in the icy air and letting the white garden landscape work on my mood, I remembered my romantic entanglement of that morning. 'I'm not a member of any race,' she had said, and: 'Some day everything will become clear all by itself.' She had shrouded her race in mystery, and played the oracle by saying that it was old and new at the same time, as well as different. What was all that supposed to mean? There is no such thing as 'no race'; every one of us belongs to a race. It is an undeniable fact of life. Bluebeard's comment that 'they don't want anything to do with us' surprised me even more. As chance would have it, the whole thing fitted pretty well with the theory of a killer race. But to hell with all these theories – something in me made me resist the idea that the divine creature I had encountered, or those like her, were killers. Yet I couldn't say what made this idea seem so wrong. It was just something deep down inside me. Had I perhaps fallen in love? Or was my unerring instinct once again putting in its twopenny worth? Finally, I cut these speculations short by telling myself that apprehending the murderer was out of the question before a motive was established.

At last I arrived at the old building. With its snow-covered roof, brightly lit windows, and picturesque, smoking chimney, it now looked like an advertisement for Irish whiskey. Unfortunately, the back door was shut this time, so I had to roam around the entire house on the look-out for a gap to squeeze through. After a long search I discovered one in the long side of the building, where there was a basement window and a narrow gravel path leading down to the street. Compulsively perfect as people like him are, Pascal's owner had found an ideal way of ensuring his darling's freedom of movement. Far down in the wall was an entrance especially designed for my kind; it complemented the highly modern interior superbly, of course. Plastic blades, arranged in an interlocking fan, served as a door through a plate-sized hole trimmed in steel that gleamed like polished silver. You only needed to bump your head lightly against the blades and they opened automatically like a camera aperture, closing shut again after you had gone through the hole.

I trotted right up to the study, but instead of Pascal, this time it was the master of the house who was sitting at the computer. I was tempted to take a closer look at this fashion junkie with his Karl Lagerfeld ponytail swinging from the back of his head, but Lord knows, I had a lot of other problems on my hands.

I finally found Pascal in the sparsely furnished living-room with the two genitalia paintings on the walls. He was napping on a large, scarlet silk cushion with golden-coloured decorative cords and tassels hanging down majestically from each corner. The entire room was illuminated by three tiny halogen spots sunk into the ceiling, which cast circles of light on the parquet floor.

The sight of Pascal made me spontaneously think of a grizzled king in a Shakespearean tragedy. And it was true that Pascal led a regal life under the protection and loving care of his very well-to-do master. Involuntarily, I started to think of all the abused and oppressed animals kicked around in this world who had not been as lucky as Pascal: animals tortured by human beings just for fun; animals bought as playthings and toyed with a little until, weary of them, their owners booted them out; animals starving in plain sight of well-nourished human beings; animals murdered brutally so that coats or handbags could be tailored from their fur; animals cooked alive by human beings who regarded this as the acme of culinary art; animals collapsing under the burdens they had to carry day after day; animals peering out of narrow cages at grimacing human faces their whole lives, or performing idiotic tricks foreign to their species; animals who raped or were raped, masturbated compulsively, mutilated themselves, devoured their own children, murdered their own kind, became apathetic and depressed, and ultimately committed suicide because they sat in a prison with the romantic-sounding name of 'zoo' – a place where they were observed and observed and observed until they did these terrible things out of desperation; animals waking up to find themselves robbed overnight of their natural environment because the human race needed more and more natural resources ... Admittedly there were those like Pascal who were privileged, who lived heavenly lives in conditions created by human beings. But this was small comfort in view of the global tragedy. The only thing that gave me courage was the perhaps illusory hope that human beings, some distant day in the future, would remember the dust-covered contract they had concluded with us in primeval times and then broken in the most ignominious manner. Then at last they would see the error of their ways and ask for our forgiveness. Naturally nothing would ever be as good as what could and should have been. Nevertheless, we were willing to forgive, would accept, would not ask recompense for all the tears we had shed because of them. It was the dream of a fool, yet I wanted to continue to dream this dream until the end of my life, because I was firmly convinced that dreams, and only dreams, would be able to triumph over the sordid truth.

Pascal gradually stirred from his sleep. When he recognised me, his old eyes opened wide in astonishment.

'Francis! This is certainly a surprise. Why didn't you let Bluebeard tell me you were coming?'

'There wasn't any time for that. A great many important things have happened since the last time we met, Pascal. Things that are linked with the murders and should help to solve them. I need your help, particularly the help of your plaything.'

'Oh? Well, I'm glad to hear this, of course. But wouldn't you like to have a bite to eat before you begin to tell me your story? Ziebold, my master, has prepared fresh heart.'

'No thanks. I'm not hungry right now. Besides, I don't want to waste any time. I want to get everything I know taken care of as soon as possible. My unaided powers of deduction are no longer sufficient to disentangle this muddle of secrets, half-truths and deceptions, and so we two superbrains are going to have to join forces. I really wanted to get over here this morning, but something unexpected turned up.'

Pascal smiled with amusement, probably able to tell by my smell what had in fact turned up.

'Thanks very much for the compliment of calling the decaying apparatus in my skull "super". But the only thing that is still super about me is my capacity for sleep, a sleep which is becoming more and more like death. There's a bright side, however, even to this. I probably won't notice the transition from the one kind of sleep to the other. But I do hope that I can help you a little anyway. So tell me all about it, my friend.'

I rattled away like a machine-gun, relating to him all the events that had taken place since our first encounter. How I had seen with my own eyes that Felicity had died, how I had returned home in shock and found the journal in the cellar that same night. What atrocities the journal had divulged, and what grave consequences they had had up to the present. Then the attack of Kong's army, and how we had all stumbled upon Solitaire's corpse. How Jesaja, the good Guardian of the Dead, had popped up suddenly, only to push open new doors to new horrors. I told him about the so-called Temple and its inhabitants who had been decorated with flowers and, to round off the story, about the mysterious Prophet who was supposedly responsible for the continuing massacre. Then I set out my numerous theories and assumptions, for the sake of fairness even taking care not to conceal their respective logical snags and contradictions. During my talk, Pascal's expression changed again and again: his face displayed dismay, surprise and bafflement, and his agitation increased minute by minute. I concluded my talk by describing my sexual exploit that morning and its bewitching heroine, as well as relating Bluebeard's views on the new race that had appeared in the neighbourhood. Pascal's answer to this flood of information was a silence that seemed to last an eternity. It was a justifiable pause, for he had to think through all these unbelievable events before he could speak.

'Hmmm . . . ' came from him at last, and I was thankful to him for breaking the unsettling spell.

'I have been living in these parts for ages, Francis, and haven't registered a fraction of all the terrible things you have found out about in such an incredibly short time. I must confess that I'm a bit old now, and no longer very quick on my legs, but your discoveries are so overwhelming that I simply should have known about their existence.'

'Well, luck aided me more than once,' I said modestly.

'That may be, but I'm the one who has the local reputation of being not only a know-it-all, but also a trustworthy confidant. Now it turns out that in reality I'm only the former.'

'What astonishes me,' I said, 'is why the hundreds of the murdered down there in the catacombs aren't in your data bank.'

'Simple, my dear friend. As corpses, they would never have turned up to begin with. Look, fluctuation is a perpetual fact of life in the district so you can very quickly lose track of anyone's whereabouts. Our brothers and sisters who die, I mean who die a natural death, are often buried by their owners in a pet cemetery or somewhere in the family's backyard. Or the owners move and take their little darlings with them. As for the other brothers and sisters, they go wandering off or switch to areas that are further away, or just vanish from the scene. However many brothers and sisters of ours may have disappeared, there has never been any reason to suppose that they were murdered. As for the six other victims in my data bank, these were found with fatal neck-bite wounds, and so were distinctly identifiable as murder victims. If, however, the murderer had been stowing away his previous victims underground with such unflagging diligence, naturally they would not have turned up above ground as corpses and consequently been registered in my data bank.'

'Did you note the brothers and sisters who suddenly, for whatever reasons, left the area?'

'Of course.'

'So we could use your data to verify, even at this later date, how many have gone missing without reason and the precise time of their disappearance?'

'Very likely, though it will be no easy task to distinguish the murder victims from those who moved on with their owners, ran away, or died from natural causes.'

'It sounds like a lot of work, but this is the only way we can determine the frequency with which the killer has been going about his business and, more important, when the reign of terror actually began. And of course there's the next unresolved question, namely, why the killer didn't deliver his last seven victims to Jesaja, the good Guardian of the Dead.'

Groaning, Pascal got up from his cushion and made a half-hearted attempt at arching his back, all the while smiling in embarrassment, as if he owed me this gesture to offset the picture of misery he presented. It was depressing to see how he sought to hide from me his weary struggle with arthritis and the degeneration of his limbs. Most likely his other bodily functions were no longer what they used to be, either. He slid down from the cushion and walked slowly up and down the room.

'That last question does indeed raise an important point, Francis. For it is a sign that our friend is beginning to make mistakes.'

'Are you so sure about that? Such an assumption has one very large flaw, in my opinion. I cannot imagine that this prodigy of horror would be able to commit even a single error.'

'But it's the only possible explanation for his changed behaviour.'

His enthusiasm for juggling around ideas and deductions was almost visible – it was as necessary to his extraordinary mind as air is to breathing, and it really had him in its grip. He spoke more and more fervently, and even his movements became faster, livelier.

'So let's assume I'm the murderer,' he said. 'I go out regularly on nocturnal raids to murder others of my kind for motives known only to the Good Lord and myself. I murder and murder, and always cover my tracks by taking hold of the corpses between my teeth, lugging them to the air tunnels, and throwing them down into the catacombs. And then, out of the blue, I give up this method, which means that sooner or later someone will find the evidence of my dastardly deeds and hunt me down. Why do I do this? Why do I do something that can only bring me into danger? Well, let's just say that I'm sick and tired of it all. Why go to great lengths to cover my tracks when I know that none of the blockheads in the square are capable of laying a hand on me?'

'Wrong!' I shouted. I loved this guesswork; it thrilled my puzzle-addicted mind. It made me tingle with excitement, setting off a chain reaction of possible solutions.

'You're forgetting that our friend is logic personified. He has a very definite goal in mind when committing his atrocities, and he kills with the deliberation of a military strategist. Never would it occur to him to deviate one iota from his normal course of action on a whim or out of arrogance. Why should he? He's been getting along just fine up to now. No, no, he has a special reason for not going on with his clever tactic. But what the devil could it be?'

Pascal froze abruptly in the focal point of one of the lights, which surrounded his shimmering coat with an aura that made him look like an angel descended from heaven. He jerked his head in my direction and gave me a piercing look with his glowing yellow eyes.

'Perhaps he wants to call our attention to something.'

'That's good. That's damned good,' I cried in delight, and jumped up.

Pascal, however, shook his head vehemently and let his ears droop down unhappily.

'No, that's not good at all. For we have no idea what he wants to call our attention to.'

'I think it's as plain as the nose on your face: he wants to call our attention to him and to what he's doing, to the fact that he's like a phantom, no, like a god, who can determine the fate of the entire neighbourhood and decide who shall live and who shall die. Respect – that's what he wants.'

'But what's in it for him? The average intelligence of the locals is so disgracefully low that they couldn't possibly understand his oh-so-very-subtle signals; they would lynch him on the spot if he were to reveal himself. He can only reap fear and hate with such tactics, certainly not respect.'

I thought quickly. Everything Pascal was saying was persuasive, and you would have to come up with some damned good arguments to make him contradict himself. Discussions with him resembled chess games, and Pascal was a grand master.

As regards the dead bodies being left out in full view, we were obviously at an impasse. But because I wanted to go on to the next question, and because nothing clever had occurred to me, I merely said: 'Well, perhaps by not hiding the bodies he's trying to call the attention of one brother in particular to what he may consider his mission in life.'

'Now *that's* what I call good!' Pascal exclaimed.

'Why?' I asked, somewhat intimidated.

'Because for the first time you mentioned a mission, Francis. Look, don't you get it? He wants his life's mission, in which he has invested so much effort, to be recognised or even to be carried on by others, perhaps by one brother in particular. It must be his deliberate intention to disclose his motives. Whatever it is that he wants to tell us, he is now looking for supporters. For some reason it's getting to be too much for him.'

'A strange method of recruiting sympathisers.'

'True. Nevertheless, his whole personality is odd. He's like a puzzle; no, he *is* the puzzle, and he's only waiting for someone to come and solve it.'

'At least he could express himself a little more clearly. Under the circumstances, it's possible nobody will be able to figure out what he's up to.'

'Don't worry, Francis, sooner or later we'll decode his signals. And then we'll be hot on his trail.'

'Let's hope so. OK, let's forget this part of the story for the time being and talk about the only suspect we've found up to now: Joker. What do you think of him?'

He plodded back to his regal cushion and lowered himself down on it very gingerly.

'A very promising suspect. He witnessed the tragic events in the experimental laboratory, and saw his chance to establish a cult of martyrdom along classic biblical lines, based on Claudandus's sufferings. As we know, it was a chance he acted on. Right away he declared himself the worldly representative of the Prophet, for the obvious reason that such a position would give him great power and special status in the area. But who else knows about the things Joker saw then, or rather became acquainted with through those cruel people? Perhaps dealing with these gruesome matters pushed him over the edge. It's conceivable, isn't it?'

'Jesaja spoke of the Prophet's voice echoing down the tunnels, not Joker's.'

Pascal put on a poker face.

'He disguised his voice. I have no problems believing that the second Rasputin would be capable of that. Moreover, he was the only one, aside from Jesaja, who knew the catacombs and how practical they'd be, so to speak, for rubbish disposal.'

'But don't forget the mysterious stranger.'

'If he exists.'

I slumped down on the parquet floor and looked off into space, stymied. As I said, everything that Pascal had to say held water; it sounded so damned logical. Nevertheless, did a case as marvellously mysterious as this one deserve such a simple, if not pat, solution? Supposedly Joker was our culprit: a religious fanatic whom I had held in suspicion ever since that infamous night when I first saw him as master of ceremonies at that ritual of pain. His whole appearance had something diabolical, omnipotent, coldhearted and downright cruel about it; so how could such a creature have played the part of the perfect killer whom nobody would ever suspect of committing murder? Precisely this primitive image threw me off. Everything fitted together too well; it was all too transparent. Without admitting it to myself, all through my many unsettling experiences I had been thinking of that despicable cleric. Like a snake that could not be trod down, again and again he had slithered up out of the deepest depths of my unconsciousness to cry at me in his awesome bass: *I'm the murderer! I'm the murderer!* But I had always refused to pay attention to that thunderous voice, even to acknowledge its existence. Now, however, Pascal had frankly and openly affirmed my suspicion, and, freed from the psychological mechanism of repression, I would have to confront the facts. If you carefully considered the pros and cons, only Joker came into the frame as the murderer. And yet something in me stubbornly resisted a solution that was simply too good to be true. I had a single trump left to play at Pascal this time.

'There's one more thing: this strange old–new race, one of whose members I came across today. According to Bluebeard they are unique to this area,' I objected roguishly.

'Professor Preterius's killer race,' Pascal said, beaming.

'Yes, Professor Preterius's race of murderers. Is there really any reason to doubt it? Certainly not because of anything as ridiculous as logic,' I replied like a slightly obnoxious child. But Pascal was not going to be provoked, and he smiled like a father committed to progressive child-rearing methods and God-knows-what signs of creativity in the most primitive tantrums of his child.

'Not only logic, Francis, although I must confess that there's something to be said for your theory. Nevertheless, it is a little too neatly put together, if you'll forgive me for saying so. You're forgetting that an ingenious breeding method, that is, one created by human manipulation, is not necessarily required for the creation of a new or an "old–new" race. In short, you're forgetting the so-called "blind watchmaker", namely, evolution, the inscrutable work of Mother Nature. For she creates a new species every day with no consciousness of her miraculous work. To put it simply, new or unusual races can arise from the workings of chance alone. You really don't have to bend over backwards to set up a clever breeding programme; this goes without saying. Look, ninety-nine per cent of our kind copulate without any control or system whatsoever. So it's only natural that sooner or later some hitherto unknown race will be created. What's the lesson in this for us? A new race is the most natural thing in the world. Hence, in formulating your killer-race theory, you are leaving out not only logic but also the role of the illogical, or chance, my dear fellow.'

'You think that the fair creature I met and her kin are the product of natural selection?'

'That seems plausible, although I can't refuse your theory because I lack supporting evidence for my own. But then I have good old probability on my side.'

The old fart was a genius – I had to admit it, no ifs or buts. For while I had been concocting ingenious hypotheses and devising abstruse reasons and justifications for them, Pascal, putting the horse before the cart and not the other way around, had started out first from probability and natural causes. I had made the mistake of erecting speculative castles, all the time ignoring the fact that things like chance and peculiar coincidences also existed in the world. In other words, Pascal had a logical but simple way of thinking; although also logical, mine was complicated.

'When will you ever be wrong, Pascal?' I sighed in resignation. 'If you don't mind, I'd like to postpone our next exchange of views until tomorrow so that I can keep at least a few shreds of self-respect.'

Darkness had fallen in the course of our conversation, and through the glass wall behind my dark-haired teacher I saw that a sombre obscurity had now descended upon the snow-covered gardens, robbing even the romantically dancing snowflakes of their brightness. I had the whimsical notion that the landscape before me, dominated as it was by the colour black, was a sort of negative film of my last dream.

Pascal noticed my dreamy look and shook his head, smiling in amusement.

'Oh no, my friend, *you* are the real know-all. Only you can contribute the decisive flash of insight that will solve this mystery. I, perhaps, possess a good grasp of the facts and the gift of sober ratiocination, but I lack inspiration. And without that, run-of-the-mill intelligence just gets stuck. The very worst scourge of our time are the many half-formed talents who so grossly overestimate themselves. But I know where I stand.'

I wanted to protest, but he was looking right past me. He got up from his cushion with a haughty expression, as if he had seen something behind my back that displeased him. I turned around quickly and saw a heavily panting Bluebeard, transformed into a shapeless snowball, come hobbling in through the doorway. Icicles of considerable size hung from his fur, and his nose glowed like a ripe tomato. I thought I perceived a mixture of annoyance and despair in Pascal's face; it could only have been caused by the coarse and inconsiderate behaviour of the intruder.

Our crippled Eskimo left behind him great tracks of slush and little pools of water on the freshly waxed parquet floor. But he carried thoughtlessness to an extreme when he stopped just before us and shook himself powerfully to get the snow out of his fur, showering us liberally in the process as well. Pascal moaned softly and shook his head almost imperceptibly. Thanks to his elephantine sensitivities, Bluebeard noticed nothing. Our host made no reference to Bluebeard's scandalous entrance and kept his customary silence.

'Where's Joker?' I finally asked him; the tension was getting unbearable.

'Not there. Vanished.'

'What does "vanished" mean?'

He squatted down on his sopping wet rear and shook himself once again.

'I got into the house through a basement window, and searched the place from top to bottom for the Reverend. Even got as far as this frigging stockroom in the attic, which was pretty creepy because the shelves there are bursting with statues of us, life-size. Tigers, jaguars and leopards too, all piled up on top of one another. Everything porcelain and real as life. But no trace of Joker. Anyway, then I went round calling and calling him and almost ruined my voice in the process. When that didn't do any good, I asked around in the neighbourhood. Everybody says they haven't seen him since our last big get-together.'

'Murdered!' I screeched.

'No, vanished,' said Pascal coolly. 'He knew that you were very close to nailing him, and skipped town as fast as he could. That would be just like good old Joker.'

'Damn. That's just like the bastard!' agreed Bluebeard.

'Now just wait a minute!' A cold anger overcame me. 'I refuse to accept a solution as cheap as that.'

'You don't have to accept it,' said Pascal to pacify me. 'It's only one possibility. But at present, and given the circumstances, it seems the most probable one. In any case, at least we now know that Joker was up to his neck in this mysterious affair.'

'He's got to be!' parroted Bluebeard self-importantly. 'That self-righteous face he put on all the time is proof enough. Though I was always dumb enough to go along with that Claudandus hocus-pocus, I never did trust that phony Bible-basher. Guilty, I say!'

Pascal could no longer bear the sight of my disappointment. He got down from the cushion and came up to within a few inches of me.

'Why are you refusing to accept this outcome? Why fight facts that are irrevocable and do not admit any other conclusion, at least for the moment?'

'Because they don't ring true and they don't add up. The information I have gathered – incomplete as it may be – does not necessarily indicate that Joker is the murderer. The whole affair is like a painting that has been put up for sale and authenticated by every specialist but which in reality is a fake.'

After we had exchanged opinions, Pascal and I decided to use the computer in the coming days to narrow down victims and to find out which brothers and sisters had lived in the area the longest. With this information we could screen out the other suspects and submit them to interrogation. This done, perhaps we could establish a pattern in the attacks. Then we would hold a meeting with all the residents of the neighbourhood, tell them what we knew, and warn them of the danger, given our knowledge of the affair. Although I too was starting to assume that our butcher was none other than Joker, who after all had vanished so neatly, I did not want to leave any stone unturned: my instincts, which up to now had never been wrong, deserved a fair hearing.

Late in the evening, Bluebeard and I took our leave of Pascal and started back home in the bitter cold. It had stopped snowing in the meantime, but in its stead a merciless frost had set in.

'You ought to watch out for your own skin,' grunted Bluebeard while we plodded through the snow on the garden walls.

'What do you mean by that?'

'Well, the way things look, this beast is still running around free, probably holed up somewhere. He isn't farting behind a warm, cosy stove any more, and he'll be having a tough time getting his belly full, too. He's going to want to even the score with the clever bastard who screwed up his plans. Shit, yes!'

'I'm not afraid,' I lied. 'Besides, I'm not the only detective who's wise to his tricks. He has Pascal as much as me to thank for his trouble.'

'Nah, he . . . ' Bluebeard's expression was glum. 'According to what you told me, the killer's only going after the brothers and sisters who want to take further classes in sex education. But good old Pascal is castrated. And besides, he's not going to be around much longer anyway.'

'Why not?'

'He's got cancer, in his gut, I think. The horse doctor gives him not more than half a year.'

I had nothing to say to that, and took pains not to reveal that the news hit me like a bullet. It was odd, but I felt as if this shattering judgement had been pronounced on a friend with whom I had grown up since early childhood. Suddenly, I was aware of how intensely I was attached to Pascal and how much I needed him as a companion, even as a beloved and irreplaceable twin brother. Yes, we were like twins, not only in matters of intellect but also of taste, a perfectly coordinated team. And now he was going to make his exit before the good adventures together could even begin. It was stupid of me to forget in the chaos of the murders that death doesn't often make violent attacks; no, usually he just stretches out his icy fingers very slowly and quietly towards the living. He is the silent presence in the background that looks at the clock and smiles.

Bluebeard and I didn't say a single word to each other the rest of the way. The insight, newly discovered, that death was present everywhere, everlastingly, had silenced us. I also knew that when Pascal died, something would die in me as well. It had already begun.

CHAPTER

— 9 —

THE FOLLOWING WEEK and a half consisted on the one hand of tricky mental acrobatics, and on the other of addictive pleasures – and ended with an unbelievably bitter surprise that almost broke the camel's back. It was those days before Christmas that smell like home-baked cakes and icing sugar, and Gustav and Archie had made it their goal to complete all renovation by Christmas Eve. Both were under such a strain that they didn't have any time for me, but that was fine because I was busy with things that were putting me through a lot worse.

What Pascal and I had planned to do quickly turned out to be a wearisome sorting not only of computer data accumulated over the years, but also of the fragmentary memories of local residents. As Pascal had predicted, it was extraordinarily complicated to sift out the 'cold sacks' from those who had died from natural causes, or left the area for unknown reasons. In the end it was obvious that we weren't going to be able to make more than a guess at how many had actually made use of Jesaja's Guardian of the Dead service over the years. Nevertheless, we did get closer to the truth with a few tricks of statistical magic, and reckoned our final estimate to be at least eighty per cent right. In this regard, Bluebeard was of invaluable assistance, for he took care of the tiresome dirty work. His detailed knowledge of the area and his vast network of contacts paid off with interest.

Pascal's data only went back as far as 1982. So at the beginning of our statistical operations we concentrated on everyone who had parted company with the area since then. On the fifth day of our investigation, we came up with a 'flexible' number of 800 missing. These, however, had gradually been replaced by about 350 new arrivals, in part because our kind – as undemanding house pets – had become fashionable with the growing number of people these days who shunned responsibility, and in part because the departures had automatically made room for newcomers. Pascal and Bluebeard knew the reasons for the disappearance of about 200 of these 800 never-see-agains. Either they had moved away with their owners or had said something to the effect that they felt uneasy in the neighbourhood or with their owners and were thinking of changing areas; most of them had probably carried out this wish at some point. Then we took a look at the ages of the remaining 600. Since our average life expectancy spans nine to fifteen years on a human time scale, and those 600 represented a solid cross-section of ages, we proceeded from the assumption that about 100 of them must have died of old age or of illnesses caused by old age – this without attracting the attention of anyone, because they had most likely been buried immediately by their owners. Pascal, of course, had kept additional accounts of the average mortality rates in the area, yet since in these cases the causes of death were all known, they did not have any logical connection with the hundreds of deaths we supposed had taken place. Given such a great number missing, we also had to allow for a percentage of unknowns, because a certain number must have simply disappeared into thin air, for reasons that we could not pin down. This vague category included, for example, the theft of pure-breds and the victims of traffic accidents whom attentive observers had promptly laid to eternal rest in the nearest available rubbish bin. We made a generous estimate of this category at ten per cent, which meant that of the remaining 500 there were fifty who might be said to have gone missing in action.

Two hundred plus 100 plus 50 makes 350. We now knew that 350 of the 800 listed as having vanished without a trace were probably not murder victims. The approximate number of brothers and sisters who had met with a terrible death from super-fang's deadly bites in the past ten years thus numbered about 450 by simple arithmetic. Nevertheless, we continued our calculations. If the butcher had set to work with uninterrupted regularity, then the number of Felidae he had dispatched to the eternal happy hunting grounds amounted to forty-five annually, or one roughly every eight days. But even allowing for inaccuracies, this figure did not conform to what had actually happened in the last two to three weeks, when the killer seemed to have managed more than twice as many victims and had struck every two to three days.

These feats of computation were, of course, ultimately nothing more than mere speculation, statistical illusions, number games flickering on the computer monitor (which we would pounce on every time Pascal's master walked out of the door). But there was no question of our having made any gross errors, if only because in the underground temple there were many hundreds of skeletons, as I had seen with my own eyes. Our methods were very likely bringing us far closer to the truth than we had supposed. On the other hand, we were as far as ever from finding a convincing murder motive.

The path to half-way realistic results had to pass through a near impenetrable thicket of detail. Bluebeard interviewed numerous residents, tracked down family members and friends of the missing, and grilled all of them about what the missing had said before disappearing, thus providing the information we needed for our computer chronology. Without Bluebeard, we certainly could not have put together a list of such size in such a short time.

But aside from the drudgery, Pascal introduced me step by step to the secrets of computers, opening the door for me to a fascinating universe full of playful logic and logical play. The data management programme alone, which so reduced the work of compiling statistics, enthralled me to the extent that I had taught myself – with an occasional tip from Pascal – how to operate it within a day. It was Pascal, too, who taught me how to install secret files. These could be displayed on the monitor only after activating a personal code so that their existence remained a secret even to the owner of the computer. Yet having at last discovered a way to gratify my perversely restless mind (condemned to inactivity most of the time) with intellectual fodder, I wanted more. The power to create a simulation of reality with a few keystrokes or to penetrate the realm of abstraction and knowledge was such a turn-on that I got addicted from the start. I would repeatedly turn to Pascal during our work and beg him to give me a new fix. He told me about the many existing computer languages with names like Basic, Fortran, Cobol, Ada and, oddly enough, even Pascal. He wanted to teach me one of these languages when the hunt for the murderer was over so that I could write my own programs.

All of these promises, delivered with an encouraging smile and shining eyes, touched a soft spot somewhere within me, because they reminded me of the brief time left to my teacher. There were so many daring, intellectual feats for us to perform, so many dark mysteries for us to unravel – if only these devilish tumours did not dwell in his bowels, growing and growing and growing while we indulged ourselves with these child-ish dreams. The pain that jabbed at my heart when I persuaded him to rave about the marvellous things he planned to teach me finally became so unbearable that I avoided every allusion to a joint future and steered the conversation towards our immediate problems. In this atmosphere of uncertainty and wild fantasising, we slaved at the computer for days on end and when Karl Lagerfeld didn't come home, all night long as well. I was pulled back and forth between excitement as we celebrated each success, yowling at our feeding dish, and the sadness that tormented me, knowing what would happen soon to my dear friend. And so the shadow of death fell on every exclamation of joy, on every smile, on every crest of happiness. Admittedly, death was still far away, no more than a shadowy outline. But you could already see the blood-red glow of his eyes.

We took only a few breaks, during which Bluebeard gave us new information or entertained us with the latest gossip. During one of these pauses, the gigantic painting of Gregor Johann Mendel again caught my attention. Since I was almost continually in the study, the painting had become an accustomed part of my surroundings, and I hardly noticed it any more. But now it quite suddenly loomed large, and I remembered that this sinister form had figured prominently in one of my more horrifying nightmares. So I asked Pascal who this Gregor Johann Mendel actually was. He replied curtly that he was a famous cleric from the past century whom his master greatly admired. Well, the answer prompted me to draw my own conclusions about his master's piety, and I let it go at that.

At long last we finished our work, and started preparing for the meeting at which we would inform the general public about our results. We also wanted to warn everyone about the murderer and explain his peculiar habits, for he was very likely still at large. As far as his identity was concerned, my frustrations were endless. Although we turned up many long-term residents, none of them could seriously be considered suspects. Either they were old dears whose chief occupation in past years had been bringing forth whole new generations, or they turned out to be grandads of evident senility who didn't even understand what we wanted to know from them. Then again, there were some who had suffered the same sad fate as Bluebeard and could be ruled out right away for just not being physically capable of committing deeds requiring such agility and energy. To my great annoyance, we had to fall back upon Joker as the only likely suspect, which plunged the whole affair back into obscurity. Bluebeard had sneaked around the house of porcelain several times, made inquiries with the neighbours, and even kept the building under intermittent surveillance, but Joker seemed to have disappeared into thin air, and the hope that he would ever turn up diminished daily. Who knows, I thought sometimes with a bitter smile, while we struggled with his murderous past, Joker might have long since departed for Jamaica as a stowaway; he was probably now amusing himself with the local ladies.

Although we were extremely proud of our work and were all too ready to pretend to ourselves that we had accomplished a miracle with our scientific procedures, at the back of our minds a sense of failure lurked. From a purely objective point of view, had we achieved anything of consequence? Absolutely nothing, in my opinion! We had no murder motive, no murderer, not even a plausible theory. We were still groping in the dark, so whenever a match sputtered into flame somewhere, we would persuade ourselves that its wan glow was the sun. We simply didn't have the glue to cement together the countless broken pieces and reveal the true form of the mystery.

The date for the meeting of all the local inhabitants was set for Christmas Eve, when our human companions would have plenty on their hands with the festivities, and we could escape their supervision more easily. The dilapidated second floor of our Villa Frankenstein was chosen as the meeting place, a location that everyone knew because it was there that those repulsive ceremonies had taken place. On the day before the meeting, Bluebeard went from house to house and from backyard to backyard distributing invitations. I had one undisclosed wish: that at the climax of the meeting Joker would turn up, just like the villain in every Agatha Christie mystery who is always unmasked when all the participants gather together. However, I had to smile at this wish, because a picture-postcard scene inevitably popped up in my imagination when I thought of it: Joker, contentedly roaming a Caribbean beach and fishing out delicious seafood from the waves.

I woke up on the morning of December 24 from a restless sleep filled with a mish-mash of all the terrifying impressions of the past weeks. In a bad mood and sleepy-headed, I began to arch my back listlessly, not knowing that this day would be one of the most important in my life, a day on which I would learn more about myself, my kind, and the neither black nor white but ultimately grey world than I ever had in those days when I had concerned myself with high-falutin philosophical matters. I was going to learn quickly, for I had an excellent teacher – the murderer.

What had woken me on the said morning was the sound of roaring laughter and clinking glasses from the adjoining room. I looked around, perplexed, because I had returned home so exhausted and depleted from the final computer session the previous night that I wasn't even sure where I had laid my head to sleep.

My eyes now perceived a bedroom – but a bedroom that made me wonder whether I was in the right house. Then I noticed the samurai on the walls, which had been coloured in since I last saw them, and guessed what I had missed out on during the computer games. The renovation of our little haunted castle had been concluded. The place where I had settled down to sleep turned out to be a so-called 'futon', which is a kind of Japanese mattress. Asia had invaded other areas of the room as well. Along the wall were screens covered with silk paper and, casting a meditative glow, Chinese lanterns with dragon motifs dangling from bamboo stands. What did all this mean? Had Gustav gone completely out of his mind? Would we soon be woken each morning by a gong? Or the murmuring sing-song of a geisha?

Archibald . . . Of course, it was the work of that walking
Zeitgeist, that trend-setting vacuum, that high-fashion jumping
jack whose strings were pulled by cultural heroes with un-
pronounceable names who elevated even the shape of their
bathroom key to the level of a moral philosophy. He had
completely corrupted Gustav, pushing on him every conceivable
junk item that could be found under the pompous heading of
'life-styles' in those interminable colour supplements. Poor Gustav! Paying off the loan for this junk meant for sure that he
would have to write 112 novelettes a year until he was 112 years
old. Sadly, Gustav was a pushover for Archie, since there wasn't
much about Gustav's taste that could be corrupted anyway.
What would have been the alternative? Some horrifying
'interior decoration theme' in loud colours from a mail-order
catalogue? I shook my head in resignation. My companion just
wasn't what you'd call a shining light, and I had to accept that
fact once and for all.

Inhaling the reek of freshly applied lacquer, I shuffled out into
the hall, half-expecting that next I would encounter a fifties
American jukebox – and blow me if Archie's décor scheme
hadn't embraced even that most tasteless cliché. Beside a small,
bow-shaped bar, over which loomed a huge mirror tilted
slightly forwards, stood that familiar reminder of the bygone
days of jive, with a 'virtuoso' saxophone croaking forth from it
– I doubted if Gustav even knew what a saxophone looked like.

Through the open door I saw the happy renovators standing
in the middle of the living-room, toasting each other with
champagne no less. They were proudly surveying the room,
which in terms of bareness was more than equal to Karl
Lagerfeld's living quarters. There was a fire-engine-red sofa and
a small granite table whose form eluded all geometric description, which stood forlornly in a dark corner. Only in one regard
had Gustav's personal touch prevailed. Proudly displayed on
the walls were enlargements of hieroglyphs, plaster-of-Paris
reproductions of sarcophagus covers, and, lo and behold, a

splendidly well-executed relief showing the goddess Bast in the form of one of my kind.

When Gustav and Archie noticed Yours Truly, they gave me idiotic grins and raised their glasses in greeting. I paid no attention to the two clowns and gave the rest of the flat a quick once-over. Compared with the trendy dog's dinner elsewhere, the study was the most acceptable. Furnished with antiques and massive bookshelves in classic library style which soared up to the ceiling, and illuminated by only one antique reading lamp, the room radiated the pleasantly contemplative atmosphere that a contemplative intellectual like Gustav needed. The kitchen, however, had also fallen victim to Archie's 'creative' mania. It was home to every piece of nonsense that lunatics sacked from respectable decorating firms had thought up, and worse put into production, and worst of all sold to harmless people like Gustav.

Well, enough griping for now. What was done was done. At least now our routine would be restored: just like in the good old days, I and my intellectually challenged friend would listen to classical music, watch those marvellous old Fred Astaire films on television and, undisturbed by the envious glances of health fanatics like Archie, gorge ourselves to our heart's delight. Just like the good old days? Not very likely – not as long as certain things that still had to be put right remained to be done.

After a power breakfast of various choice meats and scrambled eggs, which Gustav had come up with to celebrate the day, I made a short visit to the catacombs. Jesaja, whom I found asleep in the Temple and first had to wake up, went nearly wild with joy when he saw me again. After a hearty round of greetings, I asked him whether the Prophet had made an appearance in the meantime, or had even presented the good Guardian of the Dead with new deliveries, which certainly seemed possible considering that it was a religious holiday. The Persian answered in the negative, and added in his timorous, roundabout way that he was beginning to get fed up with life underground.

So, as a first step, I invited him to the midnight conference. But he backed down, reciting millions of reasons why he could not attend just on this night. The true reason for his shyness was crystal clear: the Prophet had not yet lifted his curfew.

After a few hours I left the catacombs, determined to do everything in my power to free this pitiable being from the prison of lies that the murderer had built especially for him.

Then I returned home to watch Gustav make his holiday preparations. In keeping with venerable tradition, he spent Christmas Eve alone, except of course for little me. Archie had already vanished to some ski chalet in Switzerland where hordes of jet-setters celebrated the birth of Christ in their own off-beat way – probably mating with each other and producing nothing but new generations of diehard cultural junkies. By evening, a crippled-looking Christmas tree would have been erected in the living-room and festively decorated with chocolate angels and plastic candles. Afterwards, a lamb roast would be shoved into the oven.

Although my friend was in a good mood, it did make me feel rather melancholy that, as in preceding years, nobody had invited him to a Christmas dinner. It was also safe to assume that nobody would accept an invitation from him. Once again I had to face the fact that Gustav was and would remain a loner whose existence nobody took seriously and whose death would have no other consequence than the automatic cut-off of the electricity and water. Of course there were Archie and a few others whom Gustav, in his blindness, called friends. In reality, however, they were all faceless acquaintances, and they acted that way, too. Now and then they would honour us with their company at dinner and bring a bottle of wine as a present. Now and then they would in turn invite Gustav, and he would take them a bottle of wine as a present. So the wine bottles would change ownership regularly every four months – but Gustav's feelings (for he did indeed have some) remained in that prison that holds both the lonely and their emotions captive. As a matter of fact, of all of them Archie was the most reliable, although he too only showed up a few times a year; and he had these terrible quirks. But at least he helped out my life companion in emergencies and so kept up the appearance of friendship. And I? Well, I wasn't a human being and so wasn't in a position to satisfy Gustav's emotional needs. And yet (if I may venture this sentimental confession on this sentimental day), I was the only living being in the world who really did love him. That's right, I loved that fool, that overripe watermelon in human form, that talking hippo, that cosmic twit, that all-round failure, that self-satisfied bourgeois pig, that hack author, that fat-headed lump of hopelessness, that conglomeration of inferior atoms, that total dead loss – and if anyone laid a finger on him, he'd find out what my scalpel-tipped claws were like!

Right after we had jointly devoured the roast – I under the table, Gustav on an uncomfortable designer kitchen chair that was much too small for his elephantine behind and must have cost a fortune – I slipped out of the back door. I made sure that the back entrance was open for those coming to the meeting and then trotted up the rickety wooden stairs to the next floor. While I was away, my lonely friend, as always on Christmas Eve, would listen to the pastoral harmonies of some children's choir or other on the stereo and, when he got tired of the whole hullabaloo, would once again immerse himself in research on his thirty-five-hundred-year-old goddess.

Outside the snow fell thickly, and the square, wrapped in an oversized, bluish-white cape, would have made an ideal subject for a naïf Christmas card. Yet an icy wind warned that the wintry idyll would soon turn into a malicious snowstorm. Through the windows, whose shutters had been battered to pieces over the course of time, the wan light of the street lamps barely illuminated the shabby rooms. I had intentionally arrived an hour early so that I could be alone with my thoughts, for somehow I had the feeling that tonight something decisive was going to happen. Naturally I could not expect that the meeting would bring some spectacular new piece of information to light. Pascal and I merely wanted to draw up an interim balance and perhaps make a show of something resembling collective strength. Whoever the butcher was, wherever he happened to be, we were going to let him know that all of us were hunting him down and were no longer willing to bow down to his bloody tyranny. There was a strange suggestion of something in the air that promised resolution.

Sitting in the centre of the room where everything had begun, I spent my time in a meditative frame of mind. The more the chaos in my head yielded to crystalline order, the more an agreeable energy pervaded me, persuading me to believe that I was only seconds away from solving the case. It was as if the metaphysical stillness around me had liberated my nerves from all the muck that had collected in this morass of lies and deceit, of blood and hate. I began to think more clearly and more smoothly, and time flew by . . .

It was not long before Pascal and Bluebeard entered the room, putting an end to this strange meditation before it could lead to solid results. Judging by the way old Pascal looked, the hike up here had been an enormous strain. He greeted me briefly, then, as if sedated, plopped down on his rear and gasped for air.

'When's this show finally going on the road?' asked Bluebeard impatiently, eyeing the loose electric cables poking up from the cracked parquet floor with a look of disgust. As if on cue, the first guests arrived, the first in a long caravan of the curious made up of brothers and sisters of the widely varying breeds, colours, and ages. Although the majority were the very common European Shorthair, such rare specimens as the flap-eared Scottish Fold, the proud Somali, the tailless Manx, the delicate Japanese Bobtail, and the Devon Rex, whose face was not unlike a bat's, also joined the throng. Some mothers had brought their children, who frolicked happily with each other. The most successful studs in the area and a couple of its senior citizens looked around sceptically, making no secret of their opinion that events such as this one were absolute nonsense. Yet although it was certain that they would do everything in their power to make fun of Pascal and me, you could detect a certain intentness and curiosity behind the façade of disapproval. Others regarded the whole affair as a kind of Christmas party, giving them the chance to renew social contacts. They sniffed and licked at each other in greeting, or revived ancient enmities by hissing or immediately beginning ill-tempered scraps. But the majority seemed to be seriously interested in the matter at hand. The atrocities had become so widely known about that everyone had been affected by the atmosphere of threat.

The dingy flat was filling up with increasing speed, and for the first time I got a pretty good idea of the great number of cripples living in the neighbourhood. The ones I had seen so far had been but a tiny sample of the poor creatures now before me. The many wounds that Preterius had inflicted on his victims had by no means healed completely. Long ugly scars covered the cripples' maltreated bodies; because the fur hadn't grown back right around the scars, they still looked fresh and livid. I also noticed a great many brothers and sisters who lacked either a tail or a paw.

Kong and the two obligatory Herrmanns joined the meeting, and the crowd respectfully formed a corridor for them. The massive beast strutted up to the front row, settled down with the self-satisfied mien of a pasha, and smiled insolently, as if to say that only he had the authority to start the ball rolling.

The whispering and murmuring slowly died down, and everyone sat down and looked up expectantly at Pascal and me.

'Dear friends, we thank you for accepting our invitation in such great numbers,' said Pascal, after getting to his feet with some effort. In the ghostly light, the legions of brothers and sisters looked like a very soft, very hairy carpet. Blue, green, yellow and chestnut eyes glowed here and there like phosphorescent glass marbles, gazing at us with impatience and expectation.

'Hope you got something worth saying, grandpa. Otherwise someone's going to get a bloody nose for making me miss my favourite Christmas movie on TV!' sounded off Kong arrogantly. Prompted by Herrmann and Herrmann, his comment whipped up obliging gales of laughter from the public. But Pascal was more than a match for Kong. He didn't let himself get intimidated as quickly as I, and he didn't bother to counter Kong's silly heckling with ironic repartee. Icy with rage, he went up to the idiotically grinning comic and glared at him.

'Kong, you moronic rhinoceros!' he said gruffly. 'If you had any sense of decency, you would at least pretend to mourn for your Solitaire. Save your impudent wit for yourself and pay attention to the new information we have. Perhaps it could lead to the arrest of your unborn children's killer.'

Kong's mocking expression turned at once into a stiff mask, alternately scornful and helpless. His eyelids twitched nervously, and before saying anything his mouth opened and closed several times like a fish hunting for food.

'I'm going to get that bastard sooner or later anyway, so I don't need to hear your stupid information.'

Pascal smiled coldly and took a few steps back so that he was once again in full view of the audience.

'You're not going to get anyone at all, you fool! Do you think this guy is going to knock on your door some day and ask for your forgiveness? Good Lord, how naïve you are. We're dealing with the devil himself here, not some witless idiot like you.'

Kong felt the reproachful glances of the crowd who by now had forgotten their craven attitude of a moment before, and he shifted himself uncomfortably where he sat. Seeing that their boss's authority was in danger, Herrmann and Herrmann began aggressively berating the brothers and sisters standing behind them and giving the crowd threatening looks. The big boss himself, however, was already discovering the virtue of humility.

'Surely a guy can make a joke, for fuck's sake,' he murmured finally, and let his head hang down in frustration.

'Too many jokes have already been made, Kong,' replied Pascal sadly. 'The problem is that our murderer has no sense of humour. He doesn't laugh, he doesn't even chuckle. He's parted company with laughter, having discovered a much more exciting pleasure. So let's move on to the terrible things that we have come to hear about. The most important thing you should all know about is the shocking fact that the murders in the area are not a recent phenomenon. With the greatest of probability, the murderer's activities go back as far as 1982. A culprit has to be found not for seven victims, as we previously supposed, but for approximately four hundred and fifty.'

A cry went up from the crowd, and then there was hysterical whispering. Many shook their heads in disbelief or moaned in shock. But little by little the murmurs faded away, yielding to a resigned and horrified silence.

Although Pascal's announcement must have sounded incredible to the uninitiated and given the sceptics all the more reason to question our investigation – even to dismiss it as preposterous – strangely enough nobody contradicted him. In their heart of hearts, I suspected, they all knew what had been going on the whole time. At some time or other over the years, nearly everyone must have noticed that friends, acquaintances, relations, brothers, and sisters had vanished suddenly, and for no explicable reason. They were never seen again, and never returned. That this could have happened unchecked for so long was an indication of how oppressive dictatorships are allowed to establish themselves. Evil always flourishes when it can count on well-meaning ignorance. In other words, things get as bad as they are allowed to. The desire for the false comfort of ignorance is the great evil of the world, the bane of every intelligent being, and my kind is particularly susceptible to this weakness.

Helpless rage began to rise in me the longer I watched these hypocrites, who now acted as if they were absolutely flabbergasted, although in reality they knew perfectly well what they had been putting up with for such a long time. That was the ugly side of Felidae – or the most characteristic side? Never had I been closer to giving up on the whole business than I was at that moment. As far as I was concerned, they could clean up their own damned mess. The killer had had enough time to perfect his routine. Let them try to stop him by themselves!

I was about to let myself be carried away by anger and do something rash when Pascal, as if divining my thoughts, began reading aloud from the investigation report. He described the army of skeletons under the earth, and how we had gone about extrapolating its numerical strength. Then he called the attention of his audience to the murderer's activities, which had been on the increase, and also to the fact that the murderer was one of us, someone who quite obviously enjoyed the full confidence of the neighbourhood. Brothers and sisters on the look-out for sex, and pregnant females had to be particularly careful in dealing with anyone who inspired trust, he warned. Previous experience showed that the murderer had made these two groups his speciality.

While Pascal presented these points in a manner both businesslike and intelligible to all, it was so quiet that you could hear a tail swish. Everyone was listening to him with a concentration I wouldn't have thought possible. After an initial round of whispered commentary with Herrmann and Herrmann, even Kong was spellbound by Pascal's analysis of the horror, and didn't have a word to say, probably for the first time in his thuggish existence. Before Pascal asked me to speak, he impressed upon us the necessity of dispensing entirely with nightly strolls for the time being, and of exercising reserve in sexual matters – although many of those present, as he himself knew very well, would find this an unreasonable demand.

'Dear friends, my name is Francis,' I began my speech. 'I moved to the square only a few weeks ago. Nevertheless, I have already found out a considerable number of important things, things you probably never suspected. For example, in this very building in 1980, experiments were performed on animals during which unimaginable crimes were committed against our kind. Some of you are yourselves the victims of these crimes without even being aware of it, because at the time you were in your infancy and now may no longer remember what actually happened. Unfortunately, however, the truth is this: all the maimed among you fell victim to the vile ambitions of human beings, and are invalids as the result of these animal experiments!'

A wave of cries and moans went through the audience. Everyone began to chatter wildly at once, and in no time a deafening clamour filled the room. I looked apprehensively at Bluebeard, who was sitting on the floor about five feet from me. Without so much as batting an eyelash, he stared grimly ahead with his uninjured eye. Suddenly I realised that the rogue had known, not just suspected, but actually known the whole time what was going on. He didn't exactly have the quickest mind under the sun, but he did possess one eminently important characteristic, namely a kind of native cunning – or what otherwise goes under the name of 'survival instinct'. This hidden talent enabled him to sense things by instinct that consciously he knew nothing about. And so, deep down, he had known all along that his horrible disfigurements had been the work of human beings, sadistic monsters who had treated his body as if it were a kind of animated stuffed toy. Yet he had wasted no time bemoaning his fate; instead he had bared his teeth to the world and given back as good as he got, day after day after day. Even if the human race had robbed him of various parts of his body, they could not take his stout heart from him.

Pascal tried to call the angry crowd to order. 'Quiet, friends! Quiet, please!' But the hue and cry of the guests, who were venting their fright in this hysterical way, had long since got out of control. Shock had overwhelmed many of the maimed, and they stared blankly ahead or wept openly. Friends licked one another in sympathy and spoke consolingly to one another. Neighbourhood chieftains yelled obscenities at me, as if I were responsible for the whole tragedy. Pascal made a few more attempts to bring the crowd to order until he saw the futility of his appeals and gave up, shaking his head.

When the scene began to look like turning into a riot, Kong got up unhurriedly, arched his back and stretched in boredom, then turned around to the frenzied crowd, regarding it with the kind of weary indulgence a mother shows her wailing babies.

After a moment, he thundered the command: 'That'll be enough!' His expression of brutal authority tolerated no contradiction. Everyone quietened down and turned meekly towards us.

'Do you want to blubber or listen? My God, you're pathetic. Why did you think some of us have been walking around like total wrecks? Because they happened to run into a pink flamingo in someone's backyard? Everyone knows that mice and tinopeners are the worst animals. So calm yourselves down and let this clever Dick go on yacking. Maybe he'll present us with the killer right now.'

'Thank you, Kong.' I sighed in relief, and bowed in his direction. Taking advantage of the silence that had suddenly returned, I continued. 'Unfortunately, I can't present you with the killer right now, only, maybe, with the truth. A whole bunch of you, dear friends, revere the Prophet Claudandus. As I found out in the course of my inquiries, Claudandus in fact existed and was truly someone worthy of reverence. But there's absolutely nothing sacred about him, and God unfortunately didn't protect his life in any special way. Like the maimed among you, people also tortured him in this gruesome laboratory. When they found out that his physical constitution was biologically unique, he had to submit to the very worst torture. He died in the end, but in the legends and in the cult that Joker brought to the area, he lives on . . .'

'He isn't dead!'

A squeaky female's voice. She had emerged from somewhere in the dark blanket of fur in front of me, in which hundreds of pairs of eyes glittered like sparklers at a rock concert. From the corner of my eye, I saw Pascal scowling at the audience with a mixture of anger and dismay, as if he had been interrupted while talking, not me. Again, the crowd was in turmoil, and everyone looked around in agitation for the owner of the voice.

'Who said that?' I asked.

'Me. I said that,' chirped the voice. There was a commotion in the middle of the crowd. Those who were standing there slowly fell back, forming a circle around a very young sister. They stared at her as if at a sensation.

She was a jewel, a bewitching bauble of the Harlequin race. The gleaming whiteness of her silky coat was flecked only on her nose, her left ear, chest and tail with the typically small, triangular, black spots that did in fact make her look a little like a harlequin. When she noticed that she was being gaped at from all sides, she seemed to regret her courageous interjection, for her ears twitched nervously. She tiptoed up to the front and stopped before me with a shy smile.

'Who are you, dear?' I smiled in return, trying not to make her more nervous than she already was.

'They call me Pepeline,' she answered with surprising confidence. It was clear that she would soon develop into a particularly seductive creature. The thought filled me for a moment with giddy delight, but then reminded me how far behind me were the untroubled days of my childhood.

'What do you know about Claudandus, Pepeline? And why do you believe that he isn't dead?'

'Well, because my great-grandfather told me,' she replied, looking around at the audience with childlike pride.

'Who is your great-grandfather?'

'Father Joker. He rarely visits my mother and me, and when he does come to our house, once or twice a year, he reproaches us for having skipped a meeting or two. But once I was at home all alone and bored to death. Great-grandfather came by, and the strange thing was, he felt sorry for me and let me persuade him to play. We played and hunted all day long. And because he had been so sweet to me, I wanted to cheer him up and so, just as he was going to go, I asked him to tell me the legend of Claudandus. I already knew all those stories by heart, but if you really want to make Great-grandfather happy, then all you have to do is ask him to give a sermon. He can never praise the Prophet enough. So he told the sacred legend once again, except that this time there was a slight variation. At first he said nothing unusual, just how cruel things were in the Land of Pain and what tortures Claudandus and his fellow sufferers had to undergo from their tormentors. But he was pretty sleepy after all the playing and he wasn't really paying attention to what he was saying. He said that at the end Claudandus had challenged the monster to a fight, and killed it. That's when I contradicted him: "But Father Joker, you usually say that the Lord destroyed the monster and that Claudandus ascended into heaven." Then Great-grandfather noticed all of a sudden that he had got it wrong and corrected himself. "Yes, yes, my dear, after that, of course, he did ascend into heaven." Then he made me promise not to tell anyone this version of the legend because that would be a sin. I was really little then and didn't think twice about it. But now I know that Great-grandfather had said more than he meant to on that day.'

Like everyone in the room, I was amazed by this spectacular twist in the story. Unlike the others, however, I understood its full implications. It didn't really matter to the others whether in the end the Prophet had taken a taxi to heaven or had become chairman of British Petroleum. The ways of saints just happen to be mysterious. What difference did it make whether Claudandus was alive or not? This seemingly unimportant detail, however, cast an entirely new light on the murders. For Pepeline's statement confirmed what Jesaja had said. If what Pepeline said was true, the weird voice that the Guardian of the Dead had heard in the tunnels was the Prophet's. So Claudandus really had survived Preterius's gruelling torture, and even murdered his tormentor.

And then? What had become of him then? Where was he living? Was he the killer, and if so what did he do when he wasn't giving someone's neck a going-over? And again, if Claudandus was responsible, what on earth was his crackpot motive for killing his own kind? He had Joker's publicity campaign to thank for his swift rise as the Prophet, but had his bitter ordeal also made him go mad? After he had liquidated his tyrant – a pretty far-fetched notion – had he developed an insatiable appetite for killing? No, that assumption must be false, for then he wouldn't have cared at all about who perished. But the killer clearly had special interests . . .

The whispering and murmuring in the crowd rose anew. I had to say a few soothing words now, so that things wouldn't degenerate again. I had to give my listeners the feeling that this deranged affair wasn't crazy at all but completely 'normal' – that is, transparent, explicable. Yes, perhaps I would even have to lie.

'Dear friends, I realise that you are somewhat confused after hearing Pepeline's story. But really, everything is very simple. Father Joker was secretly observing those abominable laboratory experiments at that time. He knew Claudandus, and he knew that he could turn the aura of sanctity enveloping this ambiguous martyr to his own advantage. He founded the Claudandist religion, to which almost all of you belong. It turned out, though, that the whole business wasn't so holy after all. We've just heard that Claudandus survived. That's news to me, too. Well, no matter what may have happened, except for him all of the animals perished in the laboratory during those final calamitous days, and took the secret with them to the grave. So the only one who knows the whole truth is Joker. He's also the only one who knows what Claudandus looks like, and the only one who could take us to him. But Joker was mur– '

'Joker has disappeared!' Pascal cut me short. He emerged

from the dark background, planted his impressive presence beside me, and gave the audience a sombre look.

The resolute appearance of the illustrious Pascal made Pepeline lose the little self-confidence that she had gained during the telling of her tale. She went back to the circle of those standing behind her and vanished among them.

For rhetorical effect, Pascal paused for a moment, creating heavy tension in the room. Then he smiled benevolently.

'Whatever may have happened then, dear brothers and sisters, today, given our scanty knowledge of the state of affairs, we can no longer trace back every detail of this dark story. If Claudandus did indeed escape that hell in one piece, it does not necessarily follow that afterwards he pitched his tent in this area. I likewise find it hard to believe that of all the adult animals, only he happened to survive that tragedy. The idea is simply absurd. And then there's the matter of the murder motive. How can a living creature who witnessed such cruel atrocities committed against his own kind turn into a criminal himself – overnight, so to speak – and kill his own brothers and sisters in cold blood? No, no, that doesn't make any sense to me at all. For this reason, I refuse to accept that this mysterious Claudandus is the one we ought to fear. As far as I'm concerned, someone has been skilfully exploiting this confounded, impenetrable mystery of the past for his own present purposes. Someone has assumed the identity of the Prophet to cover his traces in a fog of mysticism and naïve religious belief. And this satanic someone is, in my opinion, none other than our highly esteemed Father Joker. He's been making fools of you for years! He made himself the leader of a religion that he himself dreamed up. Presumably, he became so perversely obsessed by his cause that merely egging on his flock of believers to commit self-flagellation rites was no longer enough. Deranged by religious mania, he adopted the single-minded aim of bringing about what all religious mania ultimately amounts to: twisted bloodshed! Since his followers were not yet ready for fun and games on that level, he himself took the initiative. In order to give the bloody hocus-pocus a touch of eccentricity, he killed only those who were in heat or were pregnant. You were supposed to smell a rat, but only very gradually, then show your tacit understanding, and finally give your consent, even support, to the repulsive business. But thanks to brother Francis, his sinister plans have been defeated.'

Nobody dared contradict. I was no exception. A breathless silence followed Pascal's plausible interpretation of the facts, broken only by the wind moaning through the broken-down window shutters. Everyone was impressed by his mental acuity, and accepted what he had said all too readily. That was the impression, anyway.

Little by little, the mumbling in the audience increased in volume, but basically everyone was agreeing that the last word had been spoken on the situation and that the meeting had been brought to conclusion.

Still, something was not quite right. Though I had absolutely no counter-arguments up my sleeve, at the same time I could have more readily accepted that the earth was flat than that Pascal's all-too-neat solution to the case was correct. Then too, I didn't feel like telling him about my uneasiness. Too much had been spoken, discussed, and argued; too much thought out logically. I had to take things in hand again. After all, my primitive methods had taken me a surprisingly long way.

The meeting now broke up and the locals, still chattering excitedly with one another, left the house. Pascal beamed with satisfaction, and even Bluebeard seemed relieved. And I? Well, suddenly I had a suspicion, and would be damned if I didn't follow it up before the night was over . . .

'What did you think of my arguments, my friend?' asked Pascal.

'Not bad,' I replied coolly.

'Ha, you can't put anything over me, Francis. I can tell by the expression on your face that the cogs in your mind are turning furiously again. And quite rightly, too, because to be honest even I don't really believe that crap I was expounding so knowingly. I confess that it was a makeshift solution to calm the meeting down.'

'It sounded damned serious. Even final.'

'That just goes to show you how talented an actor I am. Maybe I should do advertising for pet food, or for the many advantages and benefits of putting animals to sleep.'

He roared with laughter. But almost at once he became serious again, and his unfathomable, glowing yellow eyes sized me up.

'Oh, Francis, I can't bear to see you go on racking your brains. Today is Christmas. Forget about this miserable thriller for the time being and get a little rest. Who knows, maybe a miracle will happen, and one of your insights will help you hit upon the right solution. I'm convinced of it. I wish you a Merry Christmas – and don't give up believing in miracles!'

He said goodbye, then departed. Bluebeard and I were now completely alone in the room; we looked down at the floor in embarrassment. I noticed that he too felt uneasy, however much he might want to believe Pascal's neat solution to the case. But the affair was still far from over, and Bluebeard knew that pretty damned well.

'A happy holiday, Bluebeard. And thanks for your first-class work; otherwise we'd still be groping around in the dark. May God protect you, brother,' I said. Both of us were avoiding eye contact.

'Shit, you deserve the thanks! Didn't exactly kill myself helping you out. Pascal was right. You have to take it easy over Christmas. Hibernate or something. Or put that bonehead Kong in his place, otherwise I'll do it. Anyway, try to think of other things for a change. Have lots of fun and watch out that old guy with the white fuzz on his face doesn't step on your tail tonight.'

He turned his back on me and limped quickly to the door.

'Ah, Bluebeard?'

He stopped, a little too abruptly, and turned his shaggy head towards me. In his one healthy eye, a knowing smile seemed to flicker.

'Do you think Joker is our man?'

'No.' His answer came like a shot.

'Who do you think it is?'

'Whoever you're going to nail, clever bastard.'

He turned and disappeared through the door.

The suspicion! The suspicion in my mind! It grew stronger and stronger until my skull felt like it was going to burst. A strange plan slowly took shape. Stranger still, I would carry out the plan, even though the chances of success were infinitesimally small. But it had suddenly become an obsession. Superstition, compulsion, mania – there were many labels for behaviour as irrational as this. I didn't care. All at once I had shed the methods of the cool statistical analyst and was once again the detective in shirt-sleeves.

'Ah, Bluebeard?'

The monstrous head craned around the door, which had been eaten away by moisture and insects. His eye, beaming in the darkness like a precious stone, revealed that he already knew what I was going to ask. He made no effort to stifle his smile.

'Where's that porcelain warehouse where Joker lives?'

Once again our tacit understanding made any explanation superfluous. My friend thought the same way I did, and wanted to see the theorising finally put to rest. Just as at the beginning, action was called for, not one long-winded, know-all speech after another. Without asking why or reproaching me because he had already searched the house from top to bottom, he told me the address. And then he vanished without another word.

In the silence I heard him slowly tramp down the stairs, cross the hall, and then hobble out of the back door. Then I waited – one, two, three minutes – until my nerves were as taut as bowstrings and I thought I would explode any minute.

Before I lost my mind beyond all hope of recovery, I ran down the steps in great bounds, left the house, and ran out into the driving snow. According to Bluebeard's description, the porcelain warehouse was at the farthest corner of the square, so I had a long way to go over the garden walls. But my obsession affected me like an amphetamine and steeled me against weariness, enabling me to cover the distance at tremendous pace. I had only a vague idea of what I wanted at the porcelain warehouse. But somehow I knew events would take a surprising turn; I would find the proof there. I remembered Bluebeard's words after he had looked around the building: 'Searched the place from top to bottom for the Reverend. Even got as far as this frigging stockroom in the attic, which was pretty creepy, because the shelves there are bursting with statues of us, life-size.'

The shelves . . . The shelves loaded with porcelain figures representing our kind – life-size! Bluebeard had climbed through a basement window and, consequently, had not made his search from top to bottom, but from bottom to top. So he must have gained access to the stockroom through an open door. Then he had strolled through there and taken as close a look at that shoddy junk as he could stand and to the extent that the layout of the room permitted. That means he had looked at all those porcelain figures that resembled us so damn well from the frog's, or rather Felidae's point of view – and that with only one eye.

So that's what happened! He hadn't the chance to look on top of the shelves.

I finally arrived at the warehouse, which, with its spotted, mouldy walls and sinister aura, looked like a corpse returned from the dead in the picturesque, snowy landscape. The porcelain store was obviously no goldmine, for the owner had let the old building go to ruin in such a negligent manner that if housing inspectors had paid him a visit he would have been presented with the stiffest fine in world history. The gutters were only half attached to their rusted supports, and hung down at oblique angles. A powerful gust of wind would have taken apart the whole junkyard, and sent it crashing down on the heads of unsuspecting passers-by. The walls were in no better condition – they seemed to be held together, provisionally, by trellising alone. An unruly swathe of ivy was wrapped around the building, and each of the many cracks it had opened up put me in mind of a yawning abyss. The windows looked like blind eyes, not only because they were completely filthy, but also because some of them lacked window-panes. A second-floor balcony had no railing; one could only guess that it was a balcony at all. I had the feeling that a brutal deployment of our tried-and-trusted assault team, consisting of Agent Archie (codename 'Kidney-Table Terminator') and Agent Gustav (codename 'Parquet-Floor Assassin') was urgently needed.

As far as penetrating the warehouse was concerned, I didn't have as much luck as Bluebeard. I circled the building once, but found that all the basement windows were shut this time. It was, however, easy to imagine that one of the skylights would afford a good view of the storage room, so what I planned next was animated solely by the aim of getting up on the roof as quickly as possible. To do this, I had no alternative but to follow a route which, though possible, entailed several deadly risks.

Back at the rear of the house, I sprang up on a tree that was about three yards away from the building, with branches formed like steps, ideal for climbing. Moreover, its highest branch soared up over the roof. With a sense of balance as highly developed as mine, and if I proceeded with special care, I anticipated being able to reach the top with a series of leaps – and, more important, come down again. However, the branches got thinner and thinner as the tree got younger and younger towards the top, and the entire manoeuvre would thus require the talent and agility of a trapeze artist.

After I had scrambled up the trunk, I allowed myself a breather on a sturdy branch, and noticed another danger. The whole tree was coated with ice, and I had to be damned careful about how I moved if I didn't want to slide down and begin learning how to fly at this late stage in life.

Executing carefully calculated jumps while sending up fervent prayers to the Good Lord, who on the birthday of His Son might well be particularly receptive to such entreaties, I finally reached the branch at roof level. It was mercifully strong and long enough to carry my weight and serve as a bridge. The only problem was the disturbing way it swayed back and forth in the icy wind. Moreover, there would be no turning back after disembarking, because the branch was far too slender to permit anything other than slow, gingerly steps forward, let alone panicky flights of retreat. There was only one way: you had to summon up all your courage and, without looking down, balance yourself on the branch until you reached the roof. With no further thought of the consequences of this kamikaze feat, I proceeded to act . . .

My kind is not cursed, thank God, with the injustice of perspiration. Yet when my paws finally touched roof tile on the other side, I had the feeling that, as far as this biological characteristic was concerned, I was a mutation. I actually believed I could sense the stinking sweat of fear under my coat while I was gliding over the branch on tiptoe, my eyes fixed rigidly on my goal as if I were hypnotised and the branch springing joyfully up and down under my paws.

Finally, standing on the secure roof, I heaved a sigh of relief, and risked a downward glance over the eaves. The seemingly bottomless drop down could have been used as a shot in Hitchcock's *Vertigo*, and I asked myself in all seriousness whether I wasn't several aces short of a full deck. Why did I risk my life for something that to all appearances would for ever remain a gory riddle? What was I really out to prove to myself and to others by doing this? That I was the cleverest creature on God's earth? How vain! How ridiculous! And, as I had just demonstrated, how suicidal!

But the defect in my brain that was responsible for my always doing the opposite of what I had just recognised as ill-advised drove me on to new abominations. Within seconds the dizzying thrill had faded away, and I remembered why I had climbed up here to begin with.

I devoted my attention to the roof. The tiles, as expected, were damaged and devoid of any kind of symmetrical order, having been flung about wildly by the wind. They seemed to be waiting for the slightest excuse to rain down on the street. But to my great joy I found a wide, multi-paned studio skylight right in the middle of the roof, though it was coated with a thin layer of snow.

I rushed up to it, and noticed that one of the panes had been shattered and replaced by a transparent plastic sheet. I scraped aside the snow from one of the undamaged panes with my front paws so that I could look down into the storage room. Despite the darkness, I was able to confirm Bluebeard's descriptions. The top floor, which had been converted in a hurry and rather carelessly into storage space, was crammed full with metal shelves and racks that held old goblets and decorative figures of ceramic and porcelain. For the most part, these decorative figures really were modelled after Felidae; they were probably intended for a consumer group having the same extravagant tastes as Gustav. I could well imagine my senseless life companion spying such a porcelain animal in a store window, running in, buying it for an outrageous price, then putting it on the mantelpiece and calling my attention to its similarity to me in his annoying baby-talk, *ad nauseam*. Yet, just as Bluebeard had said, there were also life-size versions of the more powerful of my kind. The eerie gallery of glazed tigers, jaguars, pumas, and leopards gave me the creeps, because their makers had gone to considerable lengths to make them as lifelike as possible.

Since the peep-hole I had pawed open in the snow did not allow me to see much, I proceeded to widen it. Then I went to another pane and bit by bit brushed aside the snow covering it as well. The room gradually filled with the wan light of the grim Christmas sky and slowly revealed itself. It was a long time before I had scanned every detail of the chaos in there. My frustration became unbearable, because nothing looked like what I was so frantically searching for.

Then, just as I was thinking of giving up, I noticed with a shock . . .

He did look as if he were still alive. Jammed between two porcelain brothers as snow white as he, and shielded from prying eyes by a row of long-stemmed glasses, Joker sat on a top shelf in the darkest corner of the storage room. Only the tip of his bushy tail, projecting over the edge of the shelf, would have surprised a very attentive observer below. A few thin snowflakes flurried down through a rip in the plastic sheet on to Joker's head, a picturesque touch. He sat like a sphinx on four paws, his head only slightly bowed; at first glance, he seemed to be dozing. But in reality he had long ago turned into a block of ice, because the temperature in that room was approximately the same as outside. This was presumably the reason why neither his owner nor Bluebeard had smelled the odour of putrefaction. Only when the warm weather returned would the 'cold sack' (Bluebeard's coinage was horribly appropriate this time) begin to 'perspire' and the truth be revealed.

My discovery didn't surprise me at all, for my unerring instinct had already let me know a few days earlier that Father Joker was no longer among the living and breathing. What astonished me was how easy the killer had had it this time. Unlike the other victims, Joker's neck had not been torn open. As if Count Dracula had left his monogram behind, there were the merest dimples to indicate where the fangs had been, that and a pathetically thin trickle of frozen blood. The intact porcelain figures and glasses around the corpse were also testimony to the fact that Joker had put up no resistance. Any gesture of resistance would have tipped over all that junk and made it tumble on to the floor. Yes, probably the murderer and his victim had retreated to this remote place to take care of business between themselves, in secret.

It had been an execution, and Joker had been in complete agreement with it. The reason was obvious. The Master of Ceremonies had heard that others had got wind of the fact that he was the murderer's accomplice. Sooner or later, perhaps in the course of interrogation by someone whose suspicions had been aroused, he would have broken down and revealed the murderer, and the murderer had known this. Naturally the murderer could absolutely not afford to take this risk, and so he forced Joker to take this necessary step. And Joker had obeyed, had let the beast kill him without protest. What was so unbelievably important that Joker was willing to sacrifice himself for it? What secret was more important than his own life?

Claudandus! Had he saved his own life only to take the lives of others?

Solving a puzzle gives normal mortals a feeling of pride and satisfaction, but degenerate brains like mine obey other laws, something I had known even before I solved the Claudandus case. Solving puzzles is a pleasure *per se*; the solution itself, however, is a ludicrous reward. It is delightful beyond description when a mystery is hidden within a mystery, which in turn is hidden within still another mystery, and on and on . . . Puzzle-solvers are a unique species, and it is their most ardent wish that some day someone will come and pose them a question they cannot answer. And the worst moment for a puzzle-solver comes not when he discovers that he can't solve a riddle, but when he solves it perfectly – and afterwards wishes he had left it well alone.

That's how Yours Truly felt that night when I got to the bottom of the mystery. It was at one and the same time exciting and depressing.

I was feeling disillusioned within minutes of returning to our flat. In the same suicidal way I had climbed up, I crossed to the connecting branch from the roof and climbed down. The whole time I was so intensely busy in my mind with putting together the pieces of the puzzle that I executed every heart-stopping move like a sleepwalker, not even enjoying a pleasant prickle of fear as I made the dangerous descent. Meanwhile, the snow flurries had become like icy white lava spewing from the jaws of a howling dragon. Next morning the world would resemble the kitschy landscape of a department-store window, and its picture-perfect prettiness would work Christmas fans up into orgasms.

Still engrossed in hundreds of abstruse theories, I trudged back home in a blizzard worthy of *Dr Zhivago* and slipped through the bathroom window, which Gustav had left open for me. I found my poor friend in the study, where he was sleeping with his upper body sprawled over his desk, totally sozzled. No doubt he had made a few sad attempts to celebrate the celebration of celebrations all by himself, until he realised how senseless and sad his efforts were and decided instead to spend his precious time on his work. Amid the many books on his desk were two empty wine bottles and a half-full glass, proof that work alone had not sufficed to numb the pain of loneliness.

I sprang up on to the desk and mournfully regarded the man who prepared my meals day after day, dragged me to the doctor at the least sign of indisposition, played silly games with me with a cork or rubber mouse (which I went along with to humour him), worried terribly if I were away for longer than usual, and loved me more than he loved this ridiculously spruced-up flat. Unfortunately he was snoring barbarically, which rather mitigated against my wistful feelings for him. He had laid his watermelon head on one side on an oversized volume of illustrations, open at the middle and dimly illuminated by the reading lamp.

Continuing to brood on Gustav's meaningless life, I glanced fleetingly at the right page of the book. On it was an Egyptian painting, sumptuous in its original colours. *Tomb painting from Thebes, about 1400 B.C.* was the caption. Like all such pictures, this one put me into a philosophical mood, because it was hard to imagine that such highly developed cultures could have existed such a long, long time ago. And my attention would have shifted at once back to my owner's head on the other page of the book, if something very unusual had not caught my eye.

The tomb painting portrayed a young king or deity hunting. With a white sash draped around the hips and festooned with gorgeous pendants, the young man held a snake in one hand and three game birds in the other. He stood in a papyrus boat at the shores of a lake which was rank with reeds and swamp plants. Birds and ducks of the various species surrounded him in a dazzling panoply of colour. In the background was an array of enigmatic hieroglyphs, and to the far right you could see a small goddess in a golden robe, who seemed to be giving the scene her blessing. The painting, which in accordance with Egyptian tradition portrayed every detail from a lateral perspective, was presumably the record of a hunt and therefore compressed to the essentials. What gave me the shock of my life, though, was the brother at the hunter's feet, a handsome specimen with game birds gripped firmly in his muzzle and between his paws. I knew that the ancient Egyptians had first employed us as hunters, and only afterwards put us into combat against noxious rodents in grain-growing areas. Those honourable brothers and sisters, however, were anything but the domesticated creatures we are. They were direct descendants of the original Felidae, and without a doubt the guy in the tomb painting was one of those. But what was uncanny about the entire scene was the fact that this age-old ancestor looked exactly like the sister with whom I had mated last week. The same sand-coloured coat that blended into bright chestnut on the underbelly; the same thick-set body; the same eyes that glowed like jewels . . .

Then the miracle happened: I had a revelation! It was just as if a gigantic wall in my head had collapsed and the dizzy light of a thousand suns flooded in. All at once I knew . . .

We were being re-bred – taken back to our origins, back to the earlier forms of modern Felidae, and perhaps even further back, to the proud original Felidae who had not known the chains of domestication; who, free and without ties, had ranged across the world as fearsome predators, reaping respect for themselves wherever they were found.

I had to find out more about this. I turned around with a start, and feverishly searched the bookshelves for Gustav's extensive collection of reference works. Finally I discovered the volume covering the letter G on the uppermost shelf. Using the desk as a runway, I launched myself high into the air, got the book between my front paws, tore it from the shelf, and plummeted with it to the floor.

Gustav commented on the noise with indistinct mumbling sounds, but his primitive snoring soon started up again. I leafed through the book with the speed of a bank clerk counting notes until finally I found the heading I sought: GENETICS.

As I read the first sentence my body began to shake in feverish excitement. On the one hand, I was terribly angry at my own criminal stupidity in missing this important point; on the other, I was chilled to the very marrow of my bones because I believed I now at long last knew the murderer and his motive.

With a faint heart, I looked at the entry in the encyclopaedia again:

The laws of genetics were first discovered by the Jesuit priest Gregor Johann Mendel (1822–1884). In the course of cross-breeding plant varieties, the autodidactic scientist was confronted by a problem that seized his attention and that he saw more keenly and approached more methodi-cally than anyone before him: how are genetic characteris-tics transmitted? Earlier hybridisation attempts lacked experimental precision, systematic observation over periods of generations, and logical analysis. The diversity of hybrid

generations and 'reversions' in later generations that made
a hybrid more or less similar to the paternal and maternal
lines of descent were cause for continual astonishment.
From 1856 on, Mendel conducted methodical experiments
on garden peas, and then published his forty-seven page
treatise *Versuche über Pflanzenhybriden* . . .

Gregor Johann Mendel, the priest in the painting, the giant from
my nightmare. Now that I was gradually putting the whole
story together, the details of the case whirled through my mind
like a video in fast forward mode. Only now was I able to
understand the messages encoded in them.

As each scene flickered before my mind's eye, the story began
to form into an arrow of logic whose tip pointed directly at the
murderer . . .

Right at the beginning, with Sascha, the first victim I discovered, it caught my eye that he had been aroused at the time of
his murder. When I made the same observation in the case of
Deep Purple's corpse, I surmised that someone had wanted to
prevent the victim from mating. Why didn't I ask myself which
female they had wanted to lay? Why on earth hadn't I begun by
trying to find out which females in the district had been in heat
at the time of the murder?

I should have listened to my dreams . . . My unerring instinct
had deposited magic keys in them, keys with which the steel
doors of the mystery could have been opened.

The first nightmare in the new neighbourhood, the first key:
the faceless man in the long white apron in the endless white
nothingness, which was clearly meant to symbolise that laboratory of torture, was Julius Preterius. He had no face, because the
professor literally no longer possessed a face – he had already
been dead for seven years. In the end, two phosphorescent
yellow eyes, eyes that were full of tears, had glowed in this
empty face. These weeping tears belonged to Claudandus, who

because of his sickeningly horrible experiences in the laboratory
had ultimately turned into a Preterius himself . . .

Then the second nightmare, in which Deep Purple had again
and again pushed his paw into the gushing wound in his neck,
pulling out one kitten after another and hurling them like balls
against the garage walls: this scene was meant to indicate
that Deep Purple's children were unwanted, and showed what
the killer would have done with them if they had been born.
Also, the zombie had raved about epoch-making medical treat-
ments, a further reference to those gruesome experiments of the
past . . .

I remembered what Felicity had said: 'I couldn't understand
what they were talking about. But there was one thing I thought
I could detect again and again: the stranger spoke with great
urgency, as if he wanted to convince the one he was talking to of
something . . .'

The murderer was no psychopath running amok, but an
outwardly normal individual with a sense of fairness who had
been quite ready to give his victims one last chance. He had
explained the situation to them in advance, and asked them not
to mate with members of the race that had been set aside for
breeding. Otherwise they could mate with whoever they
pleased. He had never had anything personal against his victims.
But they had not listened to him. As soon as the bewitching song
of a randy female of the 'old and new' race resounded through
the square, they could no longer control their sexual urges and
could think of nothing but intercourse with the willing singer. In
the process, however, they would endanger the murderer's
painstakingly developed breeding programme, and that was
something he could never tolerate . . .

'I think the guy who owns this place does something with
science. Mathematics, biology, parapsychology – something
like that . . .' That had been Bluebeard's conjecture about
Pascal's owner's profession when he had taken me to the old
home with the ultra-modern interior for the first time. Correct,

Bluebeard! The guy's profession was biology – and his idol? A revolutionary biologist and pioneer of genetics, whose portrait hung on the wall of his study: Gregor Johann Mendel. But what was Karl Lagerfeld's real name?

Just once, and it wasn't so long ago, Pascal had casually mentioned his name. I concentrated, trying to remember our many conversations together. Countless bits of dialogue rushed through my mind until I finally dug out the right segment from the depths of my subconscious:

'Ziebold, my master, has prepared fresh heart . . .'

Pascal had mentioned his name after I had relayed my latest information to him about ten days ago.

Ziebold . . . Ziebold . . . Ziebold . . .

I knew the name.

'I "kidnapped" Ziebold from the Institute. At first glance he seems to have chosen the wrong profession. His fashionable clothing, changed daily, and his foppish behaviour seem more appropriate for a male model than a scientist. But when he works an uncanny transformation overtakes him, and he concentrates like one possessed . . .'

Ziebold was Preterius's right-hand man in the laboratory, and had had complete knowledge of all the animal experiments almost until the horrifying end. He had known Claudandus, and witnessed his unbearable suffering. He had sympathised with the poor fellow, and the blood-curdling experiments might well have been the reason for his leaving:

'The rats are abandoning the sinking ship. Today, Ziebold departed. He never gave a plausible reason for leaving. During the sad interview we held in my office, the man spoke the whole time like a book of riddles . . .'

'Felidae . . .' Pascal had whispered yearningly during our first encounter, and his gaze had been so strange, so dreamy. 'Evolution has brought forth an astonishing number of living creatures. More than a million kinds of animal live on the earth today, but none of them compel as much respect and admiration as the Felidae. Although it includes only about forty subspecies, absolutely the most fascinating creatures alive belong to this group. It may sound like a cliché, but they are indeed a miracle of nature!'

Pascal had devoted himself to the exhaustive study of his kind, and presumably of all other species and their origins as well. How had he acquired this knowledge?

Ziebold. As biologist and Mendel fan, the man must have had tons of literature on the science of evolution and genetics.

Pascal had secretly manipulated his owner's computer behind his back; one day he must have stumbled upon this scientific material, and then set about studying it intensively . . .

My third nightmare: I was wandering through the square, which had turned into a heap of ruins, as if there had been a nuclear war. The dismal landscape was overrun with gigantic pea plants. Pea plants! The species used to provide the first scientific proof of the laws of heredity. And after a giant Mendel had brought back an army of brothers and sisters from the dead and forced them to dance blasphemously on his puppet strings, he had more or less confessed his true identity:

'Plant hybrid experiments! Plant hybrid experiments! The essence of the matter is hidden in the pea!' That's what he had babbled, telling me the title of his scientific treatise. But I had been unable to interpret the dreams, and had dismissed the signs in these visions as night terrors. An unpardonable mistake, Francis!

Even Preterius's diary contained messages that the author, without being aware of it, had set down as vague innuendos: 'Since they are primarily nocturnal, they are compelled to go out at midnight. Then the world belongs to them. It has to be seen to be believed. They more or less take over the city. I suddenly had the absurd suspicion that they feel superior to humanity and are only waiting for the opportune moment to subjugate us. It reminds me of the story of the carnivorous plant that someone brought back home as a seedling and cared for until one fine day, tall and strong, it devoured the entire family . . .'

Not only the family, Professor, not only the family . . .

The death of the pregnant Balinese Solitaire seemed to turn all my speculations upside down, proving that the killer had sought out his victims at random. This was a false assumption, for the exception had only proved the rule. Expectant females had to be sacrificed to the cause of the pure-blooded race. The males of the old–new breed had not always had their lusts under control and had occasionally amused themselves with female 'regulars'. The outcome of such inferior matings would not have fitted into the killer's plan, and so they too had had to be eliminated. At the time of her murder, Solitaire must have been carrying not Kong's children but those of an old–new male. Poor Kong had been deceived!

It could also be assumed that the killer had murdered even those pregnant females who had been completely uninvolved. On the one hand, he had wanted to prevent another race from reproducing itself; on the other, he had needed to make room for his developing super-race. He had had the same attitude towards cripples. But what was really so special about this super-race?

To cast light on the inscrutable motives of the butcher, Pascal had used role-playing methods (and what a gifted actor he was):

'So let's assume I'm the murderer. I go out regularly on nocturnal raids to murder others of my kind for motives known only to the Good Lord and myself. I murder and murder, and always cover my tracks by taking hold of the corpses between my teeth, lugging them to the air tunnels, and throwing them down into the catacombs. And then, out of the blue, I give up this method, which means that sooner or later someone will find the evidence of my dastardly deeds and hunt me down. Why do I do this? Why do I do something that can only bring me into danger?'

All at once I saw the truth: the murderer had become old.

Much too old and much too ill to drag corpses around the square and dispose of them in hidden catacombs.

I thought I knew another reason why the villain had recently left his victims lying where he had killed them. But this was a reason I wanted him to confirm for me in person . . .

The interpretation of my fourth nightmare was by now downright superfluous. I was beside myself with shame, for even someone with half a brain would have understood the dramatic symbolism and messages in that vision.

'I am the murderer, I am the Prophet, I am Julius Preterius, I am Gregor Johann Mendel, I am the eternal riddle, I am the man and the beast – and I am Felidae. All of these I am in one person, and more, much more,' the killer had said from the depths of his shifting, white form.

In reality, he had been anything but white – within or without. But he had told the truth in his ambiguous confession: he actually had been all those persons in one person . . .

'Everything that ever was and ever will be no longer has any meaning . . .'

Yes, a new age had now dawned for my kind. And in accordance with the glorious plans of the Prophet, we were all supposed to come together like the Bremen City Musicians and commence a long and wonderful journey back to our origins.

'To Africa! To Africa! To Africa!'

'And what will we find there?'

'Everything we lost . . .'

. . . Across the savannahs of Africa, among the deserted skyline canyons of New York, in the icy wastes of Siberia, at the steel feet of the Eiffel Tower, on the Great Wall of China, on the peaks of the Himalayas, in the Australian outback, in every street, lane and alley of London – everywhere they would be on the march, everywhere: caravans, armies, billions, hundreds of billions, myriads of Felidae, the sand-coloured representatives of an old–new race with glowing yellow eyes. They would tramp across an earth that would now belong to them alone. They would have shaken off the curse of domestication long ago; they would be wild, free, and dangerous. Anyone who attempted to contest their domination of the world would be cruelly eliminated.

The last human being, hidden behind a boulder, watches the eerie parade. He is in a state of complete neglect, and has tears in his eyes. And when he recognises the size of this titanic army, he loses his mind. He runs away. All too quickly they catch up with him, circle him; screeching, they tear him to pieces. The children receive the meat, the older ones drink the blood, and his skeleton is exhibited in a zoo as a warning to all living creatures in the world that nobody should ever dare again to subjugate the imperial family of Felidae. Then they go on their way, perhaps in rockets and space stations, to populate the universe, the galaxies, and even other universes beyond . . .

It was the dream of a madman!

It was the dream of Claudandus, the Prophet, who had descended from heaven to take revenge for the injustices that had been inflicted on his kind. Yet revenge was not his only goal. He wanted more, he wanted everything!

I decided to confront him that very night.

CHAPTER

— 10 —

THE END OF a story is always sad. This is, first, because at the end of a story we are sent back to a reality that more often than not is boring; and second, because when all is said and done, all true stories end sadly. The world, after all, is a vale of tears, full of sorrow, sickness, injustice, hopelessness, and tedium. A story with a meaningful end is deceptive; there is a death at the end of every true story. In this mysterious, bloody, yet exciting and turbulent story, I played my self-assigned role of detective with gusto. All the other players, too, put in brilliant performances and could be assured of thunderous applause. The story itself, however, had been written solely by the Prophet, over many years, and with inexorable resolve. He was a consistent author, who would not have omitted the final act describing his own unmasking and apprehension. That, indeed, was the point of the whole story.

Just how very much he himself wished that I would take up his ghastly inheritance and write his unfinished book to the end became clearer to me as I was hurrying along the zigzag routes of the garden walls to his home. I had to exert myself to avoid being driven back by the tumultuous snowstorm. Yet I experienced both the inclemency and my exertions as if I were in a bell-jar, for I had only one thought: getting access to the headquarters of evil and confronting the master of manipulation.

When I finally arrived at his house, my coat had donned a massive armour of ice, and I resembled a hedgehog which had just stepped out of a deep-freeze. Instead of hair, razor-sharp spines of ice grew from my skin, and even my whiskers were frozen stiff, making me afraid that they would shatter at the slightest vibration. If I had been out there any longer you could hardly have told me apart from Joker. And yet the outer cold could not compete with the inner cold.

I circled the house once and noticed there were no lights on anywhere. It was highly unlikely that the master of the house had gone to bed so early on Christmas Eve. Either he had left town, or he was frolicking right now at some wild Christmas party. The Emperor of the Dead, however, was in there: that was as certain as the fact that Claudandus was controlling our destinies. Perhaps he was even waiting for me, just as people wait all night long for a visit from Santa Claus.

Oddly enough, I wasn't at all afraid. I knew that clever bastard Francis was the only chance he had that his life's work would be completed one distant day. For whatever reason, he thought his baby was in good hands with me. But could I really allow myself to be so confident?

I paused to think in front of that ultra-stylish pet passageway. Yes, I had added one and one and come up, satisfactorily enough, with two. This fellow, however, was nuttier than a squirrel's breakfast, and I didn't doubt that his arithmetic would follow entirely different laws. In fact, he probably couldn't even do maths any more. This thought made me shake my head, and I smiled bitterly to myself. No, the Prophet wasn't exactly insane; and I had to admit that his great dream was not without a certain logic. Logic! Once again, that hateful word. The word that from time immemorial had accompanied me and shaped my life like a fetish, had, from the way things looked, shaped his life as well. The Prophet had had a lunatic but logical reason for his butchery – to the extent that a butcher needs a reason to kill at all. But no matter what the reasons, after this night, one way or another, the murders would end.

I slipped through the opening in the wall and entered the dark house. It was unlikely that he was lying in wait for me somewhere, biding his time for the right opportunity to pounce. As mentioned, he was in the habit of making speeches laden with significance before taking neck measurements. He was probably asleep right now, and would only gradually notice my presence. Nevertheless, I was gripped with a fearful excitement, and my heart began to pound like a jackhammer.

Softly, I padded through the hallway and entered the study through the half-open door. Gregor Johann Mendel looked down on me grimly from a thicket of pea plants. He seemed peeved because I had reached the bottom of his mystery. Through the glass wall I saw the snowstorm raging like an unleashed demon over the gardens. With an incessant, eerie whistling, it swept away gigantic snowdrifts in seconds, only to erect them anew a moment later elsewhere. Snowflakes swirled around making the square look like a fuzzy picture on a badly tuned television screen.

I sprang up on the desk and with both paws pressed the operating switch of the computer to 'on'. The processing unit began its familiar quiet drone. Then, like will-o'-the-wisps over a bewitched cemetery, status information on the system and the drives began to glow brightly against the impenetrable black backdrop of the monitor. After the processing unit had loaded itself its electronic memory, the cursor blinked impatiently, wanting to know what the next step was. I wanted to know that myself, and posed the crucial question: what codename would I give a file that contained the best-kept secrets in the area and should be accessible only to myself? Perhaps a name that would sum up the diabolical reason for the file itself, one that would remind me every time I typed it of the reason for my revenge, and one that nobody in my surroundings would associate with me.

My first try worked! As soon as I entered the word PRETERIUS, the usual system messages vanished and the screen reddened from top to bottom, as if a theatre curtain had fallen. Then the title of the secret program appeared in large, golden letters, while tiny, impish flashes of light danced around them: FELIDAE.

After a few seconds, this title also vanished, and then the monitor, to my satisfaction but also to my great dismay, presented me with what I had sought.

The breeding programme FELIDAE was so voluminous and complicated that only a tiny portion of it fitted into the limited confines of the screen. It consisted of a considerable number of genealogical trees, beginning at the very top with several pairs who were candidates for re-breeding. These branched off downwards, multiplying themselves into an impenetrable thicket of names. The more the diagram extended, the more the development of the species in particular genealogical trees progressed – from the domesticated type to the wild, pure-bred Felidae. The breeder had proceeded very strictly in the matter of selection, and had gradually eradicated, or presumably murdered, those generations that continued to carry the dominant gene of domestication; the old–new family tree had thus been pruned and shaped into a network of kinship relations, which overlaid the bright red background like a paper cut-out. Under every name a corresponding information box had been inserted. Each box listed details on the genotype, meaning the genetic traits each individual had inherited from its parents, and then on the phenotype, or the realisation of the individual genotype in interaction with the environment. Comments were also noted in the information boxes – on the 'dominant' hereditary factors that always expressed themselves in the phenotype, as well as on the 'recessive' hereditary factors that were second to the dominant ones, but which might 'revive' themselves. The boxes were in turn connected with one another by black lines documenting the complex system of cross-breeding. To obtain a general survey of the breeding programme, a condensed, graphic version could be called up and viewed on a single screen.

The solution, or to be precise, the principle, was quite simple. If a human being wants to breed animals, then he isolates the animals designated for breeding from those considered unsuitable. An animal that intends to breed animals, however, does not by nature have the means a human being has. The animal can only see to it that the male selected for breeding purposes encounters the right female. If an unknown animal tries to butt in, it has to be stopped. But what if it refuses to be stopped, if it insists on satisfying its lust? Well then . . .

At the lower branches of the genealogical tree were approximately a hundred names of those who had come closest to representing the ultimate goal of the bio-engineer. Among them was probably my seductress, the one with whom I had spent one of the most enchanting mornings of my life. Strangely enough, all these names were tongue-twisters. I guessed that the creator of the programme had studied not only our kind but also the roots of our language intensively. One was called Khromolhkhan, for example, another, Iiieahtoph. In fact, it did not seem all that far-fetched to compare myself with the safari-helmeted archaeologist, who, carrying out the abominable practices of his science in the mysterious burial vault systems of the pyramids, at last stumbles on the solid gold sarcophagus he has sought all his life. What I had finally excavated turned out to be a veritable Pandora's box; in time, it would no doubt come up with even more surprising secrets.

Yes, there really was much more to discover. In the lower-right corner of the genealogical table was a tiny black death's head, which I assumed was a symbol for recalling a further file of information. I moved the cursor to this symbol and pressed the enter key. As anticipated, the genealogical table faded away, and a seemingly endless list of names appeared, to each of which was appended a number, date, and time, as well as a short note. One such entry read as follows:

287 – Pascha
18 June 1986 / circa 0300
Attempted to mate Tragiyahn. All art of persuasion in vain. Tragiyahn is a problem in any case. She does not keep to the agreement and roams the entire district when she's in heat. When will they finally learn to shun the lower orders?

Another entry:

355 – Chanel
4 August 1987 / circa 2300
Chrochoch impregnated her. There were no ifs or buts about it. The owner will want to distribute the litter among friends and acquaintances. By no means can this be allowed to occur. I have great problems finding quarters for my own among the humans in the area.

Number by number, name by name, it went on in this matter-of-fact tone. It was quite obvious who was on this list: the dead! With his characteristic conscientiousness, the murderer had accurately documented and catalogued every one of his villain-ous deeds. The itemisation of horrors finally ended with number 447. No wonder that the number my intellectual twin brother and I had calculated came so close to this.

I stared open-mouthed at the monitor, and the longer I remained there in this petrified state, the more I was filled with a grief so profound it was almost impossible to bear. So many, so terribly many had given up their lives so that this fanatic could realise his dream of the one true race. It was an old dream that many other fanatics before him had dreamed, but none the less senseless for that. Four hundred and forty-seven brothers and sisters who had wanted nothing but to live and to love. That and nothing else, for God's sake!

Tears welled up in my eyes, and in my imagination I saw these many innocents whose lives had been snatched away assembled in a group, just as I had always seen them in my nightmares. They stood stock-still and had an absent expression on their faces, as if the scene were a snapshot of heaven. Yet even if they did not complain about their terrible fate, I could tell by looking at them that they wanted to get out of this cursed number-cruncher so that they could finally find some peace. At least that . . .

I decided to delete the diabolical program on the spot. It was the last decent service that I could render the dead.

'Do you know everything now, my dear Francis?'

Pascal's voice had an ironic undertone, as if he were mocking my success.

I turned away from the monitor and looked down from the desk. He stood at the door, his yellow eyes glowing in the darkness like molten gold. Then he sat down on his rear legs and smiled painfully. Impotent rage rose in me, because God knows, I couldn't find anything funny about the situation. Despite this, or precisely because of it, I returned his smile with an ice-cold one of my own.

'Yes, Claudandus, now I know almost everything. There are only a few gaps. Perhaps you should tell the whole story from the beginning. That would be only appropriate, wouldn't it?'

He smiled again, this time as if I were once again the rebellious child whose anger gave more cause for amusement than annoyance.

'Oh, you mean the famous re-telling of events by the murderer to the detective before he finishes him off – or the other way around?'

'That's right: or the other way around, as you say. But please be so kind as to begin.'

'There's not much to tell you, my friend. Most of it you've

found out for yourself. Admittedly, I slowed down your investigations a little because I wanted you to be initiated into these matters step by step. Nevertheless, you took the really crucial steps towards solving the case alone. "Winner on points" would be the right expression. As far as I am concerned, it can't be denied that I have been a loser all my life. Like every loser, I have done nothing but dream again and again of winning, just for once. Whether my dream will come true or not is now up to you, but we'll discuss that at greater length later.'

He padded to the middle of the room and stretched himself out on the fluffy carpet. The smile vanished from his face, yielding to a meditative expression. Outside, the snowflakes whirled in fury.

' "And God made the beasts of the earth after his kind, and cattle after their kind, and everything that creepeth upon the earth after his kind: and God saw that it was good." That's how God speaks of the *other* animals. But what do you know of the special animals? Do you *know* human beings, Francis? I mean, have you ever thought seriously about them? Do you know what's really going through their minds and what they're capable of, even when they're not doing those terrible things that the so-called good people condemn? Yes, yes, you no doubt believe that they can be divided into two groups, into the good and the bad. Into those who construct nuclear weapons and provoke wars, and those who protest against the slaughter of whales in the oceans and collect donations for the starving. You have never seen what it is like inside a human mind, and yet you believe you know that they fall into two distinct categories. Well, you know nothing, dear Francis, you know nothing at all . . . I will tell you a story of human beings and animals, not a detective story, but a true story . . .'

He now spoke very softly and thoughtfully, as if he were far, far away in another place and time. All the while he seemed hardly to notice me, and gave the impression that he was talking to himself.

'I was born thirteen years ago, and I can assure you that I very much liked the world as it was then. I liked life, I liked the sun and the rain, and perhaps I even liked human beings. But that was a long time ago, and I find it very difficult to remember the happy days, or even remember the feeling of happiness.

'At that time, I led an unsettled life. I was born to be a stray, as they say, and had a lot of fun. One day, I happened upon this unspeakable laboratory. It exerted a magnetic attraction on me. I don't know what got into me, but all of a sudden I was standing at the door of this cursed house. A man came up the path and opened the door for me. It was Preterius. When I realised what was going on in there, at first I wanted to get out as quickly as possible and put thousands of miles between myself and that sickening place. But then I changed my mind. Idiot that I was, I actually resolved to observe every detail of the outrageous injustice that this monster was committing against our kind so that I could alert the others outside and inform subsequent generations. As you see, even then I was filled with a missionary zeal.

'You yourself found out what happened after that from the journal of the dear professor. I would prefer not to distress you further with the repulsive details of my career as guinea pig. This chapter of my life is closed. You should only realise that what you read was reported from the perspective of the real murderer. The martyrdom that I had to suffer was in fact a thousand times more cruel than any mind, human or animal, could ever imagine.'

His eyes glistened with tears that slowly ran down his muzzle and then quietly dripped on to the carpet.

'Be that as it may, at the end of my treatment, the good old professor had started to go gaga, and all his accomplices left him. When he finally went all the way round the bend, I spoke with him.'

'You spoke with him? But that's sacrilege! We're not supposed to talk with humans. The untouchable may not exchange a single word with the impure, even if they're in danger of dying.'

'Imagine that! A believer among us! Even if this injures your religious feelings, Francis, unfortunately I'm going to have to say it: I hate God! He who created the world, He who created this human race, He who created Preterius and predicaments like the one I was in: I hate Him. If there is a God, then He is a huge, malevolent spider in a great darkness. We cannot acknowledge this darkness and the face of the spider and the vast spider's web that lies hidden behind life's illusion of happiness and goodness. Or rather, we do not want to.'

'And how did you speak with him?'

'How? Well, I realised that my days were slowly but surely coming to an end, and therefore I left nothing untried. It took untold hours of practice, but I learned to move my jaws like a human and make sounds like a human and imitate the human language. What came croaking out of my throat must have sounded rather strange, but the crazy old coot understood it. He opened the cage door to confront me in a duel. He was laughing insanely as if he had cramp and just couldn't stop laughing any more. As soon as the door was open, I summoned up all my remaining strength, sprang up into his gaping mouth, and bit deeply into his throat with my fangs. He fell down and tried desperately to pull me out of his bleeding mouth. But it was too late. In next to no time I had eaten through to his gullet and then, at last, he twitched a few times and became quite still.

'I was exhausted and thought I would collapse dead at any moment. But before I sailed on to the next world, I wanted at least to free the others and save them from being tortured further by this sadist's successors. I opened the cages and liberated all the sisters and brothers. Nearly all of them were children. Then I sank into a heavy sleep in which I actually did hear myself knocking at the gates of the next world.

'When I finally woke up, Ziebold was standing over me. He had always liked me, and increasingly often had refused to carry out Preterius's insane orders. He left in the end because he could no longer bear to witness the suffering of the laboratory animals. He had come by the laboratory that day because he had heard disturbing things from Rosalie, the professor's wife, about her husband's state of mind, and wanted to see whether everything was OK. I bet when he saw me lying like that on the floor next to the corpse he knew exactly what had happened. Yet he gave me a roguish smile, took me in his arms and, whistling all the while, walked out of that chamber of horrors for ever. By coincidence, he happened to live very near the laboratory.'

It was more or less the way I had imagined the tragic events. But this had only started the ball rolling, set the scene for the events that followed.

'What happened then, Claudandus?'

'Please don't call me that. It brings back nasty memories, you know.'

He wiped the tears from his face with a paw and then shuddered violently.

'Ziebold had me patched together, so far as possible, by one of the best animal surgeons he could find, and after a painful recovery period of four months I felt more or less fit again. But I was no longer my old self. I could no longer take any kind of pleasure in life. I had no appetite, and was seldom free of a great mire of depression. In my memory and my dreams, again and again and again I experienced the hell I had gone through; my suffering repeated itself day after day seemingly without end . . . And then, gradually, I learned to appreciate the merits of Ziebold's library. I read all those thick tomes humans had written, and learned much about their way of thinking. Most of the authors I read wrote about how wonderful and clever humans were, about the great number of things they had invented, how passionately they could love, how magnificent was their God, and what distant stars they would one day reach and grace with their unique genius. This wretched library was just one mammoth commercial for *Homo sapiens*, and I kept reading exactly the same thing in book after book: humans were and would always remain the masters of the world. And why? Because without any shame or scruple, they had enslaved or, even better, killed every other species. It was their sick pride that had given them the will and power to do this. They simply imagined themselves to be superior, and believed for this reason that they could commit every conceivable injustice against other living creatures. And the shocking thing was that they actually were superior, just because of this arrogant attitude.

'Once I realised that, I began to think about how I could turn back the course of history. I knew that however the downfall of their tyrannical rule might come about, it would have to be achieved inconspicuously. Strict organisation and clever strategy were necessary, so that the master race would not notice anything. It was Mendel's genetic theory that showed me the way. His book was a revelation to me. Suddenly I knew what my task was, what my duty was, how I could give my life meaning and at the same time take revenge on those who had inflicted so much pain and humiliation on me. But this was to be not just a matter of blind revenge; it would utterly change the world.'

'All this sounds to me like human ambition.'

'Perhaps. But it was – *it is* – the only way we can smash their systems of oppression, which have already been in existence for thousands of years. I confess that I was a mere dreamer at the beginning, and proceeded with great naïvety. I proposed my plan to some of the laboratory survivors and other brothers and sisters in the area. They refused to share this wonderful vision with me. Comfort, stupidity and fear drove them back into the arms of human beings. They said that human beings weren't evil at all and, gullible as they are, blathered about peaceful coexistence. Sure, they said, now and then you get black sheep among human beings, just as you do among members of every species, but basically . . . These cretins preferred to live as slaves and eat stinking carrion out of tin cans than to fight for freedom!

'The only one who listened to me was Joker. He had observed the gruesome events in the laboratory as an outsider, and knew what human beings were all about. And so we joined up together as a team. He was responsible for disseminating the ideology, I for the scientific side of the project. But in order not to stir up suspicions we had to get things going very slowly.

'I started modestly enough, with just one female and one male who had at least the rudimentary characteristics required for my purposes. It was a matter of eliminating the domestication gene within a few generations, and of re-breeding *Felis catus* not only physically but also with regard to behaviour and instinct. This was no easy task. Although the female and male lived very near to one another, when they got into heat they were pestered by the ordinary brothers and sisters. Or they took the initiative themselves and went to others for sex. I had no choice but to stop those who were not fit for breeding. But they did not listen to me; their sexual desire was stronger, and they behaved like brainless, lust-driven robots. And so I eliminated them one after the other, whenever they tried to spoil my complicated breeding programme. As time went by, the new ones increasingly kept themselves apart from the standards and picked lovers from among their own, but occasionally lust blinded even them and they would want to get off with standards, or the other way round. Before things got that far, I would always intervene. Joker showed me how I could dispose of the corpses without a trace. The killing will soon end, however, because the latest generations are almost all so constituted that they no longer want to mix with us normal ones. The problem resolves itself.'

'That's not quite true. Weren't you the one who was observing me secretly about a week and a half ago while I was enjoying myself with that enchantress? Well, no doubt you were able to see for yourself that your finer sort is quite capable of stooping down to the level of us standards.'

He smiled knowingly.

'Hints from me, Francis! Hints and tips I passed on to you so that bit by bit you would understand what the project is all about. Surely you already know why I did not entrust Jesaja, the good Guardian of the Dead, with the last eight corpses? I'm simply too old and too sick to drag the weight of a brother or sister over long distances. Well, actually that's only half true. Bluebeard told me what an expert inspection of Sascha's corpse you made just after you moved to the square. He said that you were my equal. Dear old Bluebeard only meant that as a provocation and had absolutely no idea that I have been waiting for a prodigy like you ever since I started carrying out my plans. My megalomania is not of such dimensions that I would flatter myself with the belief that the sacred mission will be accomplished before I die. It will take years, even decades, before the new race spreads throughout the entire world. The members of this wonderful race, it is true, have been initiated into the plan. They know that for the time being they will have to curry favour with human beings, and they will not touch them until the day when the first blow for freedom is struck. Nevertheless, they need a leader to tell them what should be done and to supervise them. That's why I was glad you came. I helped you in your investigations, but intentionally voiced doubts about your hypotheses to make you reflect on the hidden motives of the case. The very first moment I saw you, I knew that you would uncover the secret sooner or later. And for this reason I sent Nhozemphtekh to you. Just so you would have something to ponder, just so you would discover the deeper meaning of our cause and gain an approximate idea of our ultimate goal, Francis. Admit it, she's a splendid specimen, isn't she?'

I was overcome by surprise and disgust in equal proportions, and the tension nearly made me vomit. The fellow was more than just mad – he had all but turned into a human being himself!

'Well, well. Hints and wonders. And Felicity soaked in her own blood. Was she another of the treasures you put my way to make me happy?'

'No. That was a tragic matter, an accident, fully unintentional. Nevertheless, accidents happen to be a part of enterprises like this one. I admit I have shadowed you since the day Bluebeard first told me about you. By the way, that pitiful creature has nothing to do with this business. He is merely one more victim of the human race.

'I saw you flee that night from the Claudandus gang, over the roofs into Felicity's. When your pursuers finally gave up the chase and went their own ways, I eavesdropped on you and your witness at the open skylight. However, you were not yet ready for the information Felicity wanted to give you and so, after you had left with Bluebeard, I had to deal with her. As I said, you were supposed to unravel the mystery little by little; otherwise you would have had quite a bout of intellectual indigestion.'

'And what about Joker? Didn't you make a very big mistake when you liquidated your head propagandist?'

'What else could I do? Under pressure he would have revealed everything, not only to you but to all the birdbrained fools in the neighbourhood. Joker was a splendid factotum, but at the same time a terrible windbag. Sometimes I had the feeling that he actually did believe in this Claudandus crap, which the two of us had conjured out of thin air. Faith and hope: that was his *métier*. Poor fool. He would have made a much better Claudandus than I. Besides, it was his own wish to be killed. I proposed to him that he disappear from the area and settle down somewhere else in the city. But he thought that no human would ever take in an old fossil like him. And it's true that human beings like us best as sweet and playful kittens. Joker said he had neither the strength nor the desire to wander around as a stray, his days numbered. I should make it short and painless, he said. I didn't kill him. It was practically suicide, I just happened to be the one to carry it out.'

A deep sense of revulsion now overcame me. And this was someone I had once looked up to! Everything was so logical for him, so clear, even so harmless. The murders weren't personal.

No real harm had been meant. They were intended to serve a good end, and had been carried out as part of a step-by-step solution to a scientific problem. Feeling and reverence for life played no part. Only the goal existed, and that was to be achieved murder by murder, drop by drop of blood. Everything was so simple and at the same time so brilliant. How dangerous the genius of a living creature could be if put to the service of the vile and wicked things of the world. That's the way it had always been and that's the way it always would be. Preterius, Mendel, Claudandus – they truly were one and the same person.

'Now I really do know everything,' I said bitterly. 'And I wish I did not.'

He got up slowly from his seat, sauntered over to his desk, and looked up at me with a dreamy expression on his face. He seemed to be reading my thoughts. After a while, he smiled painfully, as if he had suddenly understood the punch-line of a malicious joke.

'Oh no, Francis, no. You only *think* you know everything. That is a great difference, my dear fellow.'

He shook his head in resignation.

'In spirit we are old friends, Francis. More than that, we are like twins. You certainly must have thought so yourself more than once. You think you know a thing or two, don't you? You think you're the clever one who knows what's what, don't you? There's so much you don't know. So much. What do you really know? You are only an ordinary little animal living in an ordinary little city. You wake up every morning of your life and you know very well that nothing in the world is going to worry you. You live through your ordinary little day, and in the night you sleep your untroubled, ordinary little sleep full of pointless, peaceful dreams. And I'm the one who's brought you your nightmares. Or am I? You're living in a dream; you're a sleepwalker; you're blind! How do you know what the world is really like? Don't you know that the world is really a stinking pigsty? Don't you know that if you tore down the façades of these houses you'd find pigs inside? The world is a hell! What does it matter what happens in it? The world was so created that one sorrow follows another. There has been a chain reaction of suffering and cruelty on this earth since its creation. Yet perhaps it is no better elsewhere, on distant planets, stars, and galaxies . . . Who knows? The crown of all that is loathsome in this universe and unknown universes is, very probably, the human race. The human race is so . . . so evil, mean, cunning, egotistical, greedy, cruel, insane, sadistic, opportunistic, blood-thirsty, malicious, treacherous, hypocritical, envious, and – yes, this above all – just plain stupid! Such is the human race. Oh Francis, don't you know that the humans of this world have surrounded themselves with an armour of egotism, that they are intoxicated with their vain self-contemplation, that they thirst for flattery, are deaf to what is said to them, unmoved by the misfortunes that befall their most intimate friends, and in constant fear of all requests for help that could interrupt their endless dialogue with their own desires? Truly, dear Francis, of such kind are the children of Adam, from China to Peru.

'Yet what about the *others*? What about us? I say to you, my friend, we are no different. We, who in our complacency and boredom snap listlessly at gnats, squat lazily on garden walls, purr behind electric stoves, belch, fart, doze and dream away our lives with ridiculous dreams of ridiculous hunts for such ridiculous prey as mice and rats . . . We, who trust in the goodness of the God-given order, we, who cultivate our prefer-ences for various brands of tinned food, we, who are now so pathetically far from what we once were, yes, we, Francis, of whom all the other members of the proud family of Felidae are no doubt ashamed – we *imitate* human beings, we are *like* human beings!'

'You're the one who's really a human being!' I cried. 'You think just like they do! You act just like they do! You only want to repeat all the misery they have brought to the world. You're dreaming not of real change but of establishing a new dictator-

ship paid for with hundreds and thousands of dead from your
own ranks. And tell me what kind of a role you've thought up
for the other animal species in your oh-so-very-wonderful
never-never land? Come on, answer me!'

'No role at all! They're stupid and they submit to their fate.
No will and no energy, you understand? They are born victims
and will be our servants one day, just as now they are the
servants of human beings. We could be the new rulers of the
world, Francis. Dynasties and kingdoms could arise, our power
could extend over the oceans and into the remotest deserts.
Don't be so stupid, Francis! Tear the veil from your eyes and
recognise at last what human beings have made out of us!
Cuddly dolls, amusing buffoons to satisfy their craving for
diversions, substitute love objects for their cold hearts, picturesque finishing touches for their prissy homes! That's what's
happened to us! Haven't you noticed how small we are? Any
doting human being can wring our necks. We are at their mercy
till hell freezes over, and the worst thing is, we don't even realise
we're in a perpetual state of bondage. We have grown used to it;
in fact, we even like it. Do you want your kind to live on and on
in this degrading way? Do you want that, Francis?'

'Judge not that ye be not judged, Pascal.'

'Pascal? Ha! The name of a computer language, language
created by human beings! That's human, typically human. All
these idiotic names they give us because they can't help but
project their own crippled feelings on to us. Because they no
longer have anything to say to one another, because they need us
as substitutes for disappointed friendships, and for affection
they can't find among themselves. My name is neither Pascal nor
Claudandus, nor do I bear any other name that human beings
may dream up for me. I am Felidae, member of a species that
devours human beings!'

'And Ziebold?' I asked. 'Didn't he save your life and nurse
you back to health?'

'Nonsense! He only had feelings of guilt because he himself

had been a murderer for years and because this was an easy way for him to be able to ease his conscience. They are all hypocrites, every one of them, Francis. Their own fake sanctimoniousness is their one true God, to whom they sacrifice new victims day after day. And that's exactly what they want of us, too. They want to make us caricatures of themselves!'

'But there are also good people, Pascal or Claudandus or Felidae or whoever you are. Believe me. And one day, and even if it is one distant day, all living creatures on God's earth will enjoy equal rights and live in harmony, or perhaps even in love with one another, and understand one another better.'

'No! No! No!' he bellowed, his eyes burning with impotent rage and hate. 'There are no good people! They're all the same! Don't you understand that? Animals are good human beings and human beings are bad animals!'

I cautiously turned my back on him and leaned over the computer keyboard.

'Everyone wants to rule the world,' I said, filled with sorrow. 'Really, absolutely everyone. That's what it's all about, isn't it? That's what it's always about in the end. And every species believes that it's number one. Every individual is firmly convinced that he or she alone has the right to ascend to the throne and issue orders to get rid of others. And in reality everyone is fooling themselves, because up there on the throne it's lonely and cold. We don't have anything more to say to one another, my friend. I understand the reasons why you unleashed this nightmare, and I don't want to conceal from you either that I harbour certain feelings of sympathy for your remorselessly cruel plans. But not at this price, no, not at this terrible price! I will fight you and do everything in my power to destroy your life's work. This I swear as sure as I am standing here. And I'm going to begin by deleting this unspeakable program. I'm sorry . . .'

'You have no idea how really sorry I am, Francis,' I heard him whisper with deep dejection from below.

Then, as my paw touched the delete key, I heard the sound I had been waiting for since the start of our confrontation. A loud hiss, as if the air were being ripped in two, and a violent screech of insanity. I threw myself instinctively to the side, and he hit the monitor with all his weight so that it fell from the processing unit, slid over the edge of the glass desk, and crashed down on the floor. The cathode ray tube imploded with a muffled boom, the monitor burst into a thousand shards and a broadside of sparks shot out of its insides and set the white curtains of the front window on fire.

Pascal and I now stood facing each other, as taut and tense as bowstrings, the fur along our spines standing on end. Backs arched in threat, we growled at each other in ferocious warning. Suddenly my dark opponent heaved himself up on his back legs and flung himself at me with the extended, razor-tipped claws of his front paws whirling and hissing like shurikens. I replied in kind. We met in the middle of the desk, our claws ripping in deep. We fell on to the glass top and rolled over together, attacking each other with our back paws, biting into each other blindly, tearing and slashing without mercy. Pascal tried again and again to sink his fangs into my neck, to give me that fatal bite he had mastered so well. But instead he got my right ear and bit with the full force of his jaws. A thin fountain of blood shot out of the wound and ran over my forehead into my eyes, blinding me. With courage born of desperation, I chomped my teeth into Pascal's chest, not letting go until he suddenly lurched back, yowling in fury, to lick his wounds.

Meanwhile, the flames had already consumed the curtains and their greedy tongues were panting up towards the ceiling. Molten plastic slime dripped down, burning itself into the carpet and spreading the fire. The room filled with noxious smoke and suffocating heat, and the lurid orange blaze provided us bleeding gladiators with a light that suited our fighting mood. I wanted nothing so much as to get out of this hell, but knew that the old soldier confronting me, obviously fighting his last battle, wasn't about to let me go. So we licked our wounds, snarling at each other, and prepared ourselves for the next bout while the wildly dancing coronet of flames crackled upwards, extending a thousand greedy hands towards the master's library.

Blood gushing from his chest, Pascal hurled himself at me without warning, as if a bomb had exploded under his hind legs. He sank his murderous fangs into my neck, and pulled me down on to the glass top of the desk. Scything each other's noses, eyes, and soft parts, we tumbled across the desk again and again until at last we fell to the floor, stubbornly clamped together. I felt hardly any pain, though I knew I would feel it later.

On the carpet, which was already burning away, we fought with the unyielding fervour that seizes fighters when they begin to realise that only one will survive. We hacked away at each other with our claws as if toying with a mouse, biting and ripping away at each other's bodies the way we would savage a dead rabbit. Blood from our wounds spurted into the air as if Professor Julius Preterius himself had returned from the dead to conduct his final and most cruel experiment.

But gradually we tired. Our jabs became more and more sluggish, our bites turned into weary gnawing motions, and we wrestled and scratched on automatic, in a way that would probably put an end to both of us. Then Pascal lost his breath for a moment and leaned on me. With all my remaining strength, I took this chance to etch a bleeding set of tramlines into his face with the claws of my right paw. He gave out a piercing shriek and collapsed backwards. I leapt back about four feet, squatted on my back legs, and ran my tongue over the many wounds on my body. I do not believe I really licked them – it was more of a reflex – because I had no more strength left and very little presence of mind.

Pascal, on the other hand, did nothing. Nothing at all. He merely sat on his rear and stared at me through milky eyes like a wax doll. His dark fur was now soaked with the blood pouring from his wounds in appalling profusion.

All the books that had taught Claudandus so much about humans and animals were now ablaze, and the fire was so hot that breathing was nearly impossible. In a few seconds we would suffocate, and then we would burn. And ultimately human beings were to blame. Not Pascal, not Claudandus, not us – we hadn't been the first to kill. They, the impure, were the cause of all the evil in the world, and the cause of all that had brought us to this point.

And then he jumped.

It was a suicide jump, a jump made with no thought for where and how he would land, a jump made with the very last reserves of strength, so that the jumper knew he had nothing left, would not even be able to summon up enough energy to bat an eyelid. It was a powerful jump, as quick and true as a bolt from a crossbow, and with the force of a lump of concrete dropped from a rooftop.

When he shot towards me, screeching, I instinctively threw myself on my back, jerked up my right paw, and let one single claw flash out. And when Pascal soared over me, I hacked his throat, my claw cutting him so deeply I believed I had sliced his vocal cords. He crashed hard on the other side, rolled over once, and remained lying down, silent.

I ran to him and turned his head towards me. He was bleeding horribly, and I saw that the cut was deeper even than I had thought. I could almost see into his windpipe. Nevertheless, a roguish grin flitted over his face. He opened his eyes with difficulty and looked at me intently. No anger, no reproach, and no fear were in them – also, no regret.

'So much darkness in the world,' he wheezed. 'So much darkness, Francis. No light. Only darkness. And there is always someone who will take it upon himself. Always. Always. Always. I have become evil, but once I too was good . . . '[13]

EPILOGUE

THE HOUSE BURNED down and was reduced to ashes, and along with the house, the lifeless body of he to whom human beings had given various names, but whose real name remained a mystery that he took with him to a place where neither names nor race mattered. The diabolical FELIDAE program, with its mass of data on guilt and horror, was also consumed by the flames. I myself was able to flee the inferno at the very last second, more dead than alive. By the time the firemen had fought their way through the snowstorm and opened the frozen fire hydrants, there was nothing more to put out in Ziebold's house. Once again fire had struck out a bit of evil from the world, turning darkness into light.

Yet does a story as complicated as this deserve a simple ending?

Who is able to answer that? Who is right and who is wrong? Who was good and who evil? Where did darkness end and light begin? Black and white: a fantasy of wish fulfilment, a Christmas story for children, a chimera of moralists. I believe that like every good story, this one too must end in grey. Who knows? If you were to study that peculiar colour for a long, long time, ultimately it might seem beautiful, or at least real.

I dragged myself home in a trance and blacked out in the middle of Tokyo – I mean our new bedroom. The following morning, Gustav caught sight of my numerous injuries and blood-matted coat, had a screaming fit in sheer fright, and chauffeured me in his Citroën CX2000 to the horse doctor. The doctor tortured me even more, reviving ugly associations of Preterius's cruel experiments. The healing process, too, was a dark, painful path that made me draw comparisons more than once to Claudandus's sad fate.

Since then, however, I have recovered splendidly and now enjoy the best of health.

I didn't need to tell Bluebeard and the dim-wits in the neighbourhood who the killer really was. It just didn't seem that important to me. I wanted them all to keep good memories of Pascal: hate and revenge were his aims, not mine. Gradually I was able to dispel the suspicions surrounding Father Joker's name, and I also succeeded in rectifying the nasty impression of him that the locals had been given during our evening meeting. They now believe that he wandered away to another area to spread his doctrine. Nobody thinks he was the murderer, either, although the inhabitants of the porcelain warehouse will get a malodorous surprise in the spring when it gets warm again.

Who the murderer was will always remain a riddle to the others. But nobody will concern themselves with this question, because there will be no more murders. And some day there will be nobody even to think of what happened, nobody to remember the horror. Even murderers die, and with them end the mysterious stories that keep us, if only for a short time, in suspense.

Some additional remarks to wind things up.

First, the most alarming news: next month Archibald wants to move into the upstairs flat; as he so elegantly put it, he went 'totally wild for the place' while renovating ours. In addition to the fact that I can now look forward to a further course of ear-battering renovation, Gustav and I will soon have to listen day after day to the stupidest in-and-out-of-vogue drivel that this paragon of a fashion victim can dream up. I know that. He may even get a dog and baptise him 'Warhol' or 'Pavarotti' or even 'Kevin Costner'! So, gloomy times are on their way. But if you look at it from a charitable point of view, you might find something positive: Gustav will get more human, if superficial, company, and also a chance to break out of his prison of loneliness.

Someone else has already put an icy spell of loneliness behind him. Employing our best arts of persuasion, Bluebeard and I were able to lure Jesaja out of the catacombs. We also found lodgings for him with an old and good-natured, if eccentric, bartender in the neighbourhood. When he saw blue sky again for the first time after all his years underground, he wept for joy and excitement. He has since overcome his initial shyness, mainly towards human beings but also towards other brothers and sisters. The only thing that worries me is that the bar customers will treat him now and then with alcoholic drinks and that he will be all too willing to let himself be treated. The fact that a brother drinks at all would be worth a scientific study, I think. I hope it all works out.

Pascal's wonder race has become noticeably wilder – that is, more and more of the old–news are mating with us standards, so that the coming generations will once again be of the domesticated type. After Pascal's death, it seems they lost all their inhibitions and became eager to enter new terrain. I often see my bewitching girlfriend, Nhozemphtekh, roaming the backyards, and we greet each other politely, even give each other knowing smiles. I'm just waiting for the day when she goes into heat again. Then the sweet intoxication of that magical morning will return, and together we will soar through galaxies of lust – if Kong doesn't beat me to it.

As for wishes like this one, Bluebeard and I have great plans for the future. After all our gruesome experiences, we intend to have an easy and pleasant time of it this coming spring and summer, and let ourselves be borne frequently aloft by the wings of Eros.

The sun has already pierced the steel-grey, icy clouds, showing no mercy in melting them away, and shedding the first faint rays of the new year on the computer Gustav bought not long ago. In the last few days, I have been entering into it my memories of the Claudandus case. As might be expected, Gustav lost all interest in the computer after only two days, because even after ploughing through six instruction manuals he couldn't figure it out. There is the lingering hope that when Archie moves into the house he'll give Gustav a hand.

I said that every tale has a sad ending. Well, that's only partly true, because our lives are also a story told by God. We're writing them with God. We and God are, so to speak, co-authors. Our free will and His grace work together, though they are often in conflict. So the events of this story can't be all that bad. Thus the story of Claudandus, the murderer, ends with both tears and laughter, depending on how you look at it. As for me, I'm entirely capable of adopting both perspectives. Understandably, Claudandus wasn't. He regarded the world as a fearful place. He had never been happy, and would never have been capable of happiness. He hated the human race. He hated the entire world. He said that none of us had any idea what the world was really like. No, it isn't really that bad. But sometimes you have to keep a watchful eye on the world just the same. Now and then, it does tend to get a little crazy.

Maybe I'm just naïve, and see the catastrophic conditions around me through rose-tinted spectacles because I did not have the hideous experiences Claudandus had with human beings. Despite the darkness surrounding him, the darkness that penetrated his soul, the murderer did see into the real nature of things. Much of what he said was pretty close to the truth. What he lacked was hope and faith in the light, and where would we be, we fragile creatures of a fragile world, without faith and hope?

And so we should hope – but also be on the look-out. We should remember the cruel murderer who wanted to revenge evil with evil. Or, as the satanic Preterius recognised in one of his saner moments: 'It seems to me that he's lost his innocence.' Yes, that's what must have happened. Claudandus's problem was that he lost his innocence. Just like human beings.

We, however, want to believe in innocence. In particular, human beings should never forget that their ancestors were animals, that they are, in fact, still animals, and that consequently a tiny bit of innocence still dwells within them. Claudandus said: 'Animals are good human beings and human beings bad animals.' Whether good or evil, we are all animals in the end, and so should relate to one another in loving friendship.

And so farewell from your humble and devoted Francis, and cordial greetings to all the clever bastards of the world. Go on solving riddles, even if the solutions aren't worth the trouble. And don't give up believing in a world in which animals and human beings live together in harmony, all kinds, even more sublime and intelligent species than the latter – for example, Felidae.

NOTES

1. Unlike human beings, but like certain other animal species such as deer and horses, cats are endowed with a third chemical sense which lies between smell and taste. This sense perceives certain stimuli (molecules that can be smelled) by means of a characteristic receptor, called the 'Jacobson organ' after its discoverer. The tiny organ is located in a small passage that leads away from the palate, and looks roughly like a cigar-shaped sack. To use it, the animal 'licks' the requisite substances out of the air and presses them with his tongue against the palate so that they stimulate the receptor. During this procedure, the cat adopts a characteristic facial expression called *flehmen* (a word for which there is no English equivalent), which may seem rather silly to human beings. Tom-cats are often seen flehming when they chance upon the irresistible scent of the urine of a female cat in heat.

2. Supposedly originating from the state of Maine, the large, muscular Maine Coon with its long, bushy tail is one of the few breeds of cat to originate in the United States. Its appearance, particularly its typical colouring of dark, raccoon-like tabby markings, gives rise again and again to the scientifically absurd conjecture that the Maine Coon owes its existence to the mating of domesticated cats with the raccoon. It is more likely, as many breeders believe, that the Maine

Coon, a race that is now roughly a hundred years old, was created in the crossing of shorthaired domesticated cats with Angoras introduced earlier by English sailors.

The animal, which is extremely robust, has a thick, frost-resistant, flowing coat that is somewhat shorter at the shoulders. It has made itself useful by warding off vermin in New England farms, and has contributed to preventing rats from decimating the duck population. The Maine Coon, which has a voluminous ruff, a long, quadratic skull, and an unusual weight for a domesticated cat (males weigh up to fifteen pounds), is very much a late developer: many members of the species are fully grown only after four years. It is often said of them that they are perfect house cats. Contributing to this reputation are their droll temperament, their numerous amusing traits of character, and their fur, which is easy to care for. Maine Coons have very different coat colourings and patterns. Since many Maine Coons have numerous colouring genes, it is not infrequently the case that each kitten of a litter has its own shade.

3. Following copulation, female cats behave in a very peculiar and rather grim manner: during ejaculation, they emit a piercing cry, then abruptly, almost explosively, tear themselves away from the male and turn against him in great anger. In the entire kingdom of domesticated animals, they are alone in exhibiting this radical change of mind towards their sexual partners. It may, however, be easier to understand this behaviour if the unusual shape of the male cat's penis is taken into consideration: its tip is studded with numerous thorns that provide for strong, if painful, stimulation of the female vagina. This is not a sadistic quirk of nature, but has an important and practical biological function. The stimulation of the vagina results in a torrent of neural and hormonal reactions that ends (about twenty-four hours after pairing) in the release of eggs (ovulation), thus making fertilisation possible. In the course of post-coital heat, the female rolls around on the ground, purring and snapping aggressively at her lover, who remains near by waiting for the next opportunity to copulate.

4. Cats are powerful machines and their complex musculature requires intensive care. Cats have more than five hundred muscles, while human beings, despite their comparative bulk, have only six hundred and fifty. The largest muscles in cats serve to drive the powerful back legs, but the cat also has a good deal of beef in its neck

and front legs, which are used for catching prey. Apart from these volitional muscles, which obey the commands of the brain, there are numerous involuntary muscles that are responsible for the regulation of the internal organs. After sleep or after a relatively long period of inactivity, cats therefore stretch themselves thoroughly to prevent any possible muscular damage.

5. The well-known way in which cats clean themselves is not performed merely to satisfy the dictates of hygiene. The cat rubs and licks itself repeatedly, not only to remove dust, dirt and the remains of meals, but to stimulate glands under the skin that keep its coat silky and to make it water-resistant. In addition, through his tongue the cat assimilates tiny amounts of the life-essential vitamin A, which is created on the fur by the action of sunlight. A cat's obsessive cleaning also serves as a method of adjusting body temperature. Since cats cannot perspire on account of their coat, the production of spit replaces the cooling function of sweat. For this reason, cats clean themselves especially thoroughly in warm weather, as well as after exerting themselves in activities such as hunting, playing and eating. Last but not least, cleaning also removes loose hair and parasites from their coats. It is probable that the licking process also accelerates the growth of new hair.

6. The Colourpoints, with their large head, small ears, short legs, short tail, and soft, silky coat with shades ranging from cream to ivory, represent a genetic product achieved through human manipulation. They owe their existence both to the wish to solve genetic problems through breeding and to the intention to create a cat by means of a detailed, planned hybrid programme that merges the typical Siamese markings (brightly coloured coat with darker spots on the face, the ears, the legs, and tail, as well as beaming blue eyes) with the characteristics of the Persian (long, silky coat, compact body). Despite this goal, European and American breeders have not been able to agree on a uniform designation for the racial status of their artificial creation. In the United States, the creature is regularly termed 'Himalayan cat' and possesses the rank of an independent race. The term 'Khmer cat', now no longer used, was rejected when the American cat breeding organization, GCCF, recognised these creatures under the name of Colourpoint.

The example of this cat race (and the blue-eyed Foreign White) makes very clear that breeders proceed without scruples and with great tenacity when it comes to creating a 'product' that conforms to their ideals. According to the regulations of the world association, a new race is 'official' only after it has been pure-blooded for three generations, meaning that it has a good history of pairings with its own kind. To overcome this stipulation, hundreds of cats were bred using exceptionally intensive inbreeding methods, and the race received official recognition in 1955. After this, however, breeders admitted that the Colourpoint needed to be bred with Persians to improve its fur and physical quality. It took eighteen years before it could be proudly announced to the public that the cat breeders had achieved their aim.

7. The long, stiff whiskers (*vibrissae*) of the cat, which are extremely sensitive to touch, are not meant merely to sense and brush against objects in close proximity. By means of these hypersensitive organs of perception, cats can detect the most subtle variations in air currents for purposes of spatial orientation. Cats, of course, have to circumvent countless large and small objects in the dark without bumping into them. When approached, fixed objects cause slight deviations in air circulation. Thanks to the astounding sensitivity of their whiskers, cats perceive these 'breezes' and can elegantly avoid every obstacle.

During nocturnal hunts their whiskers are essential. Intact whiskers make it possible for cats to kill by biting in the darkest night. If these sensitive organs are damaged, then a cat will only be able to kill in daylight. In darkness it would lunge without any awareness of the position of the target, and bite its prey in the wrong place. The *vibrissae* are apparently used as a kind of radar that distinguishes the silhouette of the victim when visibility is limited, and can do so within a fraction of a second; the cat can then bite into the neck of its prey. It seems very likely that the whiskers can 'interpret' the victim's silhouette in detail, and inform the brain of what steps to take next. The whiskers sprout from the tissue over the upper lip and are three times more deeply anchored than other hair. The roots are connected to numerous nerve endings that transmit every sensory impression to the brain with great speed.

8. The great amount of time that they spend preparing themselves for copulation, their sex orgies, and their promiscuous leanings – all have contributed to the reputation of cats as being sensual creatures. In

fact, their lovemaking can continue non-stop for hours, and even, with some interruptions, for days. In this regard, however, 'ladies' choice' rules. The female alone dictates the sequence of events.

To get things going, the female in heat calls to every tom-cat within hearing range. Of course, they are also lured by the special erotic 'perfume' of the female. The male whose territory the female has chosen for her overtures has an advantage right from the start, since his competition shies away from entering strange territory. In the end, however, even they yield to the seductive charms of the temptress and enter the forbidden terrain. This trespassing results in numerous fights between the competing suitors. The hue and cry that then rings out is often misinterpreted as an expression of sexual ecstasy; it is actually only a sign of justified outrage. Usually, however, interest quickly shifts to the lady, and the males leave each other alone. The male who is chosen in the end does not necessarily have to be the most dominant in the neighbourhood; it's entirely up to the female to select the object of her desire.

9. The fact that cats are real gourmets is often not given sufficient attention. For this reason, most animals are condemned to monotonous fare. As worked out by the National Academy of Sciences, the nutritional needs of cats are in fact supplied by dry and tinned cat food. But who can live on tinned food alone? It is true that legal regulations pertaining to cat food are very strict on the whole, and that cats can survive on 'cat food'. True cat lovers, however, regularly present their darlings with fresh treats. Fresh fish, fresh meat (except pork), and particularly fresh liver gladden the heart of every cat. But even cats, who are among the choosiest creatures in the world, have widely varying tastes. Like human beings, they have individual likes and dislikes, swear by certain delicacies, and reject others for the most unfathomable reasons. And, like human beings, incorrect nutrition is also very harmful for them.

Warning: Giving raw meat to cats can cost them their lives. Raw meat and innards can be infested with parasites or bacterial pathogens like salmonella. This is also true for beef, which has been found increasingly to contain a virus that is fatal to cats. Unlike prepared cat food, which is always sterile, raw meat and innards must be cooked. By the way, an exclusive meat diet is low in calcium. A deficiency of this mineral weakens the skeleton because the body absorbs the calcium deposited in the bones. The addition of qualitatively inferior protein (meat waste and table scraps, for example) can make cats die in droves. Lacking the amino acids necessary for life, the animal wastes away, acquires a dull, shaggy coat, and gradually displays symptoms ranging from apathy to loss of appetite.

The yeast thiamine, which uncooked freshwater fish contains, destroys vitamin B_1, which is essential for cats. If given alone, this fare soon causes typical signs of deficiency (for example, lack of appetite, nausea, cramps). Freshwater fish must therefore be cooked so that the B_1 vitamin remains intact.

A further warning: Even if cats supplement their food with vegetables (they can even eat grass), they still remain carnivores, and must be fed as such. The continual attempts of vegetarians to put their cats on a meatless diet is a sadistic mistake. A purely vegetarian diet causes cats to become seriously ill and die a slow and painful death. Desmond Morris, a qualified expert on cats, criticised a recently published book with vegetarian recipes for cats as a clear case of animal cruelty.

10. Before the cat became a favoured house pet, its popularity with human beings was based on its ability to catch rodents. Cats have shown that they are more than equal to this task ever since *Homo sapiens* began storing grain reserves. On a country farm, a few well-cared-for cats are enough to rule out any undesired increase in the rodent population. Before cats intervened, the human race had no protection against such pests. The champion 'mouser' is purportedly a tabby cat that lived in a factory in Lancaster, and liquidated about twenty-two thousand mice in his twenty-three-year-long life. That amounts to three mice daily, a respectable amount for a cat that received extra food from its human owner. Even more successful, however, was a female tabby that fed herself in White City Stadium on a diet of rats. Within a mere six years, she had caught 12,480 of these unlikeable creatures, an average of five to six daily. It is understandable that the ancient Egyptians did everything they could to domesticate cats, and why they punished the killing of a cat with death.

11. The astounding ability of cats to survive free falls from great heights without harm has stirred the admiration of humans since time immemorial, and fuelled the legend that cats have nine lives. Attested to by two New York veterinarians, the record is held by a cat that plummeted from the thirty-second floor of a skyscraper (more than

450 feet) and survived with only a few small injuries, necessitating a hospital stay of a mere two days.

Compared to other animals (including human beings), the body surface of cats is rather large with respect to their mass. The result is that they attain their (very low) speed of descent early, so that the impact of landing is slighter. Moreover, as descendants of predators, cats are furnished with excellent all-round vision, which enables them to adjust their fall so that they land on all fours, evenly distributing the impact of landing. But even in mid-flight cats make use of a born reflex: at the moment they reach the maximum speed of descent, the original tension of the leg musculature yields to relaxation. The cat then resembles a natural parachute, using the braking effect of air to sail downwards with all four paws extended.

12. A serious error is committed if this typical feline gesture is regarded as an act of repressive 'macho' violence. It cannot be said enough that the female cat holds all the cards in sexual affairs. In love it is always the female who inflicts violence against toms, no matter how much the latter exert themselves in conquering their queen. In the case of a neck bite, this is not an aggressive act, but a desperate, psychological trick used by male cats to protect themselves from the wild attacks of their beloved. It triggers an automatic reaction, the so-called 'impregnation paralysis', which goes back to infancy. Feeling the 'carrying grip' of their mothers, young cats become motionless. It is necessary so that the mother can carry away her children in dangerous situations without the kittens going wild. As cats age, this instinctive reaction partly, but not completely, disappears. The male cat who grips the neck fur of his randy sexual partner between his teeth thus has the greatest chance of turning her into a submissive kitten, such as she was in the jaws of her mother. Without this hypnotic trick, male cats would get quite a few more bloody noses than they already do in their amorous play.

13. The notion that domesticated cats can kill one another has a foundation in fact. In their fights, which are often uncontrollably wild, the combatants can indeed inflict fatal wounds. Although cat fights are relatively rare in the wild because it is easier to get out of each other's way there, the narrow confines of the city often cause quarrels, particularly between rival toms.

An attacking cat normally tries to bite the neck of its opponent fatally, an attack which is meant for prey. The cat does this with visibly mixed feelings because it will face bitter resistance. True combat is often preceded by impressive threatening gestures; if one of the fighters does finally deliver the deadly bite, the other counters with its front paws, attacking its enemy with extended, razor-sharp claws. At the same time he makes him feel the power of his strong back paws. In the fury of such a duel, when the fighters hiss at each other, roll over, turn, and rough each other up, it may very well happen that one animal gets killed, or suffers injuries from which it later dies.

Felidae on the Road

Francis returns as the ever curious detective when his intention to 'have an easy and pleasant time of it' in the exclusive company of Gustav is thrown into a tumult by the arrival of Gustav's new girlfriend. She threatens Francis with the cruellest cut of all, and to protect himself from the vet's scalpel Francis takes to the streets. But he has chosen to flee on a wild and stormy night and as the heavens hurl down their torrents Francis becomes caught up in the deadly vortex that leads inevitably to murder . . .

A flash, a crack of thunder, and in the glaring light a caprice of the stormy wind showed me a curtain of rain parting in the middle to reveal the mouth of a dark alley paved with cobblestones. I thought I'd come down that alley. It led to a road junction; so did the street where I now stood, which had quite a steep slope to it. I gazed at the alley, transfixed, until the bright lightning disappeared. Maybe it was my imagination, but I thought I really did recognise a familiar spot. Since the alley was on the other side of the street, seen from my present standpoint, my best course of action would be to cross the road diagonally and then turn right at the junction. It would mean wading paw-deep in the water flowing down the street like a shallow stream, but it would be worth the effort in the end.

I stepped into the water rippling by and hurried to the middle of the road. As a result I finally enjoyed total immersion, but in my present condition that didn't matter. The closer I came to my goal, the more clearly did the dim light of the street lamp on the corner show me the manhole cover in the middle of the road junction quivering as if shaken by a phantom hand. The gratings in the gutters on both sides of the street were swallowing a good deal of the flood, but things must be chaotic down in the sewers in such torrential rain, leading to the risk of sudden eruptions of sewage here and there. The immense pressure might force manhole covers off. So it would be sensible to get a move on and reach the alley before I was faced with any such unpleasant situation. Just as this thought shot through my head, I heard a rushing and roaring behind me as if the Atlantic Ocean in person was coming to town. I whisked round and looked for whatever was making the noise. Aghast, I watched as a tidal wave about half a metre high and stretching right across the street came foaming and raging round the corner and rolled on towards me at high speed. Bloody hell, had all the natural disasters in the universe just been waiting for me to take my first step into independence? No, not all of them – there were still some to come. For when I turned my head forward again to check out the best way of escape, I was horrified to see the manhole cover in the middle of the road junction tossed in the air by a mighty jet of water from underground. The paralysis induced in me by these moments of terror was my undoing. I'd lingered too long staring at the spectacle, and before I knew it, before I could get away from the middle of the road, the wave caught me from behind and flung me to the ground. I struggled to get some kind of footing, but the fury of the wild water forced my body to curl up into a ball and drove me on full speed ahead, like a car tyre come loose. The comparison with those of my kind who like sleeping in washing-machine drums was extremely apt now, for in this unfortunate situation all I could do was swallow water, strike out helplessly with all four paws and hope the wave would soon roll on and over me, leaving its victim behind like driftwood.

Although I couldn't concentrate on anything but sheer survival as I performed death-defying acrobatics in the belly of the wave, I saw out of the corner of my eye that I had now been washed dangerously close to the open sewer shaft. The latter had a particularly intriguing surprise ready to spring on me. For whereas the sludgy brown contents of its stomach had spewed up at the road junction like a liquid mushroom cloud, it was now acting like a whirlpool in a stormy sea, sucking all the water round it back down again with a crazy thirst. You couldn't call me a particularly timid type, but my bladder spontaneously emptied at the sight, enriching the waters foaming around me, for the simple reason that never in my wildest dreams had I envisaged myself drowning in the smelly vortex of the sewage system. I always expected to pop my clogs in old age, sitting on a velvet cushion, either from choking on a fist-sized chunk of liver or from fracturing my Adam's apple with shrill cries of lust while having it off with the Siamese queen next door. All this in radiant sunshine and to the accompaniment of Mahler's *Kindertotenlieder*, of course. But why so defeatist? It didn't have to turn out that way. The tidal wave wasn't necessarily going to wash me down that tiny hole – after all, it was a big road junction. No, not necessarily . . .

After what seemed to me my three hundred and eleventh somersault, I saw the full glory of the open manhole right in front of me like some creepy prophecy come true. The tremendous suction from inside created a spiralling vortex at the top, circling slowly, but inexorably drawing in all the water and rubbish near by. It looked like the glowing eye of the Cyclops himself. I'd have liked to put up a final prayer to my Creator, who for some strange reason had obviously decided I was to go to a better world by way of an intake of human excretions. But before I could get that far, the wave brought me to the edge of the whirlpool. The whirlpool promptly demonstrated its power and sucked me into its orbit with all its might. I screeched, I lashed out with my paws and tried a couple of feeble swimming strokes to escape its hellish powers of suction. I was wasting my time. Like an ant, I was washed round and round in the eddying water at the top of the manhole several times, and then I was finally dragged down into the depths.

In retrospect I see my involuntary venture into aquatics as if through a dirty, scratched plastic film. I remember feeling an urgent need for oxygen and opening my mouth as soon as I was in the water and going down. That was about the silliest thing I could have done, for what little air remained in my lungs was instantly replaced by water. Even worse than the physical shock was the feeling that in my helpless desperation I was on the point of drifting off into mental derangement. Moreover my body, like a living torpedo, kept knocking against the iron rungs cemented into the cylindrical interior of the shaft. But though I was nearly unconscious by now, and it was pitch dark inside the shaft, my highly receptive sense of sight showed me first a series of air bubbles splashing past, then the glimmer of something like a metal bar passing along the winding sewers below. Then I stopped falling, and just as I identified the bar as a hand-rail I collided with it, belly first. I stayed hanging there like a fox's brush soaked in water. The sudden impact, in its turn, brought all the liquid I'd swallowed spewing out of my insides as if it were rendering first aid. Obviously the whirlpool I'd been dragged into was the final consignment from above, because all I could feel now was a last trickle flowing down my back and then sloshing around on the stone floor.

Too badly battered by Fate to make any movement of its own, my body swung rhythmically to and fro where it lay draped over the hand-rail, until it finally dropped backwards to the floor. Once down, it curled up snake-like into a kind of spiral, and the water still in my lungs trickled out of the corners of my mouth. Although I'm equipped with the best optical system in the world, one which leaves even the residual-light cameras people use for nocturnal photography literally in the shade, I couldn't make out anything in my new surroundings at first, just over-whelming blackness. The rain went on splashing down on my fur through the open manhole, but judging by the small number of drops that hit their target I concluded that it must have slackened off. Typically, once the damage was done the per-petrator made a quick get-away. My battered body was sending me the most alarming signals of pain from every nerve ending, but I couldn't be sure whether or not I'd broken anything as I fell. However, I dared not move; I was too scared I'd find I was paralysed. And if so, what dreadful death confronted me? Unable to move from the spot, I'd be torn to pieces slowly and with relish by mice, or more likely rates who could match me for physical size. There were sure to be plenty of rats going about their nasty business down in this clammy vault. And all the time I'd be fully conscious, aware of every detail of my mutilations, watching it all *with the best optical system in the world*!

Following a time-honoured custom of the days when I woke happy, I did finally summon up the courage to shoot a claw out of the fold of skin covering the pad of my right forepaw. Gradually all the rest of my claws came out like miniature flick-knives. My wet body was overcome by a violent fit of shaking which sprayed water everywhere, and before any further tricks to get me up to starting temperature could ensue I pulled myself together and jumped up. Pains shot through my guts like demons unleashed. I held my breath, because the torment threatened to overcome me in short order. The injuries every fibre of my body had suffered throbbed and hammered so horribly that I yelled out loud. But I'd been fortunate in my misfortune. So far as I could tell from a few experimental stretches – which were painful but bearable – I didn't seem to have broken anything, and the bruises from all that bumping about weren't really too bad either. In short, I rearranged my bones and sinews and offered thanks to the Great Reaper, who seemed to have turned a blind eye my way again.

The thing now was to get away from this filthy place of perdition as quickly as possible. Slowly, and somewhat handi-capped by a numbing crick in my neck, I raised my head and looked up at the infernal chasm above, my way down to the underworld. The open manhole showed the heavens with omin-ous, towering clouds still driving across them. But occasionally patches of blue morning sky broke the darkness, allowing dim light to fall into the shaft. However, this faint light didn't seem to promise a happy ending, more like the exact opposite.

Because now I could see that the iron rungs were too far apart for me to use them to work my way up. Even if I stood on my back legs on one rung, which I couldn't anyway, for reasons of balance, my body wouldn't stretch far enough to reach the next rung above. It looked as if I had no choice but to wander around this crypt until I found some other way out. Perhaps I'd thanked the Great Reaper too soon; OK, so the fall hadn't killed me, but it was to be feared that the smell of sewage, which was getting more and more penetrating as my pain subsided, would make a thorough job of it before too long.

I turned round, and had another surprise. By now my eyes had accustomed themselves to the poor light, and I could take in every aspect of the dubious charms of my present location. It looked as it I was on the bank of a canal about three metres broad, of unknown length, a picturesque river of piss and shit bounded by an ancient, curving wall which threw back the quirky reflections of the sludge as it quietly flowed past. It was difficult to make out where this sewer began and where it ended, for the cold light falling through the shaft cast a dull glow only over my immediate surroundings. The quay on which I stood, with its rusty hand-rail, was in fact a niche; the sewage workers would climb down to this point before setting off through the tunnels. There was a walkway about a metre wide, also made of stone, on both sides of the sewer. I had no idea where this path would lead me, but it would be rotten luck if I didn't come upon a link with the world of daylight somewhere along the way. After such a concentrated set of misfortunes, the law of averages said something nice must happen to me soon.

Although the nauseating smell and the musty, claustrophobic atmosphere of my cramped quarters didn't exactly suggest Venice, this gloomy spot had a certain morbidly romantic charm of its own. Before I'd honoured the bowels of the city with my radiant presence, the stormy floods must have caused one hell of a blockage there. Now that the tide had gone down, water-drops were falling from the roof of the tunnel into the sewer as if they were dripping from stalactites in a cave, echoing again and again, making some very odd noises. The pattern of the ripples reflected on the walls was the visual counterpart of the weird acoustics, and the constant quiet murmur of the main stream provided comforting background music, putting the finishing touch to the not unattractive picture of a grisly grotto. Partly to relish my relief at finding I was still all in one piece, partly because I suddenly felt fascinated by this kingdom of shadows, I stood on the edge of the stone path, legs planted wide apart, and took in the weird scene. Somehow the hypnotic lullaby of the never-ending, echoing drip-drip-drip and the peculiar atmosphere of the unlikely place soothed me, making me feel strangely peaceful. How idyllically this little river flowed along, what meditations it induced as one stood on the bank, letting one's eyes stray over the gentle waves. Look, there was even a swan swimming in the distance . . .

Swan? Come off it, you didn't get swans in the sewage system. Crocodiles, maybe, but no swans. There really *was* something swimming in the sewer, though, something white drifting towards me, a bloated something that turned majestically round and round on its own axis. It emerged from the darkness as unexpectedly as a shining space ship emerging from the belly of the universe. At first it was only a tiny white dot, bobbing about in the pitch-black expanses of the water. It was only its whiteness that made me notice it. But the closer it came the more clearly I could make it out. Now that it was about twenty metres away it looked like a fluffy, puffed-up flour bag. My harmonious feelings of a moment ago began giving way to a vague sense of oppression that constricted my throat like an iron collar. I couldn't take my eyes off this uncanny buoy, especially as it was bobbing along straight towards me. After a while I could see that the apparition wasn't as bright a white as it had initially seemed: it was the corpse of an animal with milk-white fur which was now very dirty, and it had been in the water so long that it had swelled to twice its natural size and looked like a sodden cotton wool ball. So I was looking at a drowned body. And the nightmare showed it could get even worse. There were large wounds in the lifeless corpse, going deep into the victim's flesh and suggesting small bomb craters. There were too many of them to be counted; they had probably been caused by bites. Since the corpse was in an advanced state of decomposition, and there was no blood flowing from the wounds, which ranged from dark pink to violet in colour, I guessed that death must have occurred several days ago. Ergo, the deceased had begun his wanderings from some very distant part of the sewage system, probably right outside town, and had been floating endlessly in the labyrinth of the sewers ever since.

I'd been fearing another revelation for quite some time, and now it came. Moving elegantly, like an aquatic ballerina, a tail chopped off in the middle suddenly rose from the poor tortured body, and I recognised it as a member of my own species floating there like a grotesque lifebelt. Horror and panic exploded in me, as if defective blood vessels were bursting in my brain. Creepy speculation about what kind of maltreatment had changed one of my own kind from a clean-limbed athlete to a badly mutilated lump of flesh occupied my entire mind, and I forgot all about my own aches and pains. I expected to glean further information very soon, in particular on the corpse's breed, because it was making straight for the side of the stone walkway, so I'd be able to see its face as the body gently rotated.

However, the face turned out to be the most horrible sight of all. The corpse did indeed come closer, almost brushing against the walkway; it came so close I could practically touch it. And yes, it turned gracefully on its own axis like a drifting water-lily and showed its front view. Enough light fell on it to let me see everything clearly. But horror of horrors, there was nothing left to see! The body, resembling a cake which had risen beyond all expectations, had no head left at all . . .

Felidae on the Road *is published by Fourth Estate in hardback, price £13.99*

Martin Millar

Dreams of Sex & Stage Diving

Elfish, a woman who rarely eats and never washes, is governed by twin obsessions: her thrash metal band and Queen Mab, Shakespeare's dream fairy from *Romeo and Juliet*. To feed her dreams Elfish is obliged to lie, cheat and steal. Happily, Elfish is a compulsive liar, and fond of cheating and stealing . . .

Martin Millar's fifth novel finds him on sparkling form, racing through an urban landscape that is both as real as concrete and as ethereal as stardust.

ISBN: 1–85702–213–0   £5.99

Milk, Sulphate & Alby Starvation

'What's allergic to milk, collects comics, sells speed, likes The Fall and lives in Brixton? Alby Starvation, the first true British anti-hero of the Giro generation. *Milk, Sulphate & Alby Starvation* is a strange and wonderful story . . . I've yet to come across someone who has not enjoyed it.' – *New Statesman*

ISBN: 1–85702–214–9   £5.99

Martin Millar

Lux the Poet

Armed with only his Star Wars toothbrush and Lana Turner looks, Lux braves riot-torn Brixton to rescue his girlfriend Pearl and speak to the nation on TV.

'It throbs with street-cred, crazed comedy and flick-knife sharp jibes at 20th-century urban life. I loved it. I hated it.' – Val Hennessy, *Daily Mail*

ISBN: 1–85702–215–7   £5.99

Ruby & the Stone Age Diet

Legend has it that when the Aphrodite Cactus flowers, true love also blossoms. The narrator of Martin Millar's third novel desperately needs his cactus to bloom, for his beloved Cis has left him. Luckily for him, there's Ruby, wise, beautiful Ruby in her lilac dress and bare feet. Ruby can always cheer him up with her stories of Cynthia Werewolf and her book of gods and goddesses.

ISBN: 1–85702–216–5   £5.99

The Good Fairies of New York

Is there a place for radical Celtic fairies Heather and Morag in the urban chaos of New York? And what trials and tribulations will their human friends – Dinnie, the worst violinist in the whole world, and the beautiful Kerry, who is cursed with a terrible disease – have to endure as the two creatures hurl themselves enthusiastically into city life?

ISBN: 1–85702–217–3   £5.99

Fourth Estate now offers in paperback an exciting range of quality titles by new and established authors, which can be obtained from the following address:

Fourth Estate Limited
P.O. Box 11
Falmouth
Cornwall TR10 9EN

Alternatively you may fax your order to the above address.
Fax number: 0326 376423

Payments can be made as follows: cheque, postal order (payable to Fourth Estate Limited) or by Visa or Access credit cards. Do not send cash or currency. UK customers and B.F.P.O. please allow £1.00 for postage and packing for the first book, plus 50p for the second book, plus 30p for each additional book up to a maximum charge of £3.00 (7 books or more).

Overseas customers including Ireland please allow £2.00 for the first book, plus £1.00 for the second, plus 50p for each additional book.

NAME (block letters) . . . .
. . . .
ADDRESS . . . .
. . . .
. . . .

☐ I enclose my remittance for _____

☐ I wish to pay by Access/Visa Card

Number

Card expiry date